Praise for Hugo Charteris

....a particularly original novel. This originality consists in the absolutely contemporary, bang up-to-the-minute freshness with which Mr Charteris sees his English characters.

They are all of them, from the wily Number One, Barber, to the disruptive journalist with the chip on his shoulder, real, not faked. Their world of action and danger comes brilliantly alive.

Evening Standard

Mr Charteris writes fluently, almost casually, but this nonchalance does not disguise his skill as a writer nor his real interest in the many-sided problem he presents. In addition, he can handle suspense in a masterly fashion, making this an exciting as well as a thoughtful story.

Rosaleen Whately, Liverpool Daily Post

Hugo Charteris's Europeans are neurotic, frightened, clinging to their fragmented patterns, craving violence like morphine addicts deprived of their drug. The sheer intensity of the whole book is terrifying.

The Daily Telegraph

...whatever comes, one does keep turning the page...An admirable, idiosyncratic book...takes us with complete credibility into a world we cannot afford to ignore.

John Wain, The Observer

A cracking good novel...the tension mounts swiftly and produces a climax which is as dramatically poignant as it is unexpected.

Manchester Evening News

Conflicts of race and colour, of sex, the strain of human relationships in an uncongenial climate, the fear of publicity and of Government interference are ingredients of a story of violence that is as topical as today's headlines, and has more tension and excitement than most thrillers.

Books of the Month

...he has great narrative skill; he can hold the reader in suspense without irritation, a rarer gift than many would-be suspenseful novelists suppose, and his eye for weakness, for the flaw in character, is extremely keen.

Times Literary Supplement

Picnic at Porokorro is a new novel by Mr Hugo Charteris which, again, is a recommendation in itself. ...The times, the tense situation between the handful of white men living among and attempting to dominate a far bigger black community, the tremendously high stakes: all these make for an explosive and violent atmosphere of which Mr Charteris writes in his own taut, under-emphatic style which is yet tremendously effective. I would rate him among the younger writers today who have not only tremendous promise but very distinguished performance as well.

Sphere

PICNIC AT POROKORRO

PICNIC AT POROKORRO

by

HUGO CHARTERIS

introduced by

ANDREW LYCETT

ADELAIDE
MICHAEL WALMER
2019

Picnic at Porokorro first published 1958
© The Estate of Hugo Charteris

Introduction first published in this edition
© Andrew Lycett 2019

Published by

Michael Walmer
9/2 Dahlmyra Avenue
Hamley Bridge
South Australia 5401

ISBN 978-0-6485905-3-8 paperback

ERRATA

This edition has been created utilizing a previous edition; thus errors have been reproduced. On page 16, line 1, for *employees* please read *employee's*; on page 36, line 7, for *those choose this* please read *they choose this*; on page 66, line 32, for *if salute* please read *of salute*; on page 112, line 25, for *Sydney* please read *Sidney*; on page 138, line 5, for *gun-grew* please read *gun-crew*; on page 183, line 1, for *refer it* please read *refer to it*; on page 194, line 23, for *thinks it* please read *think it's*; on page 213, line 1, for *Perhap* please read *Perhaps*; on page 226, line 2, for *Villagers* please read *Villages*; and on page 240, line 30, for *policeman* please read *policemen*.

INTRODUCTION

With his track record of fiction exploring the fault-lines in normally staid upper-class life, mainly in Scotland, Hugo Charteris was surprisingly well suited to write about festering tensions in a British expatriate community in a West African country moving uncertainly to self-government.

Published in 1958, *Picnic at Porokorro* was Hugo Charteris' fourth novel, though only the third to see the light of day, since its predecessor *The Tide is Right* was withdrawn on legal grounds after it ruffled family sensibilities with its depiction of clannish rivalries in the Highlands.

It was one of two literary offerings that emerged from a three month safari through West Africa by Charteris and his old (Etonian) friend Nicholas Mosley, son of Sir Oswald, the British fascist leader, in early 1957. The two young men zigzagged overland from Dakar to Lagos, reaching the British colony of the Gold Coast just in time to witness its independence as the nation of Ghana in March that year.

Mosley wrote *African Switchback*, a conventional travelogue which, while well observed, was a trifle smug about the supposed superiority of British colonial practices to those of the French. Charteris took a more imaginative approach, exploring the fragile natures of the individuals involved in a major British commercial enterprise, a diamond mine, at a time of growing native unrest. All this took place shortly before the famous 'winds of change' speech by the British Prime Minister Harold Macmillan to the South African parliament in Cape Town in February 1960, which acknowledged and accelerated moves to self-rule across the African continent.

Set in an unnamed country which is almost certainly Sierra Leone (though the only geographical references are to amorphous places like Bornu Island – called after an earlier pan-African empire), *Picnic at Porokorro* centres on a diamond mining company called the British Mineral Trust (BMT) which is emphatically not one of the big cartels such as De Beers. It is one of a few independents which control approximately 5 per cent of the global market. Nevertheless in its host country it is a major presence, operating through licensed native diggers, who work under tight security and must give up any diamonds they find to the BMT – unless they manage to smuggle them out and sell them to one of the Greek or Syrian traders who offer enticingly high prices.

The country is in uneasy transition. The British retain overall control of security and finance, but, in keeping with indirect rule, a native administration (NA) runs day to day affairs on traditional lines, while going through the uncertain process of developing the trappings of parliamentary democracy in preparation for independence. A similar dynamic exists in the diamond business, where the NA has chosen to introduce a second independent mining company to create an element of competition.

The resulting pressures and divisions are mirrored in the activities of the BMT with its diverting characters – notably Tom Barber, a craggy half-British half-South African who oversees company affairs; 'Lieutenant' John Roberts, an ex-policeman with a tendency to brusqueness in his dealings with the natives; Ian Scott, an Old Etonian whose mysterious connections to Buckingham Palace help move him from a job in the diamond sorting house to one in general security; William Meyer, a Pole (and therefore an outsider) who is a buyer for an external marketing organisation; and 'Mac' Macpherson, the Scottish provincial commissioner, who is the benign face of colonial government.

The conventional action follows the kidnapping of Roberts by a rogue leader of the licensed diggers. He escapes, and the drama then centres on how to deal with a potentially explosive situation. The experienced MacPherson prevails on his colleagues to proceed with a seemingly amicable visit, a sort of picnic, to Porokorro, a beauty spot in the heart of the otherwise barren diamond mining area where this incident took place, accompanied, not to everyone's liking, by a woman (Mrs Isobel Meyer) and a child (his son Paul). The denouement comes when this party is met with surly African intransigence and, sooner rather than later, by a rifle shot from the bush which kills the young boy.

However the book is really about the ways individuals at different levels of colonial society react to this situation. The drama is intensified by the arrival of a young journalist, Herbert Warner, who exploits the cracks in the set-up in order to stand up his initially hazy story on Roberts' kidnapping.

This outrage is only the latest in a series of similar incidents, but the general response (as epitomised by the weirdly comical 'picnic') is not to over-react, but to carry on as usual in typically British fashion. Charteris proves predictably adept at observing this strange calm: "Even during a crisis we remain a very ordinary-looking lot at the BMT. I think of us at

our most typical playing cricket on Saturdays during the dry season......
The light is so intense that even sunburnt faces have, like the grass, a
white withered look; and our women are as white powdered as scones,
against sweat. The whole effect is of a party grouped for security, and a
howdah, on a raft, suddenly consoled with a mirage of cricket." Their
mixture of "unmoving inanity and umbilical rootedness" reminded the
novel's narrator of a cartoon by Pont, the pseudonym of Graham Laidler,
who lampooned British calm in the face of adversity in cartoons for
Punch before and during the Second World War.

Under this uneasy tranquillity lie resentments, frustrations and
aspirations. Charteris presents these not as massive issues, but as subtle
differences of opinion, often based on variations of class (or caste),
education, and (this being only a dozen years after World War II) varieties
of military service. So a reader needs to be aware of the perceived
gradations of the English public school system, with Roberts being
the token Old Etonian in the compound, and Barber, an Uppingham
alumnus, wanting at the end of his travails only to be able to send his
three sons to Rugby.

More significantly, Charteris shows his characters dealing (or not
dealing) with the crisis, and being affected by it. Barber chooses to
respond by virtually ignoring it. "Acted?" interposes the narrator at one
stage. "No. No one acted. That is the one thing that strikes me, looking
back on that extraordinary day. No one *did* anything. The fashion was
against it. You got round a table and a blind trend asserted itself another
inch." However, having bowed out of going to Porokorro, the normally
composed Barber feels overwhelmed by the range of problems on his
plate and wonders, "Why did he do the job if it was killing him?"

Macpherson's approach is to stress that he is an "old Africa hand" with
whom the dissenting natives will be only too happy to sit down and
discuss the issues, face to face. But he loses his only son, and is left equally
disillusioned, as he bemoans, "'It did not happen......How could it have
happened: I know these people. That's why I took Paul – because I know
them – y'see, that's why I took him. ......I was taking him to Africa – and
to my life's work; I know it's all going – but I was taking ma future to ma
past – and I gave all I had to both.'"

Women have a significant, if subsidiary, role in this environment.
Charteris has fun with Barber's absent wife, an unprepossessing former

WREN, known as the Admiral. But the 'chief' proves strangely adrift without her "four-square imperturbability" and her skill at defusing difficult situations "with one of her determined, too dry, keen little questions". Then there is Isobel, Meyer's flirtatious wife, who flaunts her sexuality, making a "tortured narcissistic hobby out of serious and vital matters like nipples and breasts", in a manner Charteris suggests is lost on Africans, whose women have a natural grace and don't need the titillations of her "Dior beachwear".

Nevertheless the highly strung Isobel proves an able critic of the soulless life within or (in her case) just outside the BMT compound. She "looked at her husband's curtains and furniture with panic. Each object tried to be bright and different, but was basically cheap, utilitarian and standardised. The house was a living unit for a producer and it came in sections, with a quota of furniture. And he hadn't altered a thing....". She searched for some mark of his personality, but there was none: "All this accommodation was partly perhaps the exile's determined and instinctive urge to adopt in the name of self-preservation the camouflage of a new milieu".

Meyer himself is another who declines the trip to Porokorro because, as he tells his wife, it wouldn't be good for his business to be seen to be on the side of the police in this 'palaver'. When he says he is sorry she is going, she taunts him that "all men have a moslem inside them....A wife takes a little initiative and there's panic. Purdah is in jeopardy. What can it matter to you if I go to Poro – whatever it's called".

Among other themes is the role of the press, both generally at home, and more specifically overseas, in fanning the embers of anti-colonialism. The opportunism of Warner, the young reporter who works for the 'Daily ------' is mercilessly exposed . His paper's name is never spelt out, but it is quite possibly the *Daily Mail*, where Charteris once reluctantly worked because he needed the money – his sister Ann was then married to Lord Rothermere, the proprietor.

Warner behaves like most journalists of his time – using his cheque book to elicit information about the earlier incident from gullible Africans. Barber feels that he can charm him, but the majority distrust him, leading to the unlikely suggestion that the newspaperman is "one of the angry young men". (The book appeared a couple of years after John Osborne's play *Look Back in Anger.*)

Although the focus is on the behaviour of Europeans, Charteris also alights on African society, which, for all its timelessness, is equally adrift – with its flashy politicians and its mission-educated guards – one of whom Warner believes is the most truly Christian person he has ever met, but he can't help feeling is "the sort of bloke you wanted to step on, in spite of yourself".

Picnic at Porokorro sparked rivalry between Charteris and Ian Fleming, author of the James Bond novels, who was his brother-in-law, having married his sister Ann after she divorced Lord Rothermere in 1952. A couple of years earlier Fleming had written *Diamonds Are Forever,* which followed his secret agent hero's adventures in the international diamond business, starting at a British owned mine in Sierra Leone. This was published in 1956, several months before Charteris embarked on his trip. However, Fleming set about writing a follow-up book, *The Diamond Smugglers,* based on a series of interviews he conducted in April 1957 with John Collard, a retired MI5 officer who had worked with De Beers on preventing illegal diamond smuggling in South and West Africa.

Although Fleming had already staked out this territory, Charteris thought he was now straying too much onto his part of it. The general ground was the great modern novel which exposed the realities of British colonialism in Africa. Graham Greene had earlier made his claim with *The Heart of the Matter*, also about Sierra Leone. But that was as much about religion as politics. Charteris' portrayal of a beleaguered British community recalls the more secular Rudyard Kipling, who wrote about the often harsh realities (and loneliness) of expatriate communities (like the BMT), and who is referred to in a comment about Barber for whom "the discipline of an assumed aristocratic equanimity and of an unfailing Kiplingesque decency, with equal bouquets for Gunga Dhin (sic) and the general, was nowadays under a mechanical strain". With his cool forensic eye, Charteris brings Kipling up to date for the mid-twentieth century. His searching prose is never less than intense, intelligent and illuminating.

ANDREW LYCETT
London, June 2019

To N.M.—in gratitude

1

THE CURRENT of the River Niele is deceptively calm, even by day.

At night you could reach the bank and think you were looking out over a small, still lake, round which the elephant grass whispered occasionally in the breeze.

In fact the whispers come from the gentle overlapping of long, thick, screwing tendons of water which sweep over the diamondiferous gravel and through the skeletons of half-submerged trees which—from Porokorro right up to Bornu Island—diggers have gouged from the bank and left to rot in the shallows.

Porokorro means " the Place of Bones."

Manga grandfathers will tell you that here, when they were children, were battles between the war-boys of the Kuru and the Manga; they can remember the painted corpses, lying out on the banks, rotting; and in the sky, small as carbon flakes above burning paper, the marks of more distant battles: slow, high, banking schools of vultures—turning . . . turning . . . the sluggish, low-geared wheel in the clock of Africa's prehistoric economy.

This was only yesterday.

The man who sowed never knew who would eat the crop.

Then came the DCs' and a short period of relative peace—sustained by Europe, even while she was disembowelling herself in scientific wars. There was peace in

Africa—it is true—but in the bush the sleep of time was over.

          *   *   *

Last month, one dawn, a shape broke the surface of the Niele's black waters and grunting breath belied the river's gentle, trickling whispers. Soon sounds of struggle broke out as though the dead branches and leathery fallen creepers had become alive under water, and were now feeding.

Splashing started, became desperate; then ceased. A feeble quadruped dragged itself a few feet up the bank and sank to the ground where for a time it might have been a flat reptile, or even " nothing "—a long bit of raised earth.

Then at last it rolled over and faced the sky—with the face of a man—a white man.

He was young and nondescript but in his staring eyes there was now to be seen that tenuous, rare perception which sometimes gleams autonomously in the muddy blank bottom of anyone's absolute exhaustion and reprieve from fear.

          *   *   *

At the camp we were all still asleep.

I have looked up the day: it was the morning after the dry-season storm. A Friday, my diary says.

Earlier, on Thursday evening, in the middle of crashing thunder and roaring rain a rumour of " trouble at one of the plants " had spread through the camp.

The way the rumour was received and quickly magnified showed to what extent people had been waiting for a " repetition of last year."

Cool, hard-working men who normally never alluded

8

to even the possibility of new trouble now said simply " Perhaps this is it," or " Here we go again."

Then as the hours passed a few facts became available; The rumour was toned down.

*   *   *

Roberts, who was recently seconded from the police proper to our own BMT Security, had carried out one of the raids which were a point of controversy between the Administration on the one hand and ourselves (The British Minerals Trust) and the police on the other.

He found, as anyone could have, any night, Africans digging on BMT ground. Encouraged by recent " bags," and BMT gratitude, he determined to break all his own records. Instead of cutting off a few fugitives, he ringed a whole crowd, including the " Cowboy "—a character, called after his hat, who seemed to be some kind of leader. The result was that his own force, of twenty African " Guards," got hopelessly strung-out, finally scattered, while he, with a corporal, plunged into the bush after the Cowboy.

Roberts (who just missed the war) was nearly capped for England at rugger. He has often taken prisoners by himself, far from his men, like a full-back tackling a winger near the base-line. The Licensed Diggers were said to be " out for his blood."

No one knows whether it was a trap. He suddenly found himself surrounded by about fifty young men armed with spades, picks and matchets—and by the Cowboy in person.

This came out afterwards. At first the bare news that he had been " captured " was brought by his African sergeant in a jeep.

This was about 6 p.m. during the storm. We under-

stood a detachment of police proper went out to Porokorro at once. But we heard nothing more that night.

None of us had had time to get to know' Roberts well.
That, of course, is one reason why there was nothing
approaching a vigil on his behalf. Nevertheless it struck
me as strange there should be so little concern. Reaction
compared unfavourably with the atmosphere in an
infantry regiment when a new officer or private was lost
on a fighting patrol. I mention this in passing because,
perhaps, it is part of the reason why the whole story
seems to me worth telling.

Roberts of course was well paid for the " special work "
he did for the BMT and he recently moved into a BMT
bungalow, inside the wire. Such a bungalow would
compare favourably with any living unit in the colony,
except the three-decker villas of the big company
managers on the coast, and one or two of the residences;
and once he was inside it he came in on BMT perks
which, to other Britons working out here, are a sort of
PX to their NAAFI.

(Our Haig, for some reason, is 22s. 6d. and Players are
three bob for a tin of fifty. We have golf course, tennis
courts, swimming pools all set in a shrubbery as good
as Kew.)

Of course, in return for this raising of his living standard,
he had to accept certain snags. We are none of us
allowed a private car and there is certainly a good deal
of " supervision " which people with frayed nerves have
gone so far as to call " spying." But what else could we
expect? Diamonds are the most portable form of wealth
in the world—and we are surrounded by the vast African
continent, where frontiers are easily passable, communications often non-existent and shelter available
somewhere for anyone, if he can pay well. Most of us

would agree the general situation, justifies a measure of control. Roberts merely made the choice we've all made.

*   *   *

At breakfast, it became known that he had " escaped by swimming " and was back in camp.

Most of what followed in the next forty-eight hours, both in the camp and on the site at Porokorro became, in time, general sketchy knowledge, but I shall tell the story as it seems to me it must have happened.

After five years here I am in the position of knowing most of the dramatis personæ fairly well.

"Number One "—as he was usually called—Tom Barber, half British, half South African, was a small man with a craggy, rather monkey-like face. He sat, as little as possible, between his huge desk, like an old-fashioned sideboard, and the vast BMT safe, which occupied the whole wall behind him. The safe glowed with three different coloured lights, hummed and was so modern it had no door. The desk had a long ivory wand.

In his high place, Barber looked like some kind of wizard, ready for and capable of anything.

This fantastic impression was reinforced by a lion-footed, tapestry-backed, gold-valanced chair—the fantasy of a big business duke, which stood amongst all the streamlined modern office equipment as out of place as a knight-in-armour at a World Hygiene Conference. It was used at Board meetings by the Chairman (Lord Heatherlake) and had been flown from London. There was a crucifixion motif in the tapestry, but the whole surprising effect was of a prop for Number One's wizardry. Swipe his chair and his wand and he'd beg for mercy.

In fact Barber (magic apart), as we shall see, was far too streamlined and alive to the ridiculous to enjoy such a piece of vulgarity. Perhaps the Board liked it. Who were " the Board "? Who was the Chairman? Sometimes we saw the word " Heatherlake " printed on our Christmas cards. But this did not put us in the picture.

We understood diamond sales were an all-but global monopoly of the De Beers group; and that we came in on the " all-but "—the six per cent which is not De Beers. Did this make our contribution " chicken-feed "? The question is like asking whether the world is small. For us the BMT was professionally vast—it was everything. And the relatively greater vastness of the De Beers empire, and of its affiliated Diamond Corporation was remote as Mars.

To most of us such names and even our own name —BMT—didn't mean much in terms of glabal statistics and so, I think, many of us, if asked about our " set-up," would have had a fleeting, crystallising vision of that extraordinary chair, which was all we ever saw of " the top."

*   *   *

Perhaps you have to be a little mad to flourish physically in high positions under a modern social-democratic system.

Barber was not flourishing, even before the trouble started.

Until recently the BMT had a monopoly of all alluvial diamond mining rights in the colony—that is except on the ground leased to the " Licensed Diggers " (natives of the colony who had paid £30 for a digging licence).

Last year a company, said to be " native owned," but in fact financed by Greeks, the Santa Barbara Native Diamond Trust (SBNDT), was allowed by the Native Administration (NA) to put up a bid for the Kaidu river zone which the BMT had already prospected and for which Barber had already started negotiating treaty-rights with the customary chiefs, and with NA.

This " native " competition caused, I'm told, a minor sensation in that stratosphere of which we at the camp saw little except the chair and the Christmas card. It was said: " Number One's having a rough time."

Our Piper Cub, Two-seater Moth, which town-cries arrivals and departures to everyone, indoors and out, was always on the buzz. Rumour was rife, though what really happened can never be known, except that the Greeks certainly got the rights.

Gossip said: Firstly it suited the Native Administration to have *two* diamond firms at work in the country. One could be played off against the other. Secondly, the up and coming politicians did not want to be tied totally to British capital when the day of Independence came. Thirdly, and most important: one of the Greeks concerned was " a friend " of two African lawyers— both prominent elected members of the NA—both of whom were soon announced as directors of the new company.

Clearly the BMT tender never had a chance. Barber never had a chance. Not that he alone conducted the final negotiations (Heatherlake himself came out), but he was, however, " the man on the spot " and we understood that his brilliant record was slightly tarnished in the eyes of those people we never saw. It was thought he should have been more " in " with the up-and-coming Africans. Indeed perhaps that was why he and not a pure South African had been appointed.

Barber, I imagine, reacts to criticism like flesh to fire, I'm sure he couldn't bear to fail. Certainly in the last weeks his blue eyes have stood out more than ever coolly and calmly, but his small, rather jockey-like, body seems a bit more craggy, his face more frayed.

He has been living about seven lives—none of them private. And as one who sees his reports I know that throughout the complex negotiation for the new zone, illicit digging here at Sangoro had been on the increase until it was reflected sharply in the production chart which hangs by the portrait of the Duke of Edinburgh, on the safe.

Only recently—since Roberts' " prangs," had there been an improvement—making the graph look something like this

—stabilised, even slightly ascendant.

Now this . . . this new trouble at one of the sites.

*   *   *

Barber switched on the fans and then stood looking out of the window in front of him. The sun was retrieving the storm as though it had been a mistake. Clouds, columns and shreds of mist were everywhere.

Already boys had started watering again, giving the huge floppy bungalow flowers the endless transfusion they need.

Barber had the expression of a man halted at a cross-roads in unknown country. There was no sign-post.

I don't think he wanted to come to a cross-roads. He knew all sorts of people in British public life by their Christian names—M.P.s, Directors, Proprietors and titled folk; even artists and writers. He did not talk of them—which leant weight to the rumour he would soon be going to London for some even higher appointment. No one in the whole camp made such effective fun of the ludicrous gilt arm-chair as he. In fact it was a passion with him. I believe he had a substantial private income. To most of us he was likeable—though odd.

The length of his jaw-line was his most striking feature, except for his eyes. His eyes gripped you—and meant to with an almost fiercely intimate no-nonsense, all-in-this-together stare—I think they meant to reveal, and perhaps did, a refulgent, tough, general decency. And yet—there were subjects which, apparently, he simply did not *hear*. Three of these were politics, and " colour," and " class." If cornered, he would say " I'm a miner " in a quiet, untypical tone.

The intercom beside him buzzed, just as Dickson the General Manager came in and took his place at a little desk, in the corner.

Dickson said, " That's Roberts now."

Dickson always spoke to Barber as though somebody might be listening.

Dickson is pure South African, and like Roberts a rugger player. He is really an intellectual of sorts and says the whites are losing their " sense of responsibility " to the African. His eyes are slightly protuberant and his frequent silence, which fits so ill with his vivid, eloquent, though bulbous stare, seems to me a restraint which has made inroads on his health.

The fact that these two men at the top are known to be " South Africans " (though to my mind Barber is much more British) often lends a submerged, nagging and unhealthy vent to the camp atmosphere, which is something like Berlin during the air-lift.

People forget that there are good reasons for South Africans heading a diamond enterprise even in a British colony. There have been diamond mines in South Africa for a hundred years, none in Britain.

But there is no end to our irrationality. I have seen an

employees antagonism to our " South Africans " become
worse the more he was exasperated by relationships, in
technical matters, with African subordinates.

And I have heard the same men who asked for the
searching of Africans' clothes, while the owners stand
naked, to be " conducted in private—for the chap's sake "
—one day, and the next, after some theft, want it done
" more thoroughly and on the spot."

And wives who suddenly wake up one morning and
feel they're in a luxury concentration camp and say
they'll " start screaming "—sometimes blame Barber
and Dickson—" the South Africans "—for " the atmosphere."

Perhaps it's easier, certainly more OK, to vent abuse
on them than on . . . what? Indeed, just what! " Out
here," people say and " they " and " they " . . . and
" Home "; and we never forget the riots last year,
which are usually referred to simply as " last year."

You can understand then how a certain conniving,
nearly furtive speech might have became a habit with
Dickson. The political wind in the colony and even in
the camp was against him . . . (against *them*, Dickson
would have insisted).

At the same time his—and Barber's—responsibilities
were vast. Unlike anyone else in the camp they were in
personal contact with the men at the top, with London
and Johannesburg; and they were sitting—when you
come to think of " last year " and the still fresh memory
of the Kuru rising in the 'twenties—on a bomb—a
D-bomb (as the newspapers called it) of light, breath-
takingly light, ubiquitously convertible wealth. All " in
the middle of nowhere " and guarded by only ten
European and six hundred African policemen—the latter
being looked upon largely as gas was in the first war:

the wind would change and then you'd have them against you.

Even loyal—it was a small force when within a radius of fifteen miles of the camp there were about 30,000 licensed—or more likely unlicensed—diggers, many of them from as far afield as the Sudan, Senegal and Dahomey, without a penny in their pocket.

" Send him in," Barber said into the intercom.

2

THERE WERE not many seconds to wait before Roberts came in.

Our silence in the BMT camp has sometimes seemed to me like the silence of engineers in engine-rooms. Of course there is the heat and sweat of an engine-room— even in the fanned offices—but that is not what I mean. There is a listening, responsible, half-distrait quality as though the silent person must keep count of some other, general all-embracing important noise—which could threaten danger within a single, off-beat tick.

Even in the mess the pause while a glass is raised, before someone says " cheers ", becomes fraught with absurd suggestion.

Is there a walrus just behind us—or something like that?

In the racing seconds Barber said, " The Secretary and the Provincial Commissioner are flying in this morning."

Dickson's face underwent a tiny convulsion and he stirred as though violently bored by the utterance of this among many certainties.

There was the sound of a step and Barber got up and went to the door.

He led the young man in like a bride.

Dickson said, " Good morning to you," in a friendly sardonic tone.

Barber was a great admirer of good generals, war

heroes and athletes. He read every word that was written about them, and knew things like where and how Lord Gort won his V.C. and even the tactics, if any, of the Afghan campaign of 1878. He himself had two M.C.s though few people know it.

He pulled out the gilt arm-chair and when it was half-way out suddenly said " Christ " with realistic agony and almost fell into it. Roberts went to help him. Barber said, " Together—NOW," and they got to it in the middle with a sudden rush.

" Have a chair. The Commode of the Vanderbuilts— the Stool of the Baskervilles. Have you had anything to eat ? " He said it all intimately as a friend.

Roberts said he had eaten " a bit." He sat unself-consciously in the chair. It was the third time in eight days that he had sat alone with these two men.

Barber took him in with eyes that were perhaps too obviously appraising—and praising; eyes that seemed conspicuously to *defer* to Roberts.

" By Christ," he said. " You're glad to be back, aren't you ? "

Roberts smiled.

Barber and Dickson had known him so far as fairly talkative.

They just waited.

But his eyes dropped; he did not talk.

Barber hitched himself up on the edge of the " air-craft carrier " and used his eyes, his personality; waited. Dickson had slewed right round.

But Roberts said nothing. He looked suddenly shy, and sometimes like a dog " seeing things."

" They got you . . ." Barber cautiously, tactfully coloured the statement with humour if that was how Roberts wanted it.

19

" Yes . . . they certainly got me," Roberts said, only half accepting the humour.

" Can we have it . . . from the beginning."

The young man made an effort. He seemed all the time to be thinking of something else. He was fresh-faced, rather ordinary-looking. Only his eyes, perhaps from fatigue, had the rather webby, " deep " look women get after giving birth, and in them he seemed to have a clear picture—though this was not produced in his words. Indeed he added practically nothing to what was already known.

When finally he said he got separated from his men Barber interrupted, " Bloody fool," in a half-commending, half-pitiless tone.

Roberts paused and seemed to think; and suffer from the novelty of thinking.

At last he said, " Well, sir . . . I thought we ought to catch this Cowboy chap . . . If there was to be any point . . ."

He petered out into a subordinate's silence.

He was 22. He had just got engaged, and had come to the colony straight from National Service Commission and Police College. To him I think the illicit diggers had been some kind of mock enemy—as on manœuvres: " Blue Land occupies this ground during the night. At 2100 hours you are the Platoon Commander of a Red-land platoon. What are you going to do? They have matchets and picks; you have staves, tin hats and a .38 which you mustn't use."

In the past Barber himself had seemed to share this attitude when talking to Roberts of his " prangs." Now after a long, long look at the young man in the chair he changed. He made him a member of the War Club.

The young man's eyes again sunk to the floor in a sign

of perplexity—and of something else, uncommunicated.

There was silence. But Barber's face fairly spoke. Some people have said that he was " false." Certainly he sometimes overdid sympathy with his juniors and subordinates. But at this moment he really was remembering a similar moment in his own life, when a bunch of Hitler's prize babies in black tank uniforms, brown as Lido boys and below the face as physically beautiful, the '39 vintage cream soon to be drunk by the Russian steppes, overran his company near Poperingue, one of the towns he had flown over as a boy, countless times, in *Chums* watching the shells burst " like tufts of cotton wool." . . . Barber remembered the first few seconds, when they got out shouting to each other, some with their Schmeissers ready—and an expression in their eyes which was a farewell to Chums. A moment of sheer balance when the thin silt of Christian centuries is at the mercy of remote, fear-warped emotions, to say nothing of a terrifying geographical privacy.

" How did you get out? " Barber said.

And strangely enough, at this directness, Roberts looked more perplexed than ever—as though Barber had changed the subject.

" You didn't use your gun? " Barber encouraged.

" No. . . ."

" Bloody good. You wouldn't have hit anything—but that's neither here nor there."

Roberts said, " It would have finished us."

Number One disregarded this. He said, " Did any of them speak English? "

Roberts said: " My sergeant spoke for half an hour. In Kuru."

" But you knew they weren't going to chop you."

" After about five minutes . . . I suppose."

" Five lovely minutes! "

" They searched us. They made us undress—and stand naked. They said they were looking for tear-gas grenades." Roberts now looked up inquiringly, as though for grenades, at Barber.

Barber said nothing, and for once his face showed nothing either—in other words remained fixed in approving attention—but on the previous sentence.

" Anyhow—you got out? "

" They said we could go—if I promised not to come back."

" Did you? "

Roberts flushed like a child. He said, " My sergeant answered. I told him to make no conditions . . . I don't know what he said. I doubt if he does . . . But they let us go."

Barber was silent. To look at, you would not have thought he had any other thought but Roberts' ordeal— and yet suddenly he stretched over his shoulder and laid his hand, without looking, on a telegram which he gave Roberts, to read:

" SECRETARY AND POLICE COMMISSIONER FLY BMT STOP THIS MORNING STOP PROVINCIAL COMMISSIONER WILL REACH YOU BY JEEP MIDDAY."

The effect on the young man of this confidence took time to mature. At first he read it as though it concerned him. When he discovered it didn't he finished it with increased perplexity and then held it out uncertainly in the air as though anxious to be relieved of what he had not, in fact, stolen.

Barber did not take the paper from him, and Dickson met his eyes with pugnacious friendliness. Dickson was happily married with grown-up children who were fond of him and came to stay with him. He liked a party and

22

had got on well with Roberts a few nights back. He used
phrases like " pulling your weight " and " fitting in "
with sincerity. I think corporal punishment, prayers and
the acceptance of injustice had played quite a part in his
education. Suddenly three of his fingers began to drum
as he stared heartily and watchfully at Roberts.

Barber took the paper back, and said, " Well—what
are we going to do? "

The young man looked vacant. He could not even
pretend to an opinion. He still wasn't sure whether he
had got his seconding business straight. Sometimes they
managed to make him feel the mouthpiece of the Colonial Police.

Barber said, " You know what they'll do. They'll
appoint a committee to make a report, which will recom-
mend an additional warden and a licensed diggers' representatives' association—L.D.R.A. And there will be
discussions and telegrams to London for six months.
Meanwhile more ground will be fouled. The best
ground."

" Yes, sir." It sounded likely.

Dickson looked round now at Barber. Roberts got the
feeling that in some way this moment had been fore-
seen, by both men . . . *by the South Africans*, he suddenly
thought.

Barber said, " If you went back in there with the main
police body—to-day or to-morrow . . . to get this Cowboy chap. D'you think . . . *What* do you think? "

Roberts' first reply perished on his lips, leaving them
open for speech, but silent.

Barber said, " They hate your guts, don't they? "

Roberts looked inquiring, and then pensive. At last he
said, " They call me Hatman."

" *Hatman!* " Barber said.

But I think he knew it.

It was curious—the idea of this fresh innocent-faced youth with his clear large eyes and frank manner being hated. The pleasant thing about him was his desire to please. And pleasing, for him, like charity, obviously started at home.

Barber now took an uneasy stroll as an alternative to speech. Dickson began to puff a silent trombone tune with his large mouth and blinked sleepily, still staring at Roberts from a few feet.

Words which seemed to need a special formula, a certain combination, like the lock of a safe, before they could be uttered waited on the edge of Barber's lips. Soon he would give them birth.

But Roberts was not aware of this. His manner was out of keeping with the pregnant silence. And so he suddenly did violence to the whole situation by blurting out, "They were on about the old man."

Barber gradually came to a halt behind him.

Neither of the older men said anything yet nor did they ask for enlightenment.

At last Dickson said, "You mean the one they ate last year."

(We had a suspected case of cannibalism last year—on a barren site where rations gave out.)

Roberts didn't seem to hear. He merely turned and looked at Barber. It was only four days since he had sat exactly where he was sitting now and amplified by word of mouth the report which he had already submitted in writing about the "old man."

So he said, "The old sentry . . . my sergeant, said they were on about him. The Cowboy chap said we murdered him. They said if I came back again they'd try me."

24

Picnic at Porokorro

He got this out as though it were the whole works.

"Try you." Dickson looked at Number One and remained looking at him. Finally he couldn't restrain himself. He went on: "Wonderful, isn't it? They must take correspondence courses."

Roberts said, "You wouldn't have thought they cared, would you? When their pals are buried alive in earth-falls they just keep digging. . . ."

Barber came back to his big desk and this time sat in it, sandwiched between the safe and the huge paper-strewn surface.

Roberts said, "I told my sergeant to explain."

Neither Barber nor Dickson seemed to hear this.

"That it was an accident . . ." Roberts went on. "Which it was, for Christ's sake . . ." Roberts ended, suddenly asserting himself, and staring them, anybody, out.

Barber said crisply, "Well, of course."

The silence which now prevailed was flat and final—not pregnant like its predecessors. The formal rank and positions of the three men seemed to creep slowly to the fore like layers of mist, shrouding individual characteristics which had looked like emerging.

And Roberts saw, in the averted eyes of the older men, no invitation to continue talking.

But Barber did say quietly, reasonably, "Your report went through to the Commissioner in the normal manner. It was approved. The matter's closed . . . isn't it?" He raised his eyes and in this last question did put that "personal touch" without which he never addressed a subordinate. Then, as though without changing the subject, he added simply, "You must be whacked, dead, aren't you? Of course you are!" He got up and now commended with his level blue eyes. "Anyhow . . .

25

bloody good, John. . . . Have lunch in bed. I'll send you some champagne. . . ."

Roberts got up and almost saluted. He lingered an instant.

Dickson drummed his fingers briefly, till he turned away to his desk; turned right away.

Then Roberts went out, leaving the chair in the middle of the room, where it looked more ludicrous than ever, the whim now of a poltergeist.

*   *   *

The sun was mounting.

Barber went across and increased the speed of the huge fans. He looked at his watch and went back to his " wizard's " place. I often noticed that he did little things of this kind with a kind of distaste which verged on violence, an impersonality, a deft objectivity which contrasted strongly with his extreme bonhomie.

He had a passion for what he called " facts."

But sometimes, when he had established a few more, as now, he looked almost ethereally tired.

3

THE JOURNALIST came, literally, out of the blue. His plane landed on the company strip and he got out with his suitcase as though from a taxi. It was mere luck that a maintenance team happened to be working on the Piper. He hailed them, like another taxi. If they hadn't been there he might have been stranded till the VIPs flew in, an hour later. But this would have suited him, also.

He was only 22 and looked less, sometimes much less. His clothes were odd—he had a sort of silk stock folded into his shirt, plastic sandals such as the Africans wear and rather ornate sunglasses in a fancy cream frame.

He gave the maintenance crew cigars during the journey to the camp and asked questions which assumed they were fed up.

We very seldom have a visitor to the BMT camp who isn't expected. Therefore we have no machinery for "reception": no waiting-rooms with periodicals, telephonists who say Mr. So and So to see Mr. So and So; will you go up now, etc., but instead just a bare bench inside the gate control-house. There a visitor must sit until an African messenger has taken particulars on an oil-grimed form, by foot, a quarter of a mile to the head office and back.

Warner could not have known that he was the first white visitor to arrive at our camp unexpected since the

Picnic at Porokorro

Seventh Day Adventists sent a Wandering Messenger through the whole colony three years ago. Sitting on the bench he came as near to showing himself "put out" as he ever did.

For the gate control-house is an unpleasant place. All heavy machinery and heavy transport lives inside the wire and must pass through the gate-house every morning, pausing only to render a complete note of driver's work ticket and a summary of his vehicle's load. The huge bulldozers, trucks and scrapes keep the spot coated thickly with dust and oil. Diesel fumes turn the air in the nose to stinking fire, and the noise from the exhausts is the same shattering roar of army tank engines, enforcing silence or yelled brevity, so that men move about in their black glasses, often with scarfed mouths and nostrils, like modern denizens of a new element—neither air, earth nor water—but a roaring void full of the stinking, harnessed, mechanical disintegration of all three.

Africans are sensitive to caste, and Warner's mere arrival, without a pass from the management, ranked him as a white without a future. He owed it perhaps to the word "Press," which he wrote on the grimy form, that he was given a seat at all and not left to stand in the crowd of Africans beside the notice "No labour wanted."

The man who took his message sloped off in a crooked course, touching things like a child and stopped, while still close, and began talking to a friend.

Warner sat in the gate three-quarters of an hour and was treated as though he wasn't there. Sometimes a special side-gate was opened and a jeep or Rover swept through with a sun-darkened white beside the black driver.

The wire, Warner noticed, was fifteen foot high,

quarter-inch lattice mesh and topped with an outward-jutting triple strand of barbed wire.

When he tried to speak to the traffic check clerk, the man seemed to use the noise as an excuse for total non-comprehension.

During the whole wait Warner looked about him with nervous interest which suggested participation in whatever activity he looked at. But he never looked at anything for long—except once: at the queue of the workless. Usually he only glanced. And he often changed position, arranging his small-boned limbs in graceful though finally tense positions. Whenever a sudden movement or shouted conversation took place in his vicinity he looked up sharply as though it might concern him.

When the messenger came in sight, returning, he watched him, off and on, all the way.

He was asked to follow.

*   *   *

When Warner announced the paper he worked for Dickson stared at him and said nothing.

Dickson has no shares in the BMT, and has worked hard all his life.

After that silence it seemed that whatever came out of Dickson's mouth would be the last, perhaps fatal excess of restraint. He finally produced two words which were quite foreign to him: " I see." Then, " Well, how can we help—I suppose that's the next thing we should dispose of," and his eyes fell slowly over Warner's person, leaving nothing out.

Warner said, " Well, I'd like to have a look round with your permission, and see a guy at Sangoro."

Dickson, I know, would have liked to know who. But he controlled himself again and said carefully and politely—in spite of the man's teenage appearance, " You'd like to have a look round would you . . . I think that can be arranged."

We in the BMT always cripple ourselves to be polite to the Press. We don't want more trouble.

" And could I see Lieutenant Roberts."

Dickson studied the girl-featured face with the great lakes of smoked glass over the eyes. At last he said, " Roberts," and then after an absurdly long calculating pause he added, " He's resting now. I shouldn't disturb him if I were you."

This was paternally put, partly to conceal a consuming curiosity, partly to keep temper.

Warner was silent, and then said, " But I've got a job to do."

He said it coolly and pleasantly.

Dickson said afterwards, " It was all I could do to chuck the little rat out." At the time he merely replied, " I've got a job to do, too, Mr. Warner."

" Well, could you give me an appointment with the lieutenant? "

" I don't think I could, no. . . . May we ask who gave you his name? "

At this moment Barber came in and Dickson said factually, " The Daily ————."

Warner had made no move to rise at Barber's entry although Dickson himself had risen.

Dickson turned to look at Warner and said, " He wants to see John Roberts: are you a friend of his? " (This to Warner.)

" Yes—I'm a sort of friend of his."

This surprising answer had the most unfavourable effect on Dickson. The very openness of the seated youth's lie was a kind of insult.

" I know his sister," Warner added and he glanced at
Barber, who suddenly came forward and put out his
hand saying, " Barber," in the American way.

Dickson said, " He flew in."

Warner now rose and shook hands.

Number One disregarded the recent tone of his
colleague, and said warmly, " How long can you stay? "
It would be difficult to know who was the most surprised
—Dickson or the young journalist.

*   *   *

We quarrel easily here. We all have to be careful—
no one more so than Number One and Dickson, who
are the most isolated of us all.

People at home will find it hard to understand the
extent to which we all feel *isolated*. (I'm talking about
the quarrelling and the way Dickson received Warner.)
It is not merely a question of being surrounded and
vastly outnumbered by countless Africans with whom
we can only communicate in a sort of baby talk. It is
in the very air we breathe. You may say we exaggerate
this, " imagine " it, just as one of us sometimes suddenly
imagines it is much hotter than it is and succumbs to
panic deciding, usually one midnight, that he can't stand
it *another minute*. Perhaps we do " imagine " things, on
the other hand it is only eight months since " last year "
—the riots—when, for 48 hours, communications were
cut and it looked as if every single inland European
would lose his life.

Not that mere risk explains the sense of isolation: the
point is that " last year," after the situation came partly
under control and we saw English newspapers, we
expected to be headline news for days. Instead the whole
affair got short front-page display for one day and then

31

half a column on front pages. After four days some of
us remember reading our air-mail editions with a pistol
on the office table, barbed-wire barricades outside, and
not finding a single mention of what seemed to us still a
hair-trigger situation.

We had 243 fatal police casualties, and 21 Europeans
lost their lives. Within a week all British newspapers had
dropped the matter—having given the impression that
it had been " labour trouble " mismanaged. A Report
came out three months later suggesting the Secret
Societies had been at the root of the matter, setting off
the first police desertions, violence and use of firearms.

We knew then and we know now that never in the
history of this colony has there been less contact with the
up-country African. This is not the fault of the D.O.'s.
They are now little more than glorified town clerks, overwhelmed with paper. But when there is talk of secret
societies creating riots the old sweats can't help harping
on Richardson—the D.O. who went through *prakka*, the
tattooing and initiation rite of the Kuru, in about 1908,
kept the oath of secrecy all his life but clearly wouldn't
have been caught unprepared by Kurus going berserk
under his nose.

Yes, we do feel isolated and you often hear people say,
" The people at home couldn't care less "—which is of
course an understatement.

In the mess the only reference ever made to " last
year " is done in the form of a joke: " I say, old boy,
have you heard: two guards have disappeared with
their rifles? " For this remark was the intro to " last
year "; one of the security officers had come in, one
ordinary evening, when there wasn't a cloud in the
security sky and said, " Two of my chaps have eloped
with their rifles."

Picnic at Porokorro

This joke was also the nearest anyone ever got to talking directly of diamonds. It was one of the few utterances which suggested the Mess was not a Thames country club, 1938.

Usually club conversation consists of talking in some other voice than your own—in the voice of a Goon or the comedian of the moment, or in aping a fruity public-school "old-boy" voice, the burlesque of a burlesque—yet still not *entirely* put on—as though the last identity desired died hard, survived real in mimicry, feeling itself intestate and without heirs; and at any rate preferable to quarrelling.

*   *   *

The arrival of a reporter from the Daily ———— might have been the last straw for Barber. But he had humour—and if ever this day became a joke, the sort of joke he told at length, with a full score for all voices, then he looked forward to rendering this particular moment when, carrying a cable which asked him to check on the number of asbestos pipe-lengths sold at half-price to a Syrian dealer last January, he found himself confronted by an odd incarnation of the Daily ————, sitting like a slim poisonous dinner in front of a hungry bulldog, Dickson.

But he kept Warner in a wry, refulgent welcoming tough smile, with mouth kept astringently still, and wrested without any kind of by your leave, the whole business of press relations from his hungry-looking colleague.

A by-your-leave to Dickson would have turned things formal—and this he didn't want.

Since his invitation to stay had turned Warner dumb,

he said, " What are you going to do to us—or can't you
say? "

Warner said, " That depends. I hear there's trouble
here."

" But there's always trouble here."

" Good." Warner was rattled by the freedom and by
being outnumbered, too. He did not enjoy saying anything, in front of Dickson, which sounded so punctured
as " Good."

Barber said, " Did you let us know you were coming?
Have we bogged it? Where are you going to sleep?
There are no hotels here . . . got camp kit? "

" No."

" D'you want to be put up? "

" I'll find something."

" But you won't. So I'm offering you a bed."

Warner stared. He was like somebody keeping his
balance in a crazily rocking boat. " Good, I'll take it,"
he said.

Barber smiled at him with a sort of calm friendly
pugnacity.

At last Warner said, " Thanks. And can I get to
Porokotto."

" You won't be popular at Porokorro—if that's where
you mean—to-day."

" I'm never popular." He had blenched slightly at the
name being wrong.

" Then you'll have to walk; forty miles."

" It's nice to know."

There was a futile silence, while Barber as so often
simply smiled, refusing to let people quarrel.

" Mr. Warner, we can help; we want to help. But
everything's a bit confused. There's a pudding already
—without extra bods on the ground. If you could just

34

wait. Till to-morrow. We'll take you everywhere. You've got no competition here. Play golf? "

Dickson said, " Anyhow I thought you wanted to go to Sangoro."

Warner turned from golf, which he had heard of, to Dickson, and said, " Is that in bounds? "

The phrase " in bounds " was perhaps intended to provoke, but he can have little idea to what extent he succeeded.

(Some of the wives talk of going " on parole " when they go to Sangoro.)

Dickson looked as though Warner had spat.

There was silence while Barber studied him, saying at last, " We live in a prison, do we? "

" You said it."

Some people would say Barber now did his " personality act " though I think that is unjust. I don't think he ever knew just how conspicuously intensely man-to-man he became—with his blue eyes eating into you second after second. " How about a beer? " he said quietly. " Meet you in the mess. OK? "

Dickson stirred eloquently and turned away to his work. Warner accepted.

Barber showed him the mess building from a window. " I'll be right down," he said.

Warner looked frail on his feet, indifferent and conspicuous. He went out awkwardly.

Dickson said, " The Jackals are coming."

Barber said, " Why? Bloody good paper, the ————.''

" Bloody good! . . . We could send him back."

" We could."

Barber turned to his desk.

Dickson pursued him: " I'd get a check on him if I were you. Anybody could walk in here and say ' I'm

35

from the Daily ————.' How did he get wind of this?"

Barber did not speculate. He had greeted Warner lightly, but now he looked at his desk for a moment as though Warner and it had won. With Dickson's help. He said, "They want this stuff about asbestos pipes. They know what's happening here but those choose this morning. . . . Could you cope?"

Then he said, "I'll have to see this chap."

Dickson said, "No comment."

Barber looked at Dickson bluntly, for now he had to carry out yet another trespass into his province, without quarrelling. "And Scott," he said. "Ian Scott. Wouldn't this be an ideal opportunity to shift him?"

"Home?" Dickson said.

"George Gordon said he'd take him when he needed another pair of feet."

"He's got feet, has he?"

Barber tried to humour Dickson, tried to agree with him enough to get a little leeway. He smiled almost obediently and said, "He hasn't stopped many runaway horses, has he . . . I know! He's your pigeon, Dick. Do what you like. I just thought he might cost you a six months special medical treatment if you leave him where he is."

Without a word of agreement Dickson at last signified that he would co-operate with this further subtlety in the general waltz of British insanity by catering for Scott's social sensibility, as though it could have a bearing on a balance sheet or anything else either, and to-day of all days.

He wrote a fast note, which Barber did not seem to notice till he said, "Thanks, Dick," without looking up.

4

AT TEN A.M. on Friday Ian Scott must have been the only European in the camp who still had not learnt of the trouble at Porokorro.

He was our Old Etonian. If a visitor from one of the sister mines said " Who's that chap? " then most people replied, " That's the Old Etonian." Or " He's an Honourable and an Old Etonian," as though he was half holy. I mention this because it tells you something about the camp.

Scott worked in the separating house, the last stage of the extracting process. There the finest gravel containing the diamonds, is sluiced over greased slopes on which the diamonds stick and the gravel doesn't.

When the stream is stopped you are left with the three black banks of grease, starred all over with diamonds. An African kneels down in nothing but a pair of pocket-less shorts and with a wooden implement removes the grease, diamonds and all, and scrapes it off on to the edge of a tin. Following him step for step, eight hours a day, there must always be a European; Scott.

Naturally " the House," as it is called, is a place of great responsibility. The two Europeans who work in it have to be not merely " above suspicion " (we are all that), but something more, something monk-like.

Brown, who grades the diamonds after they've been boiled and sieved out of the grease, is skilled. Scott isn't.

37

Picnic at Porokorro

The House is wired in with the kind of wire which in zoos is used to insulate animals you mustn't feed, and there are security guards all round it. The few Africans who work inside must strip naked before going in or out; and this meant that while Scott followed the slopes to the bottom there was usually a naked man, near enough to smell, standing in front of an African guard who searched his mouth, anus and the seams of skimpy shorts with the bullying ostentatious slowness which African officials, high and low, delight in.

*   *   *

The noise of the pumps and the mechanical sifting trays seldom lets up and is loud enough to make speech a considerable effort. Brown seldom speaks. He has twice in the last ten years been away for " a rest." He sees and touches enough diamonds to buy a Rolls daily, but must by now have broken himself into regarding them as just grit.

None of us know much about him—except that he once bred Dalmatians in Holland. He is sallow from lack of direct light. People think he's deaf but it isn't true: he's simply not interested. He never comes to the mess. After Meyer he is the person who could most easily store up thousands against old age if only he practised extreme moderation.

No one had yet succeeded in quarrelling with him, even in bedlam and 100 degrees of heat, and that is the reason, I think, why Scott was originally sent to him.

Although bowed over his stones, Brown always knew when a stranger had come into the House. He would look sharply up, take in the identity of the visitor, and then go on with his work so as not to waste the time it took the new-comer to cross the floor and climb the little

dais where he worked. Only if the visitor were very
senior he put his ear in a hearing position, before the
man arrived.

Scott, on the other hand, never noticed if someone came
in even though the opening of the door affected the
temperature of the air and altered the resonance of the
machinery. But then he also often didn't notice when
the African scraper, on the ground in front of him,
reached the end of a bank and was waiting for him, the
European, to take the tin out of his hands.

So when Jepson-Snailes came in with the note from
Dickson—for Scott—Brown glanced up like a card-
sharper and then went on grading, and Scott, unconscious
of new company, continued to retreat step by step with
his head set in the angle of vigilance but his eyes sometimes floating inwards like a person listening to a long
dull speech.

Jepson-Snailes had a huge amber scar down one cheek.
He got it in a Gold Coast (as it then was) sister mine—
from a Licensed Digger. Only a year ago. He had come
to us straight from hospital and the UK, without taking
any leave, reaching us on the Wednesday, only two days
before the trouble started.

Brown hadn't seen him for five years. He looked up
and said urgently, " All right again, old man? " as
though he had been absent five minutes having just
pinched his finger in the door. The inquiry was not
unsympathetic—merely urgent, welcoming the end of an
interruption.

Jepson-Snailes shouted, " I'm coming in here with
you."

Brown said, " Good show, old man—what's this? "
and he took the envelope as though it were an enemy.
" Y'know I haven't got time to play at this sort of thing."

He meant reading which he now did with passionate and resentful care. "Oh—hey!" he said thankfully, "This is for young Scott—give it to him . . . that's right then . . . that's right."

Jepson-Snailes had met Scott in the mess. He handed the note as though he had been presumed upon and turned away. Scott began to open it and then remembered the fleet brown hands darting out beside his feet. He nursed the note backwards till the end of the bank. Then he read:

Dear Scott,

I understand Mr. Gordon has room for you in Security. Jepson-Snailes will take your place in the Sep. House.

Please report to the Security office straight away. You're expected there this morning.

R. E. Dickson

The brevity made Scott's eyes glitter. Two banks still to go, but he turned round and looked at Brown, who, with Jepson-Snailes, was stooped as usual, sorting like a squirrel. There was no reason why either should ever look up, judging by their positions. The noise of machinery ruled out shouting. So against all regulations Scott walked over holding the tin of mixed grease and diamonds, leaving the African by the next bank. Twice he looked over his shoulder and pretended to look at other things besides the scraper, who grinned amiably the second time.

" I say! What's up? " Brown said reproachfully.

" I'm frightfully sorry, but I've got to go." Scott showed the letter. "Jepson-Snailes will be taking over from me."

Jepson-Snailes, after a glance at the deserted bank of

diamonds, returned his gaze to the stones on the table as though Scott had never spoken.

"Well. . . . Good-bye, Mr. Brown," Scott said.

"Oh! Well, good-bye, old man, all the best. See you around."

And Scott went—as he did go from things.

At the door he had to pass close to two superbly muscled, naked Kuru who were waiting to get their shorts back from a guard.

Search, this morning, was unusually ostentatious, for the guards, unlike Scott, knew there was "trouble."

As Scott approached one of the Kuru was told to bend over. The man's body tightened in a reflex reaction as the search was consummated. Scott smelt excrement.

*   *   *

Scott had come to us, believe it or not, from the British Council and it was said he'd had another job before that. He was the younger son of some earl who had big diamond interests. This made sense. Only contacts in the stratosphere could account for his radical but easy switches in employment.

He was tall, boney and almost laughably good-looking —like an Italian male model for evening dress. His expression was of morbid gentility—and even morbid gentleness. A sweetness gone bad—how bad was seen in his eyes which brooded as though he had just been insulted and could only save himself from answering with bitter self-control. His speech was slow, whispy and sometimes faltered as though he were trying to remember the point. I believe he was analysed after the war by a fashionable Freudian in the West End. Before that he had wanted to be a missionary but his father had stopped him—one imagined for Edwardian reasons of social

41

prestige. The Freudian finally put paid to the vocation and had probably been responsible—in a nebulous way —for Scott's marriage, which was sudden and to a typist in the British Council. This, as a social liaison, fell so much below the father's hopes, further even than holy orders, that he fell ill and wouldn't go to the registry office or see the girl. Since then Ian had wandered, mainly abroad, perhaps with every excuse for being " a mixed up kid." To crown all I learnt from a friend of theirs that Ian's wife sometimes said openly, in front of strangers, that she had married Ian for his money, only to find he hadn't got any and never would have any. I doubt if she wholly meant it—but the bemused look which came into his idealistic face when she " twigged " him (as she called it) was terrible to see. She aggravated it by taking his ear and, swaying his head back and forth, saying fast, " Poor, poor Bunny—it's lucky I love you —isn't it—isn't it—well, isn't it ? " and at last he would say—and this was the most terrible moment of all, " Yes " gratefully and bend his big head nearer her, even though her tones had not been conventionally those of love.

The mining job had been got for him after he had quarrelled with his British Council boss in Barcelona (over the use of the non-Spanish lavatory. The quarrel was conducted in heroic couplets by letter, although the two men worked in the same room). He had come to us expecting that the word " executive" meant something different from supervising, year in year out, a black man scraping off " *graisse praliné de diamants* "—as he once described it. Couldn't anybody do that, he said innocently to Barber after he " had marched himself in." Barber was silent and after a time said, " Apparently not." Then, " It's a position of trust. Perhaps you should cling to it."

Scott had flushed. Barber knew people in London whom Scott knew, yet in the mess paid no attention to him.

Scott had been careful to march himself in· when Dickson was on leave. He stood before Barber looking shocked, betrayed; he lingered.

" Well, is it for ever? " he said and a sort of febrile irritation meant to be desperate dignity crept into his voice. He understood, so to speak, a token period of six weeks " in the ranks."

Barber said, " It's a bloody job—is that it? " and smiled at him almost " on the old-boy net "—in the manner which he was so quick to adopt with people of a very different social milieu.

Scott relaxed at once, gratefully. He laughed a sort of glad social, snort-laugh. " Well, it *is* rather bloody." Now they were getting somewhere: *entre nous.*

Barber, still smiling, said, " Well—why did you come into it? " Scott was mentally winded. He just stood. Then Barber said people had to go where they fitted; there was "no margin to play about in—is there? . . . I think you'll find there isn't now—anywhere. And if there is there probably shouldn't be—and won't be, much longer."

Scott stared and thought of the enormous play-life Barber was known to fit in: deep-sea fishing off Santa Barbara, air-trips to cricket matches and home for the last Test. He felt a desire to associate himself ex officio as it were with this man and his life and yet also somehow to despise him, he didn't quite know why. Barber gave him a blank liquid blue stare. Scott was beginning to go when Barber said suddenly, " Do you shoot? "

" Yes."

" Have you tried the pond by your bungalow? "

43

Picnic at Porokorro

" The pond ? "

" I got forty teal there one morning. Try an occasional flight. It'll take your mind off the graisse parline—what was it—*praliné*. . . ."

Scott had not supposed Barber even knew which bungalow he lived in. And he himself didn't know there was a pond anywhere near it.

He said, " Oh . . . really ? I might try it. Thank you."

The truth is he could not talk to anyone—even to Number One—except in a voice that sounded patronising even to the point of " understanding." It was there in his larynx and vocal chords like the fixed limited range of a primitive instrument.

I suspect Barber reacted to this tone more than he would have cared to admit. And so perhaps it is to his credit that he kept his eyes open for a place where Scott " could be used "; and now had found one at last in Security as soon as the trouble at Porokorro placed that branch under strain.

But was it a wise move ?

I shall never forget an incident which happened when Ian Scott first came to us, in 1955—a time when the evangelist Billy Graham was drawing bigger crowds than football in England.

Several of the younger executives were talking about this phenomenon in the mess—partly because someone's wife had witnessed it and partly because a copy of *Life* lay open on someone's knee. The usual points pro and con were being made: mass hysteria, genuine feeling, supply and demand, convertion skin-deep, exhibitionism, Billy Graham's healthy physique and exemplary life —all in the chatty trivial way which is more than half echoed from feature articles and casual conversation, perhaps with someone whose aunt had been to Wembley

44

and come back "transformed." Scott had contributed very little but I noticed he gradually leaned forward with his exquisite hands devoutly folded and his eyes, normally so soft and distressed, positively shining with pent-up emotion. I expected at any moment an outburst—one of those embarrassing high-pitched outbursts of a man to whom outbursts are foreign by nature.

But not a bit: his basilisk stare was for some spot on the table, between the beer mugs, and at last he spoke with the sort of wheezing quiet effort which is associated with a baser function. " I don't understand," he groaned and everyone stopped talking, partly because a display of real feeling even when incoherent is in itself an event in our society and commands attention, like the pyramids —by rarity and relative difference.

" What don't you understand, Ian? " someone said, nearly frivolous.

" I think . . . it's . . . awful . . . *awful* . . ." and he was clearly quite unable to say more even though driven in that direction from within. His face was clouded with real pain and his speechless plight gradually created a tiny disturbance—as though he lay there arched backwards in the throes of epilepsy, in danger of biting off his tongue. People stared at him in dumb surprise.

If people had known about the missionary zeal and the analyst I think their perplexity might have been not less but greater. For surely Ian Scott would have had us all believe he had put away childish things, God foremost, and could no longer get worked up about the finer shades of sincerity in religion.

" If he helps people . . ." someone said.

Scott said, " He *doesn't* help. . . ."

There was silence.

" OK, Ian . . . It's awful," someone allowed in an

agreeable tone. "But you don't want to cut the chap's nackers off, do you? He's not that bad."

Scott managed to smile as though he had caught himself for an instant through the eyes of others.

Someone said, "Billy Graham's just the religious version of U.S. spam—the label's on the outside, the ingredients are clearly marked and the stomach powder is included in the recipe, also two coupons to get another next year."

I remember then the way Scott laughed—his sudden unreal guffaw so completely at variance with his recent taut fumbling for even the smallest sound.

"That's it—canned," he shouted. "Well, that's what I meant: Its CANNED."

Was that what he had meant? I'm sure he didn't know, any more than the rest of us.

He finally knitted his fingers in the most relaxed and sacerdotal position and smiled at us with the fragile, tender graciousness which was his stock social smile. But I could never forget the intensity of his original expression, when he leant forward at the mention of Billy Graham.

Sometimes this huge beautiful creature—whose long hair in some extraordinary way was beginning to look like a wig—stared into the faces of people at the mess who called him Romeo (when they got tight) and heard, "You ought to be a TV announcer." Then I think he wondered if it were not all a bad dream from which he would wake . . . where? Behind some curtains moving like lungs in a slow breeze scented with wallflowers and stocks, and clicking gently with summer noises. That feeling of wholeness and belonging and of being who he was should somehow have continued . . . Dr. Speers, the analyst had always sat behind him . . . like something surfacing,

blank, blanker than the place from which it came.
Eyeless. . . .

Sometimes in the mess his speech came slower and
slower, his smile more elusive and less connected with
what was said to him and the little " Cheers " he uttered,
after a pause of taboo overcome, caricatured all those
other " cheers " which were joyless enough as it was.

He told me once that what he remembered most about
his analyst were his eyes—or where his eyes should have
been. He said the man always wore glasses so thick you
couldn't see through them.

" I once had a dream that he took them off and then
I saw that he had no eyes, not even sockets." And he
laughed, adding, " But of course it wasn't a proper
dream. It wouldn't have counted."

*　　　*　　　*

He made his way over to Security as though already
responsible in a new, more serious and suitable
capacity.

He had memories—suddenly comfortable ones—of the
army where he had been an officer in the last month of
the war, and these were soon strengthened by the sight
of jeeps and trucks drawn up outside the Security Office.
There were even Guards loitering about in an orderly
way like men waiting for Company Orders. One group
contained a few diggers with a twist of dried grass round
their waists—the token which made them prisoners.

The scene was familiar. And so was the way Mr.
Gordon asked him to sit down.

Scott scarcely took the man in, so intent was he on
the fact that he, Scott, was joining Security.

" You were in the Grenadiers, weren't you? "

" Yes . . . as a matter of fact I was." '

Gordon was silent, letting the implications expand. His mouth was lifted with the hint of an accomplice's smile.

Scott approved the question—and the answer; the whole situation.

Gordon said, " Number One thought you might like a change of scenery."

" *I would.*"

Gordon had been up all night keeping in touch with the post at Porokorro. He had gone down there at dawn and brought Roberts back. Scott, he thought, probably knew the whole picture. So he merely said, " We've got a lot on our plate just now. . . . We could do with another cop. Are you game? "

" Yes—indeed. If . . . er . . . you're satisfied with my qualifications."

Gordon was silent. Then he said dryly, " The qualification is common sense." Then more agreeably he said, " The screw will be the same, I'm afraid. That's nothing to do with me—but you might find the work more interesting."

Scott was grateful for this language, and positively moved when Gordon added, " I'd go round the bend in a week in that Separating Hole. Or start stuffing my pockets."

He was moved because the handy worth and stealability of diamonds was suppressed so deep in the BMT that you could go a year without hearing a joke on these lines. It was therefore a mark of extreme trust—and also perhaps a social shibboleth—a secret sign exchanged. Gentlemen could utter it. Others would choke.

Ian laughed loud, he guffawed. He found tears in his eyes. It suddenly seemed to be months since anyone had spoken to him at all.

Gordon scarcely smiled. " We've got a show on at

48

present. You probably heard. Good moment to join. I think the thing to do would be to get down there with Roberts this evening. There might be some fun. All depends on the VIPs. Anyhow, go down with Roberts. He's flatfoot proper but he knows the form now better than anyone."

Oh it was a relief. That sophisticated, calm ironic face instead of the pale tortured sweat-gleaming urgence of Brown, grading stone after stone, silhouetted against the vast windows like grammar school windows. And there was " a show on". . . . He pretended he understood, had heard all about it.

He " fell out " and went to the mess—which was unfortunate

*   *   *

Ian Scott had often stood in messes alone in midmorning. The predicament was beginning to feel familiar. He stood with a cold beer, watched by an African polishing glasses.

But as a result of his interview he raised the beer in a practical, authoritative way and looked at his watch as though it chased him. He laid the glass down and the slight clank drew his own attention.

Things were better. Who, he wondered, should he ask about " the show." . . .

At this moment a stranger walked in with fancy sunglasses. He seated himself on one of the high bar stools and having ordered a drink said to Scott, " Well—what is it? Same again? "

" Oh. . . ." Scott got up as though shamed. " No," he said, " this is mine. You must have one on me." And he smiled with great gentleness and welcome.

Warner had no personality. Every crystallisation in

49   D

that direction had been upset. He had started as a son without parents; he had been trained as a culture executive—a don, failed the grade and become a reporter; he was lower middle-class but in adolescence had been poorer than working-class; he would have chosen to be proletarian but was soon debarred by education and (he imagined) physique. In fantasy he would have liked to be aristocratic but was debarred by birth . . . and " the time of day."

The only places he turned to without negative intensity were Poland and Yugoslavia—places where people like him, young yet without past, had power, and were perhaps forming a new élite, " without personality " if you like; places where Communism was OK.

Warner said, " Go on. Sit down. What is it? "

" Well, I mean. . . . You're a visitor, aren't you? "

" Two Carlsberg," Warner said to the barman and then looked round about him and at last at Scott's close clothing with as much licence as though the man were asleep.

" Have you . . . come to join us? " Scott's smile put the man at his ease.

" I'm a reporter."

Scott was shocked; he said " Oh " as though he had asked a man what was eating him, only to hear " Cancer." His smile died slowly of sheer penitence, and then revived desperately. " How extremely interesting. What paper? "

" *The Times.*"

Now he laughed for the second time that day as though reprieved; he guffawed. Now he mocked himself, admitting his first impulse had been to commiserate. The word " reporter " had been responsible. While his face was still radiant he said, " I thought you might have

been for the ————," and he said the name of
the man's paper.

Warner looked at him.

" What do *you* do ? "

Scott became immensely reserved. His eyes narrowed.
He folded his long-fingered beautiful hands on the bar
and there they made a little group which they both
looked at. A signet ring with crowned swan was upper-
most. Scott turned it slightly as though correcting an
imperfection. And he said softly and with a suggestion
of importance, " As a matter of fact, I'm somewhat in
the air at the moment—however . . ." He smiled gently
at his hands and then looked at Warner with responsible
reticence which asked to be let off, a little coy look of
charm and tantalisation. His eyes shone with simple
sincerity.

Warner said, " Careless talk costs lives ? "

Scott guffawed. Life was getting better: the lids were
coming off. " It is rather like that, isn't it ? " he said.
" No, I'm a ' cop.' A lay cop. But I have yet to see
really—what that means." And Scott roared with completely disassociated laughter again as confident of
universal approval as a child. " When I know I'll give
you some copy."

" Christ! And what was your last racket, if it's not
intruding ? "

Again Scott examined apparently a vistaed attentive
church beyond his folded hands. Suddenly serious, so
serious and trapped. " I've been working in the
Separating House."

" What's that ? "

" It's part of the diamond process."

" The mining of diamonds ? "

" Yes."

51

" What happens? "

" How? "

Pain crept into the large, exquisite face. " The supervision," he said evasively. " It's just the supervision of a
largely mechanical process. But I'm not—I'm not on
the technical side. They have Africans . . . and an
English engineer."

" You're Dutch, are you. Visiting? "

Now as though woken in the middle of a bad dream
the mothy, pitch-black eyes dwelt on Warner with that
occasional bitter gleam of which certainly Scott himself
was unconscious. The gentle rarefied voice tailed off into
a monosyllable which like that of a drunk had a sort of
metaphysical ring as though it asked the nature of God.

" What . . . ? " he said, and his brows lowered on
Warner.

" Christ! " Warner said. " No wonder there's wire
round this camp. The local population has a right to
insist."

After a silence Scott said very slowly, "I'm not sure I
understand."

" Brother, let me assure you: you don't."

I suppose it was as well that Barber came in at that
moment. The bar-boy had prepared the book (no money
transaction is allowed) and was holding it in front of
Scott and Warner. Barber took it out of his hands.

" You're not allowed to do this," he said.

" But *I* am . . ." Scott said.

Barber, signing, said off-hand, " I hear you're a cop
now, Ian." Scott was framing a reply which would do
justice when Barber picked up his beer and said, " Shall
we go over there? "

Warner followed but Scott did not. As they began to
move he looked at his watch and murmured something

about " getting on." When he went through the door Barber was opening a window with violence. " They think we smell," he said, " yet they never open a window."

*   *   *

" *The Times!* " Scott felt slightly sick and faint as he went through the flowery bushes. He took the *Telegraph* but he had heard someone say, now he came to think of it, " Auntie Times is wearing quite a Red petticoat since the war." The report of the Midszenty trial . . . Duff Cooper had spoken out.

Well—no wonder, if that was one of their Foreign Correspondents.

He felt seared, shocked. *The Times* . . . ?

" Darling," Penny sang, " you *are* a pale old thing."

His brows knit as he concentrated and remembered. " I've got rather good news."

" It *must* be good. You're trembling, Bunny. Are we posted Home—are we? *Are* we . . . I *don't* believe it . . ."

She held him by the upper arms and stared into his handsome face as though together they were posing for an advertisement. Caption: Happily Married.

And she kept repeating, " Are we posted home? " knowing well that he did not want to go home, since such a posting would amount to another change of employment, another failure.

" Are we really . . . I *don't* believe it."

She was giving him pain, on purpose, just a little.

" No, darling," he murmured graciously, while his tender, too tender eyes glittered away from her, with a kind of objectless hatred—as though too proud to include his chosen wife in the emotion she provoked.

" Then," she said, " before you tell me the good news, tell me: is the riot bad? Should I hide my ring? "

53

" The *riot* . . ." he murmured.

Then he laughed, guffawed and generally got his own back. At last he said gently, " No, darling—there's no need to hide your ring. There's no riot. Just a little trouble."

" What sort ? "

" Hardly anything."

And he turned away with a sudden twinge, realising that he had forgotten to find out.

"What have they been telling you," he asked indifferently.

5

TRIALS BY ordeal in African tribes are often preceded by long harangues. The witch doctor, exhorting the fire, the boiling oil or the poison to punish the accused if he is guilty, makes much of the concern of relatives, compatriots and even dead ancestors; he dwells on how they are all watching, all interested—until of course the boiling oil or poison either mesmerises the accused to a fatal agreeing apathy or stimulates him to a keyed-up physical state of contradiction, goading his muscles to react in the way which will save him—by vomiting, exuding a glandular secretion—or darting a hand like a snake striking, too fast to burn.

Even the detribalised African is prone to such suggestion, and carries within him the huge load of the collective conscience. If he does succeed in hardening his heart he becomes a much more obvious berserk devil than his European counterpart. But usually he does not succeed. More likely his heart will break.

When this conscience and yearning gets transferred to Christ, the upheaval in the individual can be total. Such an event was the birth of the Negro Spiritual and hence of Jazz; and the reason for the many negro " Messiahs " who so " got the point " they cried out aloud, imitating Christ.

When an African heart does break from guilt, exile or any dejection no one can find a piece big enough to start the business of reconstruction. It has to grow again out of nothing, absolutely nothing, and while that is happening the man can lie as though dead and is useless as an employee, as many whites have found.

On the morning in question this was the state of Security Guard John-Jesus Amanda, a product of the Late Methodist missioner Craig, who sowed real Christians in the colony like land-mines, with his torrential preaching and at last desperate example.

Amanda had refused to leave his bed when ordered and since Lieutenant Roberts wasn't there to decide what to do, the problem fell on the shoulders of Sergeant Kahn, who had long disliked Amanda for opting out of rackets which depended on unanimity.

He had an unpleasant bearded face, this sergeant, and had got Roberts his biggest bag when he shouted in the night "We got Sergeant Kahn—we got him quick quick." A crowd of illicit diggers then sprouted out of every patch of night and rushed exulting straight into the arms—and staves—of Roberts' men. Kahn cracked them over the head as they came . . . to finish him off.

The sun was well up but Amanda still lay curled on his mat, in the middle of piles of equipment, rations and the long peeled wands which were the normal weapons.

"Sick parade," Kahn shouted.

There was laughter. A table was set up and a bottle of Dettol and dead lizard put on it.

The cry created a diversion.

The men round about were in high spirits as they always were when there was promise of action. Most were Manga—a warrior tribe—who, before the whites came, had done a brisk trade in Kuru slaves. The whites had stopped that but instead had made them policemen and

given them an occasional outing like to-day with sticks
and tin-hats against the traditional prey—the painstaking
Kuru who made up half the total number of licensed
diggers.

They were disporting themselves, half self-consciously,
as physical élites are apt to do. But the game of soccer
with an old tennis ball was a mere apéritif of things to
come, and the cry and tone of " Sick Parade " at once
attracted several players.

A small group formed, laughing, round the figure who
hadn't made his bed up but still lay on it, dappled with
high sunlight. Others now came up and stared.

" John—Jesus," the sergeant called.

The figure on the bed made no move, and at the second
sound of his name turned away.

Suddenly from rage the sergeant turned the whole
incident with one sharp shout to duty.

" No. 4232 Security Guard John-Jesus Amanda. Step
for-ward."

The laughter stopped. Some men moved away from
before the sergeant.

" Come here. That is an ordah."

The penalties for refusing to obey an order on active
duty have still some archaic variants such as being tied
out in the sun. They are dead letters—but perhaps only
white custom prevents them from rising from the dead.
How thin that custom was in the sergeant everyone
knew.

The silence was long and filled with the eternal fluting
of the African forest.

At last Amanda got up in his denim trousers and,
holding them to him, came in front of the sergeant.

" Attention! "

He put his hands down, managing still to clamp his

trousers to his side. He was not Manga but from the coast.

" You sick man? "

Amanda said nothing.

" You no like police patrol? "

The man had sick, dreamy, inturned eyes.

" What's wrong with your tongue, man? "

A parrot phrase on African lips, learnt from some white man recently or perhaps long ago, often strikes a strange note like knocking a hollow wall. It reverberates and wakes harmonies in other African English phrases— in the ablest African editorials and political speeches. Have we sold them a house with dry rot and don't they know it? When I look into their eyes I often see a quick furtive parrotry at work—though perhaps behind that, something larger, both much better and much worse from which will be born their real future. The worse aspect is never more obvious—and unconsciously angry—than when they are most engaged in our kind of professional talk—litigation, military procedure, customs, drainage, etc. This sergeant now was a conflagration of just this anger as he took almost sensual pleasure in again rolling out Amanda's number.

" Four two three two eight nine Amandah! "

" Yes, sah. "

" Take two days special patrol duty at old site Poro-korro. Owing to present circumstance and man shortage you will occupy the post alone. "

There was a pause before the wretched figure answered.

" Yes, sah. "

I don't know much about Amanda. He had nearly gone to Santa Barbara university college. The others had amulets round their necks, he had a crucifix. The African alone in alien country can be the African dead. And here

58

the country was not only alien in the traditional metaphysical sense of vast unpropitiated forest, but also hostile in a concrete modern way: full of illicit diggers.

When a child is broken with sorrow the face makes no attempt to conceal the self-pity, but there's still hope; an African in sorrow looks at death and believes it. There can be no addition to his suffering.

So Amanda's face did not change.

He had already touched the bottom.

Why?

As he turned away he muttered, " I done one thing wrong," and he kept repeating this as he gathered his kit. " I done one thing wrong, I done one wrong thing."

6

THE SUN mounted, lost its sharp perimeter and became a glare. Round the BMT camp the tippers and plants clanked, creaked and crashed; bulldozers snored and gouged; lorries revved and clattered. Business would have seemed as usual had not the occasional white, meeting his own kind in the road, paused for talk.

* * *

Gordon, the Security Chief, came into Barber's office. He glanced at Dickson's empty chair and then at Number One.

When the door was shut they smiled at each other as though they shared an unspoken understanding about life in the BMT. Number One chucked down his pen in pleased surprise like a boy at school. Sometimes these two spent their first ten minutes bringing each other up to date on the latest activities or utterances of certain favourite characters—black as well as white.

Barber was a good mimic, but Gordon revealed his talent for human observation only here in the company of Barber. He did so coolly, sparingly and without comment, and partly, it seemed, out of polite emulation. These two, together, became very much British army officers who had secretly enjoyed the war and regimental life. In the BMT they had preserved, in use, certain capacities and attitudes which they could never have preserved in the post-1945 army. Here they had, and took for granted, the decent power they were brought up for.

Barber said thankfully, " George," and then, " Did you get my present? "

" Scott? "

" Yes."

Barber's eyes rested with tough relish on Gordon—and yet also with curiosity. He was tilting his chair back. It was the prefects' room. " I thought he might climb into the grease or something. You can give him some spuds to peel to-day, can't you? "

Barber now talked of Scott as though he were really in the forefront of his mind, though to his face he scarcely recognised him.

" He'll do," Gordon said, with only slight interest.

" I'll get you a rise if he does. I get letters from Buckingham Palace about him written on a sort of shirt-front notepaper and signed Dorothea de Something."

Gordon smiled non-committally.

" I've had one made into a collar."

Gordon remained silent, almost smiling to be polite. Then he said, " Have you seen La Meyer? "

Barber got up in glee. " D'you know who she reminds me of? Come-and-fetch-it."

Even now, in mid-gag, Barber gauged Gordon's face curiously and seriously. Why had he come?

After a vacant moment Gordon smiled. It was years since he had heard that name or thought of its bearer: the girl who did the coffee at the Pirbright Mess—where he had first met Barber—on a course for the Boys' Anti-tank rifle, sixteen years ago.

" Come-and-fetch-it," he said.

" We 'ave 'ere the Boys' Anti-Tank Rifle. It is easily

er—air-cooled becorse, 'aving fired one round, you f——'in won't fancy firin' another."

1940. The mood collapsed as though they themselves suddenly felt it an act, too far-fetched by half.

Gordon suddenly broached business apologetically, with awkward seriousness. "Where are your VIPs, Tom?" He was older than Barber and had once been his C.O. though never in battle. He spoke Kuru and had been among the Licensed Diggers disguised as a Syrian. Four years ago he had killed two men who attacked him. He had done the sort of things Barber would have liked to have done.

But within the BMT Barber was in the clouds above him and soon might be out of sight. Barber's attempts to conceal—even *reverse*—this discrepancy were sometimes so excessive as to embarrass Gordon. The Come-and-fetch-its and gags were unnecessary. Gordon wished Barber good luck, but sometimes with a cool ironic smile, yes, with a sort of smile that got home—without meaning to.

Barber sat down, flung himself down, feet elaborately out. He was now humble, deferring to his subordinate former C.O., whose job he often said he "envied like hell." And he said quietly, confidently, "They're on their way. And the press is here. Daily ———."

Gordon laughed, honestly.

Number One said, "I don't know quite what to make of him. Red as a baboon's arse, I think."

"You mean as a white Managerial arse with prickly heat. But what else would you expect?

"John . . . What have you got for me? Something—I know," and Barber's blue eyes, wide and sensuous as a tree lizard's, bore swiftly, certainly on Gordon's, who smiled for a moment before saying simply, "Yes, I have.

Picnic at Porokorro

Three of the Nungoro guards have disappeared—with their rifles." And a moment later as if in answer to Number One's thoughts, he added, " We've kept some down there—since last year."

The noise of the tips and bulldozers dominated the room as though it had suddenly became empty.

At last Barber said, " Rifles! "

He washed his face, as it were, with one hand, crushing the skin downwards from his forehead till finally he looked over his cupped chin.

He said, " You saw Roberts? "

Gordon's affirmative went without saying. His eyes refused to change the subject but remained fixed on the rifles, on Nungoro . . . on Barber.

There was a hint now on his face of that fastidious irony with which he sometimes congratulated Barber on his ever greater successes within the BMT. He added coolly, " Nungoro is ten miles from Porokorro." He was quite unperturbed.

Both these men now knew well that the situation was getting more and more like " last year "—but both of them knew, too, that in the last ten months there had been other episodes which had never reached the newspapers or even the BMT mess, which were identical with the early stages of " last year." ·

" Any details? "

Gordon said reluctantly, " I think one of them fought for two days on the wrong side—last year. But it was never proved. The witnesses never turned up."

" But you kept him on." Weariness sometimes made Number One sound sarcastic.

Gordon said, " If we believed every accusation there would be no BMT Guards."

" I know . . . I know. . . ."

After a few moments' silence Gordon said, so easily as
to sound almost frivolous and thus, in the circumstances,
sadistic, " Why worry? Government made this bed: let
them lie in it. When they started Native Diggers' Licences
in 1947 a fourteen-year-old moron could have predicted
to-day's situation. Probably they thought of it themselves,
but they didn't think of preparing a solution. Why? "

He answered his question cuttingly: " Partly because
the two solutions are simply unmentionable. Withdraw
the licences—or the BMT." Into his voice there had
crept the suggestion of ironic challenge and he smiled
faintly at his superior.

Barber suddenly said, " In fact they're bloody good
chaps, the licensed diggers. I know them. They kill
themselves in those holes. . . ."

" Kill is correct."

" I don't really agree with your either/or business."

Gordon was agreeable. Barber said vehemently, " All
we need is adequate police and less woolliness. The diggers
are tough. They respect toughness—and decency. Facts.
Tell the diggers the facts and give the law some muscle.
Roberts can't be expected to be *decently tough* with a
handful of Kuru boys with sticks. Government wants
waking up. The thing is they don't *know the form*."

" Can't you show them the form? " Gordon ventured,
on another tack.

After this remark I think now that both of them must
have been thinking very different things.

Gordon said, " It's rather odd that since the Native
Company was formed the activities of illicit diggers in
this area have just about doubled."

Barber said nothing.

" When the Native mine starts up—will *it* have trouble
with licensed diggers? "

64

" I should think twice as much," Barber said. " Until Independence. Then the laws may change."

There was silence again.

Gordon said. " What are you going to tell the top brass? " It was clear that even when recording BMT history he had, in his own mind, never left the subject of the rifles.

Barber said, " This: mining fresh ground we average one carat per cubic yard; mining ground that has been dug over by illicit diggers—for instance at Mglongo— we averaged half a carat per cubic yard—*at twice the cost.*"

" I mean about the rifles," Gordon said.

But Barber continued, " In other words, Government ought logically to be prepared to spend on police anything under a quarter of what they took from us in profits tax two years ago, before illicit digging started. That is, up to five million pounds per annum."

"At present the Government security bill for the whole colony, £200,000, is only twice what ours is for this mine."

" Does Britain or does Britain not want 5 m.p.a."

" Could the whole thing be put more simply? Yet trust them to consider appointing a Commission. Anything to pass the baby, procrastinate—call a spade a trowel . . . Buy time to-day with to-morrow's money."

There was the noise of a plane.

" Pip, Squeak and Wilfred," Barber said. Then casually, " Have you reported the loss of the rifles to the police? "

Gordon was surprised into a moment's silence. Then he said, " I did a short report. It's being typed now."

" Well leave it for the moment. Sit on it. They may have gone duck-shooting." And he added, " They

wouldn't hit anything if they did let fly—would they? "
He smiled and added " Duck . . . or anything else."

Gordon was silent for a second and then smiled with
that air of remote sophistication and experience—an air
which I think none of us grudged him. And he said,
" Probably not."

It was Barber s turn to be silent. His eyes lowered to
the table.

There was no sound except for the rasping note of the
Piper Cub.

Gordon stared curiously. At last he said, " Whatever
you say."

There was an uneasy moment in which Gordon made
no move to go. Barber's face could scarcely have been
believed to have been the recent mask of a sergeant
instructor on the Boys' Anti-tank rifle or of a subaltern
wanting Come-and-Fetch-it as well as a whisky; nor
that of a man in the presence of a great friend. Now he
looked like Brother Barber, an old ascetic who had never
had an intimate; only a private achievement.

" We don't want a flap," he said.

The noise of the aero-engine became loud as it banked.
Gordon said, " Then . . . is that all? "

The question echoed, seemed to roar as though the
acoustics of the room had suddenly yawned. But it was
something to do with the aero-engine above.

" G'bye, George."

Barber raised his eyes and for a moment caught those
of Gordon. His expression conceded something remote,
private, for Gordon alone.

Gordon did not respond. He nodded deferentially—
a kind if salute—and went out.

7

EVEN DURING a crisis we remain a very ordinary-looking lot at the BMT.

I think of us at our most typical playing cricket on Saturdays during the dry season, when the grass is bleached. There we sit waiting our turn to bat, under a palm leaf shelter with rather blank, uniform expressions, all wearing white linen, watching the efforts of our two representatives at the wicket.

The light is so intense that even sunburnt faces have, like the grass, a white withered look; and our women are as white-powdered as scones, against sweat. The whole effect is of a party grouped for security, under a howdah, on a raft, suddenly consoled with a mirage of cricket. The faces are set in that moving inanity and umbilical rootedness which Pont used to catch in his cartoons.

It is half past three. Perhaps the banker from Bunandu is bowling . . . the clapping comes now and then like the desultory creaking of the old clock before it strikes. Soon the lemonade will come and, when it is cooler, a few children.

There is one person among us, however, whose face always seems to me to reflect our predicament, even when he's watching cricket. William Meyer. He is a Pole who has lost everything—the friends of his youth,

67

his family, his home and property, his nationality and, on the day in question, was said to be losing his British wife and so probably his child, too.

He is a buyer for one of the big marketing organisations and as such hasn't got a house *inside* the wire—but outside. He deals entirely with the Licensed Diggers but has undertakings with Government and with the BMT only to buy and sell at a certain limited profit. He really has no protection except goodwill. His house actually touches our perimeter wire and yet he, I know, wouldn't mind being a hundred miles away, even when his safe is full of diamonds. But it wasn't he who selected the site.

Some people find it hard to account for Meyer's popularity with the BMT and the whites in general; with the blacks it is understandable enough, for he gives them good prices and regards the diamonds as African gravel —theirs if anybody's.

He is rather a death's-head to look at: very tall, pale, black-eyed, beak-nosed with huge, high salient cheek-bones and eyes that are an odd mixture of main-chance acumen and metaphysical despair. The slowness of his speech is merely due to his eternal act of memory with a language learnt late in life but it gives the impression of great prudence, and sometimes since he is so often right about Africans, of second sight. He stoops slightly, too, as though looking into a crystal, perhaps of his own past suffering (he was in Buchenwald), or perhaps simply to be geographically on the same level as other people. I have heard him called Jew, gipsy and aristocrat and it's possible he might have been all three.

You would have thought he was too " foreign," anarchic and pessimistic to be liked in the BMT. Our pilot once said of him, " The chap seems sometimes to have forgotten his scythe and hour-glass." But he said it amiably, even respectfully. And that's what's so strange.

Perhaps the thought of him soothed whites with property—as though he had survived an operation any of us might have to undergo; or perhaps we liked him unconsciously because of his peculiar relationship to diamonds.

He buys direct from the licensed diggers but takes thumbprints or "marks" as receipts. He himself is an expert valuer; he buys from the ignorant. He could collect gem stones like pebbles and yet we would all of us, I think, bet our last shirt that he has never rendered anything but a true account to his employers.

I've seen him squat beside a digger, over the ankles in mud, and go through a sieve-full of gravel saying in his Charles Boyer screen-lover's sad, sensuous voice, " Com—I bring you luck."

And then he is unique, too, in possessing a private car, which wags have said is why he looks so melancholy, there being nowhere to go in it.

Some of the women last year worked out that he was " really a prince " and I believe his beautiful morose face was often the talk of the wives who imagine themselves making him happy and replacing Mrs. Meyer—Isobel— a mysterious figure who provoked speculation and jealousy by living, it was said, in the West End—" with the child "—in any kind of sin that came to hand, but who, the week before the trouble, had electrified camp conversation by arriving unexpectedly at Meyer's bungalow " without the child " and four pigskin ward-robes with handles which she called her " suitcases "— thereby provoking more disapproval, guesses and jealousy than ever before. She had come, it was decided, on business: i.e. said the women—to get a divorce.

Picnic at Porokorro

But had she?

Of course, eyes ate her when she turned up for our Friday night dance (exactly a week before the trouble) in white satin and *shimmering with diamonds*. She had rosy radiant flesh and showed as much of it as possible. She had, you would have thought, " everything "—but her long black eyes had a hungry active look which fed upon people as though something ought to be happening that wasn't. She was so self-conscious she involved everyone else in being more conscious of her than they anyhow were. The result was she could not have got more attention had she come naked. But wasn't this what she wanted? Meyer looked very glum. Diamonds are almost never worn in the camp and no one knew which taboo to look at most—her flesh or the stones. She made a dead set at Number One—at Barber, who was nearly rude—probably because he had noticed the way in which she had looked round the room at the other wives, and because already he must have heard (as everyone had) what she said in the stores the day she arrived: " I'm going to see how long I can stand it "—" it " being obviously more us than the climate.

Curiosity didn't starve. It became known in the middle of the dance that she had once been proposed to by the King of Siam—perhaps fortunately, for it provided an alibi for the diamonds.

Then she disappeared, went home to bed—it was said —with a headache. But Meyer came back and drank and talked as usual, about other things.

*　　　*　　　*

On the morning of the trouble, when telegrams were flying in a crazy triangle to and from the BMT, Santa Barbara Residence and Whitehall—Meyer was driving

his Rover bleakly fast to get back to Isobel, who had
said she " would go mad and walk through the camp
naked " if he wasn't back by lunch. Such a threat from
any other woman might have been discounted, but you
never knew with Isobel.

He was then still ignorant of the trouble at Porokorro,
having been one night in the bush buying at Nanuma,
another Licensed Diggers zone.

His used, sensitive face showed no pleasant anticipation
as he drove.

Already the sun had drunk up the storm and the dust
rose from his back wheels in a boiling wake which showed
in the driving-mirror like the entrance to a vast dirty
tunnel.

When he saw the car in difficulties, with the African
feet sticking from under it, he braked sharply before asses-
sing the colour of the owner. A breakdown here can
be an ordeal and it is extraordinary how many " progressive " white people who would be furious at the
accusation of colour prejudice never stop when they see
an African car broken down (a fairly common sight)
but would rave if an African car gave them the go-by
when they were in trouble.

And the penalty for stopping is usually only to be
asked to take a message or to lift one person to the next
town.

In stopping Meyer did not even feel a pathfinder in
common-sense and mutual insurance. He felt no different
from what he always felt; he just stopped. The trust of
Africans was the spine of his job and he kept it, even in
his thoughts, naturally, without effort.

Now he looked backwards out of his window.

Memory, for Meyer, selects unaccountable, simple
vignettes for its filing system. A big place, a long period

or a complicated situation is found under a single seemingly haphazard, not very typical tableau which is at once complete to all the senses—so that the whole war could be a man looking over his shoulder at first light in a nest of soiled blankets; and a whole love affair a face on the stairs or the noise of an arriving car. But at the moment of the picture there is no presentiment that that particular moment has been selected as an essence of memory. Meyer did not know, as he looked through his window, that for the rest of his life he would remember the sight of his friend the Provincial Commissioner and his son by the roadside, even though (dressed as they were) the scene was strange enough, in that place, to be a candidate for eternal memory without the help of still unborn events.

In places unknown to Meyer—on the children's links at North Berwick or in some hotel near a Scottish private school, such a pair, so dressed and so equipped, would have fitted in. The blazers, the open shirts, the boy's butterfly net, the holiday complexions and the general air of the bored bread-winner getting away from wife and work in the direction of some sporting instinct, however, faded, and his own youth, would have made sense—and so of course would have been the almost belligerent Scottishness of the father's wind-scoured whisky cheeks, spectacled radical humorous eyes and electric grey hair which seemed to have shot up in horror at the world's "non-sense" and stayed there sustained paradoxically by the spirit of the kirk.

Here the compact little group struck the eye as the trade-mark of insanity—made more conspicuous, more touching to Meyer's deprived feelings by its obvious family-ness, in the best sense: the still half-telescoped continuity, big blazer into little blazer, and by the butterfly net—a sort of flag—of people who enjoyed life and could still go after something which had no bearing on their pay or power.

But why here—in the dust and dereliction of gouged-out swamp and wayside grass furred over with red dust . . . ?

While MacPherson was walking forward, Meyer thought, against all appearances, " There is trouble at the mine."

The P.C. came up as though he couldn't believe his ill-luck turning to worse, in the shape of William Meyer.

" William Meyer! " he said grudgingly, and his eye, straying to see what space there was, fell on the iron box in the back. " And his loot."

" Spot of trouble, Mac? "

English colloquialisms and nicknames sounded strange in Meyer's throaty accent. They were unsuited to his earnest personality, but he seemed to persist in all forms of camouflage out of an exaggerated sense of courtesy and indebtedness to his foster country.

" I'm wanting a lift to yer Eldorrado. That's what. And just as quick as you were going."

Mac was an unconventional Provincial Commissioner but even Meyer had never seen him. " I think you are hitch-hiking lost," he said, smiling.

" Ahm on holiday with ma boy," Macpherson said. " Paul—say howdydo to your fairy godmother, while I tell Jacko what's what."

The boy had an angel face. He was about eleven—the same age as Meyer's own child. He shook hands bluffly, smiling with sophisticated assurance—and got in as though land-rover backseats and all Africa were old favourites with him.

Then the father followed.

" Trouble ? " Meyer said.

" Well, where've *you* bin ? "

" Nanuma."

" Ai, *they* think there's trouble. The diggers have confiscated a policeman."

" A BMT guard or a policeman ? "

" A b—— BMT policeman."

" Roberts."

" Ai, Roberts," MacPherson said critically.

" He is not a bad boy."

" I bet he's a surprised one. ' Your ignorance find not, till it feels.' "

" Porokorro ? " Meyer said.

" The beauty spot of yer Eldorrado."

" My wife wanted me to take her there to-day ! "

" Well, take her. Take her to-day. Take your children too. To-day."

MacPherson was staring straight ahead. He went on: " One something hour more—and we'd've been out of reach. Up-river. Paul here and my old woman and me. Then the telegrams. ' Gladdest you cancel your leave . . .' —well, it's good somebody's glad, isn't it ? When I heard what the trouble was I said, ' Right—I'll take my leave in the trouble because that's what the trouble is: it's no trouble. It's a beauty spot plus a lot of youngsters in uniform playing at soldiers.'

" Meyer ! "

Meyer turned at the sharp utterance which seemed to come from a different person. He found a finger pointing at him.

" You're going to tell me something. Is there one policeman at Sangoro who speaks a word of a native language ? Right. Question two. Is there one of them has been here more than two years ? No. Question three.

74

Picnic at Porokorro

Is there one of them has ever done duty outside a dance hall and learnt tact removing drunks? No. They've come straight from service commission and the police college. They missed the war and they're out on their own—one of them got the M.B.E. last year, now the rest want one too. They couldn't remove my mother without making her violent."

"You've chosen a weak instance, Dad," said the boy.

"Oh God, pray for stupidity," he said quietly to Meyer, having lost his train of thought, "in yer offspring," and then to his son, "There's no fool like a clever fool."

Meyer smiled with sad pleasure.

"No, Meyer—seriously. Bring yer wife—and if she's got a good figure, let her bathe. Crocodiles are exaggerated. And if there's any other women and children in yer El-dorrado who're wanting out—then bring 'em along and have a picnic right in amongst the Licensed Diggers. Nan would be here if she hadn't her gynaecology class for witch-doctors. Though you can leave out "doctor." Just bloody Harley Street witches. They threw away the forceps she gave them because if their patients see government implements they refuse to pay. They think it's free from then on. Have I got to have lunch in clink?"

"You can come to us if you like."

"Is Mr. Tom Barber still there?"

"Yes."

"Tom! I'd better take lunch off him," and Mac-Pherson added in a reflective tone, "Mr. Tom Barber is very good at his job."

The Rover raced on while MacPherson sat sideways on to Meyer in an attitude which had affected carelessness but which had become rigid.

Meyer at last said, "And your son?"

75

" Will you take my devil for lunch? " MacPherson replied, as though he had suggested it.

He was controlling things. All details. Staring ahead. The rest of the journey was passed in a certain kind of silence. It was work. In spite of the butterfly net, the similar holidays shirts which father and son wore as conspicuously as flags, MacPherson looked keenly, intensely, even painfully ahead. Twice he did not answer when spoken to and once when Meyer spoke of the new Native-owned diamond company, he said, " I moved forty penniless thousand Mandingoes and Sudanese over the border—with five picked D.O.s—men just out of school—armed with walking sticks. I don't get it. God give me the grace to know when I'm getting old. You pipple in that Eldorrado merely make me feel young. In ma ruddy prime."

And then " William! I've not had the pleasure of meeting Mrs. Meyer—but she's coming to Porokorro. *And you are, too, d'ye hear!* No, seriously, William." MacPherson's eyes spoke while his tongue paused. . . . " Seriously—you'd be doon me a favour."

Meyer smiled, which annoyed MacPherson.

" I'm telling you something, Mr. William Meyer—it would do *you* a power of good."

They left it like that. At that time Meyer did not realise the invitation was serious. Very serious.

8

THE DAY of the bush telegraph has passed and the very phrase become white jargon; yet colony news still travels among Africans up-country at about the speed of sound.

By eleven o'clock the storekeepers, idlers and all kinds of wayfarers in Sangoro were looking at any car that contained Europeans with a little more interest than usual.

The Gulf, you might say, was more to the fore in African eyes. Events at Porokorro, of which no two reports were the same, were published in a broody, no longer ambivalent, stare.

Some whites went so far as to imagine it was " getting like last year," and " took precautions." The Swiss chemist and general storekeeper at Sangoro left for his holiday with his wife and children a week before he had planned. He left on the spur of the moment, I heard afterwards, with only half his luggage, and drove 200 miles—straight to Santa Barbara Air Hotel.

But this was exceptional. Mainly the place was much as usual that morning. Ugly, untidy and garish in spots like something diseased; full of people doing very little.

It has changed a lot since MacPherson first saw it forty years ago. The old nucleus of beehive huts has sprouted arms of tin-roofed shacks along the red, dusty road. Most of these sell beer and sardines and some have in front of them a crowd of recent British or American

77

cars with perhaps one wheel, a radiator, or some vital part missing. These were once owned by Diggers who found a few diamonds—and then no more.

The scene suggests a sudden end to the world's motor industry: what there was continued to roll—an ever diminishing number, surviving by cannibalism, until only one or two stood as now, pointing down remote, dusty roads; the rest being herded and stranded, chaotically, in that shabbiness which overtakes modern gloss, in an instant, as though it had been waiting.

Among the metal carcases naked children play while their mothers sit, each with her little " market " which by native custom she may exact from her husband . . . perhaps two shillings worth of cigarettes—in piles of three; beechnut pellets in twos, spread on a vast leaf; three beers and a brilliant bowl of rice. The mothers sit with their chewing sticks rolling in their gums, or smoking pipes all day—bright as parrots in colours from Manchester or Hong Kong, and sometimes as garrulous.

They, at least, didn't care about the rumours. Porokorro was man's palaver.

In front of one tin shack there were more disembowelled cars than anywhere else for hundreds of miles. Some of them still had running-in notices on them, or " Another Morris " in the back window. One wheelless land-rover bore the tattered ambiguous legend " Experience " and the shed itself the words " Tim Amadeus Amfookha, Cold Beer—Councillor—Stringer—Repairs. Consultations."

*   *   *

When the BMT Rover—trim as a military vehicle before a GOC inspection—drew up and dropped Warner, Mr. Amfookha, who was sitting on a tilted chair with a billiard cue between his legs, showed no sign of being impressed or even interested. And as Warner came towards him Mr. Amfookha angled his head and the field of his view to one side so that when Warner addressed him he was able to bring it back with a slightly affronted jerk.

It was an odd meeting. Detribalised black and detribalised white. . . .

Warner was thinking of Dickson and Scott; Amfookha of money.

When Herbert Warner went to get his present job he had a Second Class Honours Degree in English, that is to say no relevant credential except the way he came in, sat down and confronted the news editor, which was the same way as he had this morning confronted Dickson.

After a few exchanges the news editor, a cripple with eyes of almost dreamy tenacity, said, " So you wanted to be a professor," and his eyes mocked the youth; then he said, " What do people want to read about? "

Warner said, " Sex, money, food, drink, crime and rank."

There had been a silence during which the huge presses below drummed like a ship's engine and screw. Then the cripple said, " Your order's cock-eye. Where d'you live? "

" Number One, Nowhere."

" What cash have you got? "

" Two quid."

The editor threw three pennies on the table. " I'll increase it. Bring me a story before midnight."

I knew of that news editor. He himself probably did only once have three pennies. It was big talk, a man acting even to himself—but the act, apart from being symbolic in a small corny way (with which Warner had at once collaborated), also contained a certain hard sense: it obliged Warner to find something without any of the usual helps. The story he brought was not published, but it got him the job straight away on the big national daily, without a day's grind in the provinces. He started at 500 a year, plus expenses, or the " sauce," as they were. called.

He began now to speak but Mr. Amfookha seized the opportunity of interrupting him: " Well, what can I do for you, Mistah."

Warner held out a card—waiting all the time to be recognised as at least a friend. Amfookha read, conspicuously.

Warner said, " Christian Manders." He was thinking of Dickson and Scott, and how probably in years they had never entered an African dwelling.

" Wel-come" said Amfookha.

He got up and held back the bead curtain door of his house.

" Wel-come wel-come. Go in."

Warner went in. A woman vanished like a shadow from the back. There was oilcloth on dirty wood, flies, a pair of Victorian scales and a lot of tin advertisements —one of bathers in long bathing dresses, for Clacton-on-Sea, another of an air-liner whose propeller arcs spelt " Coca-Cola " and, in the middle of all, like an ants' egg in the midst of dusty twiggy dereliction, a huge fridge.

" Mr. Christian Manders, my friend," said Mr. Amfookha. " We help each other. When I go to the coast I stay with him. I am Ledge Co. candidate."

Mr. Amfookha made a considerable speech which Warner was only able to derail at a further mention of the name Manders.

Picnic at Porokorro

"Mr. Manders," Warner said, "thought you might have something for me . . . I'm . . ."

"Of course I help. You want anything, I have it. The election is in thri months. The Peoples Democratic Party—PDP work for thri things. I tell you what," and he extended three fingers, one of which he selected with the finger and thumb of his free hand.

Warner said, "Diamonds are my line. Diamonds . . . and murders. I'm . . ."

"I got no diamonds. Here is no diamonds. Porokorro —diamonds. I don't touch diamonds. I say take them away: I don't want to see them. Here I make the laws— I don't break them."

"I'm a journalist, Mr. Amfookha . . . and a friend."

"Journalist—which pay-pa. . . . Ah, from London! Will you take beer—or whisky?" and he shouted a voluble torrent into the back and was answered by a single gentle bleat on one note with a drop of a semitone at the end.

Warner leant forward and said, "Look . . . We're right behind you people. Now Mr. Manders said you had a story . . ."

"You want stories I give you murder stories, you want beer and I have it cold, you want a friend—I have guaranteed sister."

"You've got me taped, Mr. Amfookha," Warner said, as though he were in the reporters' room. He was getting impatient. Time might be short. He stared at the man as though at a lock.

"I got everything taped," and as though his words were at the moment on trial, Amfookha shouted even more imperatively into the back where he was answered by exactly the same noise.

"Then let's start with the murder," Warner said.

" Mr. Manders said just go ahead: ask him straight:
about the murder.

" Straight! Of coss. You come from Mr. Manders—
so I trust. I tell you white man murder. Ha ha—you
think I laugh. But I'm stringer for the Santa Barbara
Times. I string it already. African scoop."

" Frankly, I'm beginning to doubt it."

Mr. Amfookha leant forward. His eye-whites gleamed
and shifted fast.

" Was lawful arrest in any way implicated? Was the
admitted permission accessory after the fact? Could a
granted lack of aforethought invalidate manslaughter?
Thank you, thank you—oh no, well then, thank you
very much."

" I wasn't there so . . ."

" Oh no—then, thank you."

" So could you . . ."

" No—you were not. Well, here we are lawyers here,
politicians and Christians. I know you are in the dark
that is why I'm lending you a torch so you can set fire
to your pay-pah. There is no frid-dom in a prison however well administered. It is episodes of this kind . . ."

" *What* episode? "

" Ha ha. You say ' What episode? ' You want to
drink what you like drinking. But Councillor Amfookha
gives medicine. He tells you Episode BMT Murder.
Old man. I have eye-witness report. There will be a
question in the Grand Council. Right Honourable
Johnson will place it. Drink that, my friend."

Warner took off his sun-glasses. It was almost dark in
here.

It was the first time he had shown his eyes, indoors or
out. They were small gems of intensity.

His words sometimes had an almost laboured ordinari-

ness as though they were no part of him, having been
learnt from a book. But his eyes looked like eyes behind
a rifle.

Why, I wonder. What forces combined to put this
young man amongst us?

People often say " the future is uncertain " and " it is
hard to see what kind of world will emerge," etc., etc.
Many turn for comfort to the past and point to times
when attitudes and values were widely agreed on. I
suspect Warner remembered no such time—either in his
own life, or—except as schoolman's cant—in history. He
was several kinds of orphan. In the past there was the
present; and in the future, too, there would be the present.
For words like *moderation, stability, continuity, respect, self-
discipline, restraint and traditional values* you could pass the
basin. He knew close-up, that vocab of a racket by no
means dead, and as to the past he'd need an introduction
if possible from someone who knew it as well as he. All
he had ever known was the present, the naked present
and the reasons for it as plain as a bloody sum on the
one hand, and on the other phoney solutions, " wombs."
Because a man was *out*, wasn't he? Perhaps if masses,
everyone, everywhere dedicated themselves to this screaming admission of being out, his own mind would have an
anonymous relief, a catharsis. And he would be less
" out." They would all be *in*. Big, and in. He cried
He often cried suddenly like something unstrung, cried
and cried.

It is true, of course, that his definition of " phoney
solutions " and " wombs " was apt to be applied to
anything—not only material things but even feelings—
he hadn't got and had never had; but could you really
call such a comprehensive passion by the little word
envy? It was capable of religious leverages and if the

hateful figure of Christ arose he would leap into the grave of humanity, a political Hamlet, and say " Forty Thousand Christs with all their . . ." then, yes, then his tongue clove at the next word. He knew a discord and turned away weeping. And he switched: shouldn't we all take a course in hate before we start prating about " love."

Contradictions rose like murder in his breast until they reached in the name of relief the last satisfaction of the angry child—denying anything—anything offered; denying at last everything, even pity.

This—the out-denying of the denied was sometimes a lust with him—to the point of self-extinction; it sought power in amorphous anonymity in the masses, who would remove his cross of inferiority not only in its most obvious manifestation, class, but more his whole personality, his " background," his " culture," which he had been fed late as a possible trade, not born with and which was, yes if you had to use the word—his Cross, because impossible and yet desired. Perhaps even life was his Cross—for sometimes this unhappy youth longed, like his most hated philosopher Nietzsche, never to have been born.

Only drink balanced him and made him feel human. It was an obsession with him, almost a symbol.

But don't worry. Let no one worry. Put away the handkerchiefs. On top of all he was as cool, as rational as a machine and conducted his job like a surgeon. His face was impersonal, even bland and empty like a tailor's model. He'd settle for common sense. Only his eyes were private, and gemlike with the concentrated pressures of his chaotic unrevealed self.

*   *   *

" Mr. Amfookha," he said, " I'll buy your eye-witness report, and an introduction to the eye-witness, for ten quid."

His voice was slightly changed. He had not fully believed Manders. He leant forward, holding his fancy glasses like a bait.

Once in a while his job could be aligned with his bent. That was the pay-off for the other whiles.

Now he produced money—like waste-paper.

He dated the feel of a money wad in his pocket from the week after his feature on Palace Public Relations. The headline had been " Do We Smell " and the opening words, " Let's get this straight: who's yellow—the Press or the people who daren't meet it."

The way Warner now threw out the money—and then took some of it back—suggested a certain physical fascination for it. He had a *roll* of notes, an uncountable sheaf—and yet when he separated them into a few individuals he developed a suddenly almost sensual relationship to the feel of them, and became suddenly both bitterly reluctant to part with them and yet contemptuous of them. He even flicked the ones he was losing venomously with his finger-nail and fitted the ones he took back with care into the ball. He still had no bank. The office sent him letters about it. Sometimes I think he gave a whole bundle to someone he liked, who needed it—and then, truly grieving, recouped half on the next expense sheet. No one in the London office went too carefully into his expenses, even when they included such items as hiring an aeroplane. Provided he turned in the goods in the flat, racy, factual deflationary style chiselling accurately at the heart and ovaries of the approved Aunt Sallies—then that was OK. Up to a point, of course.

85

But he knew where the point lay: round about 30 per cent high, which when it came to air taxi would keep him in shirts.

Christ, he had company: money was now on the house. It was his kind of five per cent. Happy days. All in it together now. Even Amfookha—if he'd pull his finger out and know a friend when he saw one.

He patted the sheaf and said, " All yours. You tell me all you can: who kill old man, where and when, what time . . . eh?—what with? I give you plenty money."

" You want change? " Mr. Amfookha said unexpectedly. " You get tired carrying all that small coppa? "

" Come again? "

" You like bigger notes—£5 West African Currency. Omos? Say omos you want."

Warner smiled. " Stinking, eh? "

" Yeah—I got plenty stink. And I tell you all I can."

" OK. Let's have it."

" OK. I have it. I give you good report, full details. Here is my election address in which it is mentioned. ' Grievous rumour.' "

" Now look! "

Warner wanted it, he really wanted it. He tried. For an hour. Language sometimes took on the quality of a pot boiling: the sounds altered but said the same thing. Always at the last moment a name turned into a group, a place into an area, the date into a month and the detailed action into a blur in the dark which soon became a blur of language regaining its balance at last only in a legal peroration where the eighteenth century sound was so exactly right that Warner's mind chased the sense desperately, with a feeling of exasperated inadequacy.

At last Warner interrupted. " Oh, for Pete's sake.

You're not a kid. . . . Roberts, *Roberts* wasn't that the white policeman's name. . . .?"

A moment later he thought he understood. He had raised a mocking index-finger at Amfookha's face: a finger so naturally and genially mocking as to be the finger of an equal . . . Suddenly he caught a glance in which he saw himself focused as it were for the first time: the man who had arrived in the BMT jeep. A white, BMT, man.

" I forget the name, Mistah. Yes, sah. I forget."

Warner's finger fell.

" OK—I get it . . ." and he sighed the words out like a slow puncture: a final comment: " You win."

The beer was already equally distributed in the form of sweat all over his clothes. A silence outside told the time and the height of the sun. The face opposite became hateful—a piece which wouldn't fit; the language business impossible. What was this baby talk he heard the bosses use to them. Krio. He couldn't get the hang of it. Yet the Pongos got somewhere with it.

Amfookha sat watching him.

Warner lived off his tension. When it collapsed it left him a sudden ruin. The top spin of his conflicting passions had physical symptoms: heat in the head. Then probably certain glands packed up. He was left with a flatness which defied description and which took the form, if he was in company, of infantile selfishness and total sadness. His immediate necessity, however trivial— or large—became imperative and excluded every other consideration in the world.

" Oh F—— " he said.

The crisp notes had been working on Mr. Amfookha, though his hunger was really a habit, not a necessity.

One of his nostrils twitched slightly, for chicken-feed;
but it was still feed.

He leant forward. " I tell you what. I tell you name
of other eye-witness."

" Well—for crying out loud—what've we been asking
for? "

" Name of policeman . . . OK? "

" I could tell you the name of a policeman too—but
I wouldn't charge you a tanner."

" I—tell—you—name—of *nother policeman*." The fat
black man looked ominously into Warner's eyes.

" Go ahead."

" He's on duty Porokorro Ferry. One man. Wait.
I write his name."

" How do *you* know he's on duty at Porokorro? "

" I don't know. He may be. His wife my sister. My
boy take her rice to police lines. She says her husband
absent. OK? "

Mr. Amfookha wrote laboriously, with letter-by-letter
satisfaction. "Very good man. Mission boy. Never tell
a lie. John-Jesus."

" Sorry I couldn't give more than a quid for Jesus.
Here: one now—six later," and he took the piece of
paper. " I'd make it ten bob if I had change." He had
lost his temper—but there was no medium, no object for
his rage; just the heat, and those disconnected, rolling
eyeballs in the dark, and flies.

" Much trouble down there? " said the Councillor,
bowing the reduced fee into his pocket, as though he
didn't care.

" There are diamonds down there and white capitalists
and coloured men. Can you add? "

Amfookha laughed—so spontaneously he felt he might

have betrayed himself into other sincerities. He stopped and started again, laughing differently.

"Very good. Very good. Diamonds plenty trouble. I say to Father Jessup: Amfookha wish there were no diamonds."

Warner stood on the edge of the bright light putting on his glasses. "I remember a woman in furs who used to 'visit' me when I was a kid. She said diamonds started as tears. I forget just whose. And froze. She must have been perished."

"Ha ha. Good day, sah. Here is my card."

"Good day, Mr. Amfookha." He raised the other scrap of paper. "And now I turn unto Jesus—is that it?"

"Ha ha—good luck. Come back. I tell you election date and place. Full schedule."

"I even might."

Warner must have had some presentiment Amfookha knew more than he had said, because he stood moodily beyond the beads, reluctant to go. In front of him the BMT truck with its vast scarlet B.M.T., circled in yellow on the door, confirmed his earlier suspicions. He wouldn't get anywhere with that.

He said, "Where is this place Porokorro?"

"Very far very bad road."

"Can you hire a car here?"

"Yes—sah. I have very good car. Land-rover. Porokorro one hour. Low gear. Five pounds."

The BMT driver was reluctant to be dismissed. He had been told to take "this master" to lunch at the mess and until he had done so there would be a pain in his mind.

Warner scrutinised the alien face and thought the man had been sent to keep a watch on him.

"This master stay," Warner said to him, getting the

hang, " you run back to that master and tell your little tale. OK? "

" Yes, sah."

" Well? "

The man stood there. " Yes—sah."

Suddenly Amfookha bellowed at him in his own language. He still stood. Some of the stall women laughed. Then he went.

The dust settled—on the beer bottles, and the beech-nut, and the children playing.

" You got BMT pass for Porokorro? " Amfookha said.

Warner said, " Don't worry, I've got a pass for every-where."

" Everywhere! Ha ha very good—you like Mr. Meyer? "

" Who's Mr. Meyer? " Warner said.

" Walk, any place—no guards, no hat—just little case full of diamonds. Just one mill-yon, ha ha. Meet the Devil: Devil say Good morning, sah."

" Mr. Meyer of the BMT? "

" Oh, no, no, no. Corporation Buyer. You want introduction to Mr. Meyer you come my place Tuesday night. He stop for cold beer on Tuesday nights."

" Just cold beer. Just cold beer. Is that it? "

Warner was silent with his back to Amfookha, per-haps on purpose, for after a time it goaded Amfookha into a torrent of information, spoken rather contemp-tuously, as though for a visiting journalist to stand there *thinking* about Mr. Meyer when he knew nothing to think about him, and when he was in earshot of stringer Amfookha, was a piece of irritating presumption.

" Some people very ill-informed. Mr. Meyer good to diggers. Give them good prices. Syrians only people no like Mr. Meyer. BMT like Mr. Meyer, Africans like

Picnic at Porokorro

Mr. Meyer, Civil Administration like him, Diggers love him, yes, sah. Very good prices. When you come Porokorro alone like that to-day and they see one man in the distance with guide, they say, Mr. Meyer."

" John-Jesus and Mr. Meyer—the heavenly Daddies."

" Not John-Jesus. Mr. Meyer. White man. Tall man —sleepy face—so "—and the vivid vital bulbous face of Amfookha suddenly seemed to see a lizard far, far away and became drowsy from the fixed sight of it. " Walk alone like you."

" I'm Meyer the Buyer," Warner said. The sun sapped his desire to speak or to question. It left jingles in his head. It reduced everything to meaningless jingles. He was as near nothing as made no difference.

Amfookha went on but he scarcely heard.

The Rover came, with " Tim Amadeus Amfookha " written in red ten-inch caps on the door in a circle and bigger than the BMT of the camp vehicles.

" Good luck, sah, good luck."

When he got in he lay back with his knees up and as soon as he was out of sight closed his eyes. He had got up at four and been sick in the plane. The sun, in the last few minutes, had traced out the big black circumference of his eyeballs in faint pain and made one shoulder feel fizzy, bruised and dead, so that he moved it to prove the contrary.

" Meyer the Buyer. Amfookha the Crook-a and Scott the Upper Class Clot."

They closed up behind a lorry, accelerating blindly into its boiling wake till they saw its silhouette like a ship in a fog and two scarfed Africans in the back jolting about like gagged goggled corpses; then they drew into the clear light and air.

Picnic at Porokorro

Warner tried to blow the dust out of his nose. He thought he might pass as Meyer's new assistant.

He needn't worry about fouling this particular nest because after to-day he would never come back to it.

After to-day it was for the fire.

9

THE HANDS of the clock in the head office were gathered aloft in one vertical, appetising half-gash but none of the VIPs allowed himself to be seen knowing it. They read the make of their Biros before they knew it was 1 p.m. The fans feathered and feathered the air and the voices, dwindling and becoming formal as they became bankrupt, gave to moral fear the tones of moral responsibility.

For Barber, Joint-Hicks representing the Governor (a man like an advertisement for officers' mackintoshes), Police Commissioner Fadden, formerly of Birmingham, and MacPherson had been in conference an hour. Now they avoided each other's eyes as though they had been joined by a hypnotising Chairman called Nothing whom each thought visible only to himself.

Only MacPherson seemed occasionally free of that terrible Chairman, yet to the others his " view " seemed so mad they lowered their eyes out of friendship.

For MacPherson kept repeating " There *is* no trouble."

Barber let it pass two or three times as though it were the " façon de parler " of an amiable man; and then perhaps he was really answering it when he suddenly said, " Of course . . . the diggers are perfectly decent ordinary chaps: that's just it: we want closer relations with them. . . . At the moment there's simply no contact —none whatever."

" Except between your sticks and their skulls," Mac-Pherson said.

" And why does that happen? Because there's no other kind of contact. That's a last resort. Where are your public relations, Mac? " Barber said critically.

" You mean Mass Education units with loud-speakers? "

" All right, whatever does the job," Barber said.

" Well, it's that or an honours degree per digger, isn't it? "

" Well . . . you're saying it."

" No, I'm not saying it, Mr. Barber. I'm saying it for you. I say there *is* no trouble . . ." and this time he leant right forward and said, " *What* trouble is there? " right into Barber's face, who returned the look calmly and with smiling deference—as though he had only tested the expert, the man who really knew.

" Mac, I shouldn't have thought it needed describing."

" My! That's just what it does need. Descrrription."

MacPherson's " r "s had begun to roll. It was hot. They were beginning to be hungry; some of them incoherent.

" There's *no* trouble. There's *bin* no trouble. Ye've got to convince me, Tom, that there *is* any trouble —except boys in uniform who missed the war and want medal-palaver. I know these people—diggers you call them, and I knew their fathers. They're *not* bloody good chaps—they're bloody rogues, like you and me. But treated right they're not going to take people prisoner and make 'em—what was it, undress— and search their skin for grenades." He shook his head wearily.

" You're saying what I said. Except I can't agree

94

about our guards. They have a job to do. Approved by
Government."

" Ai. But *how do they do it?* I still say there's bin no
trouble."

" Were you there, Mac? "

" If I had been we wouldn't all be here now wasting
our time. I'd be chasing butterflies with my son up the
Nuna. Five hundred carat bloody butterflies." Mac
browbeat them, each in turn. Then skilfully, sym-
pathetically he relented. His voice changed to a minor
key:

" Mr. Barber, four months ago I moved thirty thousand
illicit diggers back over the frontier with five D.O.s—
young men with walking sticks! "

The silence was ambivalent.

" I wish there'd never been any diamonds," said the
Secretary smoothly. " A.G.'s hair's turning grey."

Everyone thought, for an instant, with extreme
reluctance of the Governor's hair.

Fadden said, obediently and rather restlessly, " Well,
what's it to be? Do we collect the ringleaders and this
—er—Cowboy? "

Had he been asleep? Someone ought to try and
crystallise the various points of view, if only to save
people from the appearance of having slept.

It was probably for the Secretary to sum up, but
seniority was confused by the fact that all their ranks
were different in kind. After various looks and one or
two polite noises they all by tacit mutual consent deferred
to confidence and experience—to MacPherson, who had
been in this very spot before Number One was born.
There and then they deferred to him even though
privately they thought his view " mad."

And no one was keener to defer to him than the

95

Governor's representative, the Secretary who had been frightened by Fadden's recent summarising remark: " Do we collect the ringleaders? " This seemed to be in flat contradiction to the whole trend of the last hour's discussion and agreement. Or had he misunderstood? Not for the first time in his life the Secretary fell back with gratitude on the generous role of second fiddle: " Yes, Mac, you go ahead. I think this is your pigeon."

Fadden, whose genial freckled face had first been seen officially on a Birmingham beat thirty years ago, had in fact nodded off once or twice. He had been at a party the night before, slung by the rep for Carlsberg lager. It had seemed to end in an aeroplane with the Secretary. In fact it must have.

MacPherson now addressed him in words he didn't understand: " There's no ring to lead, Mr. Fadden. And I'll tell you another thing. There'd have bin no trouble if *you'd* bin there either."

Fadden felt a compliment had been paid to him. But he couldn't decipher it so he belched politely which somehow saved him from the need to reply; and he looked patiently, responsibly and obediently at his blotter. He thought his chaps did do their job, and he looked quietly pleased.

The Secretary said, " Then over to you, Mac."

MacPherson's strongly personal manner had by now dominated the room. He had capped Barber's own unusual technique in official relations, yet Barber seemed grateful and admiring, and now said, " You want a bathing party—is that it, Mac? "

Everyone wanted a summary, a decision, and lunch.

But Mac said, " Well, why not? Don't your wives go there and bathe? "

" A bit higher up . . . they have done."

" Well, to-day they can disport themselves with a sense of mission. While I talk to the boys."

Barber's eyes were footlights for the lone figure of the Scotsman. Was this all? A picnic? Would there now be the curtain and applause?

Silence. People wondered why MacPherson didn't get to his feet and give instructions.

Barber tilted his chair back and said, " Mac'll tell them their mothers were baboons and he'll hang them up by their balls if they do it again—all with a great grin and they'll love him—what? " Barber made everyone smile. " Damn' good."

But he isolated MacPherson further with his footlight eyes. " And that's that," he said quietly. " And after-wards life goes on, as usual. And in a few years the BMT will find its plants bogged down in a waste of unlicensed craters like the Somme battlefield."

" By God, the Somme craters *were* unlicensed."

" But we don't want them here," said Barber.

" The BMT, Mr. Barber, is doo'n OK."

Barber smiled.

MacPherson pointed in his face and said, " Poor Tom —how you'd love to agree with me. I always say: There's a man I'd like to rescue."

Then turning now at last to everyone, and talking specifically, he said, " So if the Secretary agrees I shall go down there first and speak to the boys. Afterwards " —he tossed out his hand theatrically—" have tea on the river."

Was that all? Was that the plan?

The silence was uneasy until Barber said, " At present the illicit diggers are in possession of ground which is leased to us and which they took by force last night. Are you going to talk to them while they remain in possession?"

MacPherson flushed. He had thought the answer to this so simple. He had answered it in his own mind and surely hadn't he spoken it? A hesitation of age, of pure age and perhaps of alienation in this new atmosphere made him frown and he said in anger, which was sharper for being unconfident: " No . . . No. Take your whole army, tanks and all, bazookas and machine-guns—but *with me in front*—and walk on to the leased ground. *But no more.* You'll probably find they've gone anyhow. But from *there* . . . I'll proceed alone. Thank you. . . . Hat in hand, Mr. Barber. *The violent fit of the times craves it as physic for the whole State*, Tom, isn't that it? "

Barber, I know, thought he knew precisely the pattern of what would then happen. He imagined MacPherson sitting on a gilt chair in the market-place of Porokorro with the chief bowing to him and the silent crowds pressing round to hear their fate. Those strangely *chic* boys, many of them from French territory, who had travelled some of them thousands of miles in the hope of getting rich quick. Often MacPherson talked of them movingly (Barber remembered this), describing how white men in such a minerals rush, in such under-fed, over-worked, continually tempted thousands would be ripping each other up nightly—but how somehow they, with their tribal customs and home-made courts, had avoided chaos in spite of there being no legal social framework, too much palm wine and beer, and few women. Mac-Pherson sahib would sit wishing for the days of the King's Messenger—a lonely brilliantly dressed unarmed African who walked in the middle of a seething tribe, put his hand on a troublemaker and said " Come with me."

Picnic at Porokorro

It had been enough. It had been more than a hundred ex-subalterns with tommy-guns who had never been to war.

The silence was long, defeated and confused.

People had given in—to Mac and to the desire for lunch.

"Tom . . ." MacPherson said appeasingly, "there *ain't* no trouble."

It was getting boring, as well as indeterminate.

Barber saw the bluff old Scot rise from his ceremonial chair and walk towards the most arrogant-looking of all the youths with the widest hat, the sauciest switch, the most knife-edged trousers; and after a moment's intuitive pause hit him almost enough to hurt, but just not, just enough to shock, on the side of the face.

"You Kuru man?"

Silence while you could hear a pin drop. Then at last sheepishly the boy would reply, "Mandingoe Sah."

"You there yesterday . . . catch policeman."

Silence. Then: "Mandingoes talk plenty sometimes."

Silence.

"Plenty copper, eh?" MacPherson might pull out his trouser pocket and rescue from the material three enmeshed copper shillings, look at them cryptically—while the eyes of the Mandingoe dropped upon them—with contempt. MacPherson put them back without a word. Then after a few steps. "I still got more copper than him."

Laughter—uncertain, watchful.

Then suddenly he would round on them and abuse them in their own language as fools. Only fools wanted trouble—gun-palaver. Then no diamonds, no cars, no wives. No more licences.

One of the men would be wearing the clean hefty
dressing of the local dispensary. Underneath would be
the creamy sulpha paste clogged against a damp cherry-
coloured sore that would, if left, at last reach the bone,
cause osteomyelitis, perhaps cancer and so death.

" Can you make that? " he shouted, pointing. " Half
BMT profits go for that. And you dig one hundredth
part of BMT diamonds."

Of course it was all convenient, much of it back to
front, half a music-hall turn, half cunning. . . . Barber's
mind closed down on what else it was, closing simply on
one certainty: out of date. Something else was needed
. . . *was coming.*

" Have we anything else to tell each other? " Mac-
Pherson said.

Barber began putting away his papers.

" Have we? " MacPherson repeated, " I was on
holiday. Yet I've been the one doing the talking. Why?
Because the rest of you don't want to say anything."
And he added after a few seconds, " No—you don't."

The pause was short. Barber's eyes lifted to Mac-
Pherson's, humorously, " giving him best."

Then the Secretary said, " Personally I'm dry as a
kiln."

A moment later, in the passage, the same voice could be
heard fruitily assuring Fadden that when he'd pumped
ship he'd cable A.G.

And on the tone of that voice the meeting closed as
though returning to key.

Some of us heard it in the distance, that day, without
surprise. It still echoed in a thousand clubs and gun-
rooms far away. The old cool echoes never faltered.
God (Oxon.) was an English gentleman and the estate
was entailed. The Secretary thought it wasn't, of course,

but he *felt* that it was; yes—in spite of every proof to the contrary, the feeling lay in his voice like the keynote of a still unfinished symphony.

He pumped ship and then he did cable A.G. to the effect that the situation was being explored and was already " calmer."

10

Ground exhausted by the Licensed Diggers is stricken as the Somme and Ypres of pictures, and beneath the surface almost as full of bones and rusty metal. An area of it may, like the " Mad Mile " of Monte Cassino, get a nickname. Then the number of people who died there becomes the boast of the diggers. The name sets off the fable which they are still living. They like and foster the fables. The history of their own risk perhaps makes more credible the chance of getting rich.

The site west of Porokorro is called the Valley of Death—and referred to as such in English.

Trees that still stand there are silver, dead. The ones on the ground show roots that look gnawed through. And in a sense they were gnawed—not quite by teeth— but by spade, pick and matchet. Trees bigger than any in England were dug up, and if iron hadn't been available they *might* have been gnawed and torn up, with teeth and hands.

Some of the brown hills of waste have returned to green in the rains but in the dry season it is still a kiln of brazen rock and sand interspersed with craters that stay flooded. At dusk the mosquitoes whine and whirr like violins over the teeming slime.

No one knows how many men have died on these sites. There are no inquests, no news stories. Officials say " thousands."

Picnic at Porokorro

When a crater has been worked out, diggers tunnel towards the neighbouring crater. They pass the gravel back to be sieved. They penetrate deeper and deeper without props of any kind. The soft earth falls in such volume that sometimes no attempt is made to dig the trapped out. What would be the point? Why dig them out to bury them again? The real digging resumes, often, before anyone is dead.

In the early stages of a crater chains of men hand up buckets of water from ledge to ledge. Boys with ten-foot, small-headed spades fling up repeatedly a pound of earth with a rhythmic incessant 200-degree swing—from the lowest level to the next—and so on till the earth is scattered on top.

Some of the men wear coloured shirts, but some add a more beautiful, a more infernal touch by slaving naked like models for an anatomy class: the weave of their every muscle, because of under-feeding and over-exertion, is visible almost by strands.

Toil is rapt, silent and ceaseless. No singing and no commands.

MacPherson finds, in movements which once could not have been done without singing, a mark of illness, almost of doom.

And I remember he talked of the exhausted ground, the waste land, like a mounting bill, though in fact at the time of the trouble he hadn't seen Porokorro for two years.

Lately the used sites have become never wholly deserted.

At sunset you usually see a few bathers or still a few groups washing the gravel on the edge of an exhausted crater. These are people who have not enough money to rent a new patch from the village chief—or perhaps no more energy to dig. They inhabit the waste. They pat out the fine gravel in neat cakes. No one speaks. The weakest fetch heavy baskets of gravel, while the biggest drifts the knife across the cakes of tiny stones, again and again, layer by layer. They are the ascetics of one fanatic hope and the low sun throws their shadows far. In the distance others, naked, are washing off mud before going back to their *shimbeks*—palm-leaf shelters.

Here and there along a causeway a little party moves home in single file shouldering their long spades. In front is often a youth more strongly built than the others wearing a sombrero, carrying a switch and sucking a long piece of grass. Everyone is engrossed in one single common hope.

Dickson, the general manager, has filmed it all a good deal in colour. And he is right—it is strange, photogenic, perhaps even unique. But I don't understand the expression in his face when he talks about it. He is smiling. Perhaps because now it was all boiled down to one and the same thing—his thing, the BMT's thing.

*   *   *

The police post for Bornu Island ferry used always to have a couple of BMT guards in it until the BMT plant had finished working the ground on this side of the river. It stood opposite Bornu island about a mile upstream from the main crossing-place to Porokorro village, and in the heart of what had been one of the most fertile areas for Licensed Diggers, now an extreme example of used ground.

On the skeleton trees to-day a party of vultures, drying their outstretched wings, occasionally did little dancy steps and shuffled their feathers without disturbing their formal attitude; and a hammerhead with its great browless beak provided the landscape with what it seemed made for—a touch of Dürer's diabolic grotesque.

In the far distance from the direction of the river there was a ceaseless sound of voices.

It was here John-Jesus Amanda was sent with his bed-roll and small pack, Sergeant Kahn having an instinct for torture.

Amanda picked up the edge of the *shimbek*—which the recent storm had ground into the mud—and then let it drop. He stood staring round with his huge sorrowful eyes. He was tired of the sun, of life and light and what it showed. Let God take back what He had given. He made a sort of shelter under one of the trees, moving languidly, sometimes listening to the voices, sometimes staying quite still, listening, his hands hanging like a dancer's.

Bornu, where the trouble had been the day before, was in the middle of the river and slightly upstream—about 500 yards away. The air was still, and though the voices could be heard clearly the thick bush on the island shielded the diggers from sight.

Amanda sat down by the path's edge. Three men carrying provisions came by and got into one of the dug-outs drawn up on the bank. They took no notice of John-Jesus, merely calling out the customary string of greetings which tapered out in gentle echoes like a marriage service tit for tat—with grunts dividing the responses—the last being almost inaudible from a distance.

All this was customary and helpful: it covered what they were doing, and it covered what had happened to him, to be in that place alone.

Hours passed. The heat, the loneliness, the distant boisterous voices and his thoughts crushed him into an ever more dismal congruity with his setting. He became that man of dust and apathy, the Forlorn African.

Then a single girl came by with one of the large brilliantly illustrated Japanese basins on her head. It was full of rice and heavy enough to oblige her to keep facing forward. But she saw the figure crouched under the tree, recognised him and slowed.

The first phase of the greeting fell with a different intonation and in reply she made the sound which is half acknowledgment and half sigh and signature of absolute anonymous womanhood—an extraordinary noise that seems to come at one and the same time from the belly and the nasal arches of African women—but which affects only most men's loins.

She stopped. He asked her where she was going and she said to the island to sell rice. Her husband was there.

When he had finished asking she didn't go on but remained standing opposite him, facing forwards. Then she took the basin down. He came forward with his mess tin. She spilt him out some rice, while he squatted with his knees by his ears.

She undid a leaf and took out some kola nuts. One of them was white—the sign of friendship. He gave her money for the rice but not for the nuts.

He lifted the basin on to her head. He was a mission boy.

He said the diggers were still on the island. She said, yes, there was a lot of palm wine drunk there yesterday when the whites went. And then she said a lot more—a catalogue of facts, but without particular emphasis.

There was silence.

He said, " Three guards came there to-day? "

She grunted in the affirmative—but still with that wooing femininity as though the topic, to the extent that

it was to do with her, were love. By now she was facing
away again, under her load. It was difficult to believe
that either of them knew of any drama under the sun.

" With rifles ? " he said.

" *Ainh*," she said as though confirming the health of
her mother.

John-Jesus bit into one of the nuts.

At last he began the valediction. She began to move,
replying. The valediction continued—ending with that
chord of hers—her whole body, her essence in a sound.

11

ALL THE way from Sangoro, right past the gates of
" Whipsnade," as he now called the BMT camp, Warner
sat loose, in a slightly lopsided position, seething with a
to-and-fro match of thought. For it was a sort of match:
they hit the ball, he hit it back and so on till the latest
they—Dickson, Scott and Barber—had all been promoted
and invested with all kinds of special knowledge—even
of newspapers—and put in positions they had never
known—only to be trounced by his superior intelligence,
his final scoop which had overtones of the Dreyfus case.
White-man murder.

Matches like this had been going on in Warner's mind
ever since he could think, but particularly since he
landed in the colony three weeks ago. In the colony
there was so much to react from. In that way the place
was pure uranium.

Yes, he knew now that it paid him to go around reacting
like a cat on hot bricks. Distastefully he knew it was
why they had sent him. The gimmick-crazy generalising
moles upstairs had discovered they actually had a live
" Angry Young Man " on the premises; a young man
that much angrier because he himself had *failed* to
become an English " red-brick " don. The Moles' minds
clicked—on the usual tuppeny ticket: " Angry young
man looks at Africa," and sent him down the west coast
to write angry young pieces which readers could quarrel

over in the letter column. He had said to the moles, in
so many words, couldn't they stuff it, because wasn't it
dead and *who* was angry? He got the impression the
young men who were really angry were the ones in bowlers
in the Kings Road whose children really would go to
public schools, and the middle-aged professional classes
and small private-income group. Except that these last
knew better than to lose their bait: the strength of gilt-
edged lay in keeping cool, as the Tory Minister of Labour
knew damn' well.

When he reached Africa he at first became more surprised than angry. He started off being surprised by the
Santa Barbara Times.

After all, Wilson, the " Advising Editor " (the only
white man on the staff), had been a star performer at
home. He was famous in a small way, in the Street.
A millionaire's daughter eloped with a traffic cop:
Wilson kept both of them in a roadhouse near Gretna
Green for ten days. He claimed he, not the cop, persuaded the girl to marry. He got " bride's dawn rush"
photos, including a close-up of the speedometer showing
sixty in a build-up area, while other reporters were
watching the Channel ports. Then a year later he got a
scoop on the divorce too.

Big title print had been flown out specially with Wilson
when the *Santa Barbara Times* was bought. Warner had
expected to see it in daily use—splashing the old 200
monosyllables which had built his own papers' circulation
in England—Queen, girl, probe, Red, ban, beer, sex,
drive, peer, speed, tax and the rest. Or their African
equivalents. But to his " astonishment " (he did not
really go in for astonishment) he found the format the
same—but the headlines smaller and the text usually
straight, provincial or dull.

Apparently the stuff that sold at home didn't here.

He noticed, too, that here one or two reporters were allowed to " write fancy "—even repeat the same word five or six times in one sentence. He approved this as the verbal equivalent of jazz exuberance. He went to some of the reporters' homes and took a hand with the drums. There wasn't much talk and the African men and girls jived differently from the people at home. You could say absolutely differently. He couldn't quite get it. He thought them rather up-stage.

What was the wave-length?

With Councillor-stringer Amfookha you could perhaps legitimately despair. There wasn't one.

But this John-Jesus. What would be *his* wave-length?

" John-Jesus," Warner murmured, and added, " Christ! "

Yet he easily identified himself with this young African policeman hired to stop his cousins and brothers picking up their own grit. In spite of his name he should be a piece of cake.

And then Warner thought of the big young man at the mess with the ring and the crowned swan on it: Scott. There were still people about who enjoyed *being who they were*, who sucked the sweet of their own identity come cancer, poverty, neurosis or death.

A flame of blood licked through his brain and he thought they f—— f—— loved their own individual identity. Well, he would introduce them to an ungarbled version. Verily a sparrow would not fall without Herbert Warner getting out the facts, and ditto for Scott. Because the fact of a sparrow falling was only that fact: one sparrow less; and the fact of Scott was that he got a nice feeling from being Vespasian de Scott or whatever he was, and there was no celestial ticker tape for either event. sparrow, Scott and God were all for the bird.

But when Warner got to Porokorro and looked at it, he not only forgot about these people, he almost forgot about the murder too. He stared and stared and could not believe that such a sight had never been in headlines.

Well, it would be now!

Some of the diggers looked up curiously from their craters at the white man and his African guide. And he stared down at them through his sun-glasses as though they were specimens, which they were, as he was. He wouldn't go in for any mateyness, which they would naturally mistake for the nauseating variety, so he waved briefly and—of course—honestly. But they did not respond.

The driver went in search of a Security Guard while Warner stayed by the car watching the vast infernal scene. At last the driver returned with a Guard who said he would guide him to John-Jesus Amanda.

" You from BMT, sah? " said the Guard.

" From Mr Meyer's office."

The Guard hesitated, then turned to lead the way.

It was two miles to the Ferry Post. Long before they reached it the craters became less and less populous, then ramshackle and deserted, finally flooded, level with the ground, so that they threaded their way precariously over narrow causeways or made detours using fallen trees as bridges.

The guide stopped suddenly and said, " There, sah," and pointed superstitiously to a cluster of surviving vegetation.

Now, near it, a man in denims emerged from the shade. Warner went up to him: " You speak English? "

The man stood to attention. " Yes, sah—all words."
" You know where I find John-Jesus Amanda? "
" Yes, sah. Here, sah."
" You John-Jesus? "
" Yes, sah."
" Let's sit down. Smoke? "
" Not on duty, sah."
They sat down. Warner had planned shock tactics.
" You go many raids? "
The man hesitated and looked up at the distant guard,
who still came no nearer.
" I not know your name, sah."
" Your friend, that's my name."
" I not know you friend . . ."
Amanda had a beautiful face and voice, and yet for
his country and his time he was relatively-speaking an
intellectual. He had only just missed getting into Santa
Barbara University College after leaving the Methodist
mission school.

It was above all the voice which " got " Warner. In
an Englishman it would have made him reach for his
mental gun; as it was he looked into the enormous,
webby, sensitive eyes and wondered: What the hell . . .
Police Constable Jesus, M.A., Third Programme
Announcer. Or was it Sir Philip Sydney reincarnated
black?

Fear can give anyone temporarily the eyes of a poet, of
a saint, of a mystic—and perhaps these categories were
always only people who had a fearful, an unforgetting
attitude to death which intensified life. Amanda was
afraid. His apprehension stood in his eyes, clear as a
hoarding. But Warner thought: He knows about the
murder.

Amanda said purely, " What are you, sah? "

The seriousness and calm confidence with which this question was put betrayed Warner into a flicker of anger; he damned the officers' tricks the poor blighter had picked up like a parrot.

When he spoke it was not as he had planned to speak. He said simply, " Mr. Meyer sent me."

" I see, sah. You got Corporation jeep, sah? "

" Back—at the post. . . . You want to see papers, photos; you Customs man? Or you Mission Boy, John-Jesus? You believe me? "

" Yes, sah."

" Bad trouble yesterday."

" Yes, sah."

The man was still suspicious.

" Mr. Barber very worried. Mr. Meyer away—buying. Mr. Barber send for me. Say: Go ask John-Jesus what happened. We must know what happened. . . ."

" Mr. Roberts and Sergeant make report in full."

Warner paused, then he said coolly: " D'you think I'm a spy man, John-Jesus? Why you no tell me . . . when Mr. Barber says Go ask John-Jesus. And Mr. Meyer say, Good man, John-Jesus. We believe John-Jesus. Very good man. Mission boy."

The emotion which suddenly flooded the all too transparent face of John-Jesus gave Warner the handle he always looked for in dealing with people. But nausea almost prevented him using it, and his bodily tension increased. He began chucking stones. He half aped himself talking, as though the words, even as a subterfuge, were intolerable.

" God see all things, John-Jesus. God everywhere."

" Yes, sah."

" Diggers bad men? Good men? "

" All kinds."

" Mr. Barber want to know how old man was killed in troubles yesterday."

" No one killed yesterday, sah."

In the silence Warner felt defeat. But he had an ally he did not know: the place, Porokorro.

It ebbed in on them from the great red brown waste all round. And John-Jesus had already been four hours there; he had never forgotten it. Perhaps Warner was one of its apparitions.

John-Jesus said, " Old man sentry die every day here."

Warner, not looking at him, thought he meant the deaths of old men were common on the sites—but then in the silence he looked round and saw him holding his heart and looking ill.

The man was acting; he must be. Warner said, " So it gets you down? "

" Yes, sah."

" Well, now you just tell us all. Unburden."

Amanda said nothing. Warner selected another stone. He held it and turned it over in his fingers.

" I am the Way and the Truth, isn't that it, John-Jesus? "

He flipped the stone and wondered was it worth listening to a religious maniac in a jungle back-lot.

" Yes, sah."

The stone struck a tree and bounced back.

" *Who actually killed him?* "

" Manga prisoners actually kill him, sah."

Warner said quickly, " We know the prisoners killed him but *how*? "

" With blows."

Warner pretended to have been misunderstood, to be searching for clearer ways of expressing himself.

"Yes," he said tolerantly, "Mr. Meyer knows that. He knows that, John-Jesus."

He stopped throwing stones and said, "Where was the old man?"

"By the tree, sah, he was sentry, sah."

"By himself?"

Silence. Warner turned his great sun-glasses at the youth.

"With me, sah."

"With you?"

"Yes, sah. With me, sah. I talk to him. He is French man from Bamako. Very old."

"Why were you with him?"

"I guarding him till others come back."

"Who come back?"

"Guards with prisoners."

"Yes, OK. They came back. We know that. We know that quite well. What is not clear is what exactly happened next."

The man's head swayed and hung away. "I no tell lies."

"Mr. Meyer knows that. That's why he sent me to you."

"I no tell lies. I no want to wash my hands any more. I bin too frightened to help Jesus. Diamond palaver no good. I say send me Balu. Gordon masta promise Balu. But Sergeant Kahn put me here. Now I never leave. Never more."

"Quoth the Raven." Warner took up another pebble. "Mr. Meyer good man, Christian?"

"Yes, sah."

"He say John-Jesus know in his heart what happened. He give witness for Christ."

At last John-Jesus said, "Mr. Roberts masta good

man too. Very kind man. Comes to my house. Dance high-life at Christmas after guard sports. He no kill old man."

"I know," Warner said quickly, "it was all an accident. But how did it happen?"

"He say, 'Let four of them have a go—to give old man sentry something to remember.'"

"Prisoners?"

"Yes, sah—illicit digger prisoners: four were let free."

"So they give it him good?"

"They think old man sold them. I know they will kill him. But I say nothing."

"Well?"

"Diggers very strong. Old man like old stick . . . breaks . . . little bits."

"They killed him."

"He cry one time. To me. And one time to them: I done no wrong thing. He give me cry for my life."

Warner relaxed. He said indifferently, "What the hell could you have done?"

The man was weeping. Slowly he held out his hand, offering something. Warner opened his palm and felt fall a few tiny bits of gravel.

He again thought the man was mad. Then he saw one pebble, on one side, gleam with fires.

"I no one," Amanda said, "no one, no one."

"I should hang on to these if I were you, chum— you'll see it differently when you want a shilling for the gas."

But Amanda's hands had disappeared. "Tell Mr Meyer one thing I know. Gun palaver to-night if Mr. Roberts come back to Bornu Island for Cowboy. . . ."

Warner looked up from the diamonds. "What . . . what was that?"

" Ndongo, there."

" Ndongo? "

" Three guards took rifles to-day. One man corporal
very bad man. He hire out BMT ground every night, get
plenty diamonds—like those."

Warner restrained himself. He crouched forward in
silence by the sobbing man. He opened the palm with
the diamonds in it as though he would dribble them
down at the man's side.

" Ndongo? "

" Bad man, sah."

" What you mean ' bad '? " Warner said.

" Corporal Ndongo bad man."

" He done murder thing? "

Amanda's eyes were full of hopeless knowledge. Such
pessimism Warner had never seen in a human face.

Warner said quietly, " He kill someone too? "

" I kill old man. John-Jesus kill old man before
Christ."

" Let's put on the other side, shall we? " he said.
" Ndongo kill someone too? "

Amanda said, " Last year. Big trouble."

" *Last year?* "

" No one knows."

At last Warner said, " So they'll shoot, will they,
to-night? "

" Ndongo has bad grigri."

" Grigri? "

" White man's eye skin from last year."

Warner said, " And a toad's eye. Why you tell all
this? "

" To-day I see Christ there like a white bird. To-day
I tell all: I no one. He say John-Jesus one time come

unto me. At his feet old sentry lay and Christ say Behold
—you done this to me."

Warner said, " That would make a difference."

" Difference come like lion and show claws for ever:
I say Christ save me: John-Jesus no can bear such
difference. Take this cup from me. But Christ leave me
with the lion alone."

" Big of him."

There was a long silence. Then Warner said, " What's
this Ndongo going to do? "

" You tell Mr. Barber, sah, wait. Wait one day. Then
palm wine finish and Cowboy and Ndongo and rifles go
to France."

" *France!* "

Seconds passed while Warner thought the man truly
mad. Then he got it: French territory.

" Tell Mr. Barber, sah. Diggers not bad men. Only
two bad men. Tell him wait."

Warner looked up and around, and again down at the
wreck of humanity at his feet. Suddenly he knelt and
cuffed him lightly in an incongruous, gauche way.

" Hey," he said, " Jesus—or whatever your name is—
pull your finger out. Cheer up. Change your name. It's
later than you think. I've got to go."

There was no response and after a long stare at the
bowed head, Warner said, " Well—I'll do something for
you. And it won't be pap."

He dribbled the diamonds down on to Amanda's
thighs . . . the dribble became slower. Before the last and
biggest could fall, Warner's fingers curled. " I'll unburden your conscience this much," he said. " I'll do that
for you." Since the man paid no attention Warner
kicked him lightly. " Well—*look* . . ."

But Amanda didn't hear him. Perhaps the swamp had

produced many phenomena, many visions already and
he was already preparing for the next, after Warner.

Warner, turning to go, suddenly noticed a lopsided
cross a few yards away in the shade. The two bits of
wood were tied together with a bit of webbing.

" You've got it bad, haven't you? " he said. " They
really took trouble with you." And he thought the BMT
could probably pay twenty per cent with a few more
like him.

And he turned back thinking he had met a Christian
for the first time ever, the kind of chap who put the
whole BMT in the palm of your hand. Yet the sort of
bloke you wanted to step on, in spite of yourself.

12

LIEUTENANT ROBERTS could not sleep. His mind kept revolving on all that had happened in the last week, trying to impose some sort of pattern upon it. Heaven knows, he didn't set up as a brain but he usually saw what was what.

The letter he got written to his fiancée before turning in had tried in vain to ease his bewilderment. " Boy ! " he had written, " is this a cat's cradle or is it a cat's cradle. Keep your fingers crossed for yours truly. They no like that cop man."

Now, as he lay, fragments of the last days kept intruding and he found himself re-living situations to a different end.

He had made the mission boy John-Jesus come out again on the patrol yesterday. He had made him get up and come. A month ago he knew he would not have done this. He would have believed in the man's sickness and left him in his blanket. But the laughter of the other guards had found an echo in himself.

He was glad he had checked Sergeant Kahn. . . .

How those boys laughed before a raid ! How they enjoyed the raids, with their long pale wands and tin hats. Ruses, ambushes, brief successful struggles—sometimes booty. They were all Manga—and had been doing this for the last billion years. Not white-man's war, " oh, no, no," laughed the ones who'd been in Burma, and they rocked with laughter, " white-man's war no good."

Picnic at Porokorro

The mere idea of it made them roll—because imagine!
They had been in it—*yet were still here. Still here*, to roll
on the good earth, and slap its fat body.

In fact, the raids were a good party. The tuned-up
keenness of those fine chaps all round him. The way
they crouched slowly from the upright, like big cats,
when they had finished spying. And the way they listened
at night—with eye-whites gleaming.

Then the yodelling charges ending in the vicious
thwacks on all who " resisted arrest " (the prisons were
full). Yes—he knew they broke bones every raid.

There had been enough danger in it to give it a tang.
And no more. Give them fifty years and they'd wipe the
floor with us at rugger. All Blacks—change your name,
perhaps your game too.

Then the business of that old sentry—and then yesterday. . . .

He felt shame—the deep shame of being caught cheat-
ing. Why. Childish in a tin hat. Real danger had been
different. He should have understood.

He turned in the bed.

There he stood naked in front of fifty of them while
ten in turn searched his clothes . . . his shorts: a loving
cup handed round. He had thought they wouldn't
stop there. . . .

He turned over on his pillow—pulling back the guards
who were holding back four prisoners and he shone his
torch down at the old man with the dainty little deltas
of blood branching from nostrils and the corner of his
mouth.

He had put his hand under the shirt and felt for the
heart. The Sergeant had wanted to leave him but he
had made the prisoners carry him.

How had it happened? When he had said, " Let four

of them have a go," he should have known how Africans hit—even their children.

It dawned on him that the prisoners saw the old man standing *with guards and no one holding him. They thought he had sold them.*

John-Jesus had wanted to help carry the man . . . the little creeper.

The thing was—he hadn't thought at all. Not till now.

He had a headache. But he didn't feel much guilt. He thought you could drive yourself barmy once you started. " So if it's just being found out I mind—that's just f—— undignified. So I don't mind. Besides, there's no blame: Barber and Dickson are right behind me. . . ."

He got up and had a drink of iced whisky. The house was still but he knew his three boys in spotless white were in the kitchen and aware that he had left his bed. Their silence was OK in the proper place, but sometimes—coupled with the general incommunicado—it got on your nerves.

" Moses," he called.

His voice died flat—but he was sure it had been heard. There was no answer. He looked through. There was a pair of sandals by the door. The fridge hummed.

He went back to bed and stared at the ceiling. How much does a chap care . . . if no one lets on. Just how much. The world felt dead, pointless. They wanted to have a go at him. Let them. He thought of his girl.

For some reason he wanted to go back. *To-day.*

He dropped off surrounded by silent faces—Barber, Dickson, The Cowboy, John-Jesus. Trouble was nobody ever said anything.

To look at you'd think everything was hunky-dory. Like the bed, the food, the fan, the pay, the health . . .

13

ISOBEL MEYER thought she might be in Newtown Harlow
on a hot day with nothing to do. Or in Hell. It was
the same thing. Hell with black stokers who trod softly
and gave you frights.

She looked at her husband's curtains and furniture
with panic. Each object tried to be bright and different,
but was basically cheap, utilitarian and standardised. The
house was a living-unit for a producer and it had
come in sections, with a quota of furniture.

And he hadn't altered a thing. . . .

She stared round for some mark of his personality,
some tiny sign of rebellion. But no: even a tablecloth
was an official cousin of the curtains and both were
relations of the Council for Industrial Design. And there,
she supposed, was the *couch*. . . .

She smoothed her hair from one temple and closed her
eyes as though coming to terms with an impulse to faint.
For in a sense this was the story of their marriage:
the dream at dinner with the Galitzines had turned into
this.

It is true, of course, that we ourselves had often
remarked on a certain clash of personality between Meyer
and his house.

He himself might have loomed out of the shadows of
a Gothic castle library heavy, almost life-weary with the
old concept of the immortal individual soul, and steeped

in the long hours of kindred study which lie in trellised light on the wall above Rembrandt's St. Jerome.

I suppose some of us expected an old icon or something like that, lying about—saved, as so often miraculously happened with these expatriates, from an amputated past; saved or bought again. Or at least some emblem of his former existence. A gesture of value.

There was nothing of the kind. On the contrary, he had equipped himself with the very accessories which in their way were most uniform and typical of the new alien milieu, a small cheap camera and projector for taking and showing coloured photographs—likenesses of people so literal and life-like as to make the previous decades of black-and-white photography seem an abstruse art-form.

All this accommodation, on his part, was partly perhaps the exile's determined and instinctive urge to adopt, in the name of self-preservation the camouflage of a new milieu, but I think it was also something more: a kind of faith, and a refusal to allow himself any spurious relief.

Perhaps it was also due, quite simply, to the £1,500 a year which he sent to Isobel for herself and the child. Not much was left for interior decoration. And then he was out, five days in seven.

"But how can he *bear* it?" she asked herself, and suddenly there and then at 12.50 in the Corporation Bungalow she wondered how she would get through the next minutes.

In any house containing Isobel Meyer there was always a state of emergency. At any moment stairs, kitchen or more likely sofa might become the stage for a sustained aria, revolving round a new or an old allergy—all in the tones of " reason."

For there was Isobel Meyer and there was Isobel Meyer's

body—and the two did not agree—in fact she told one of the wives, during her short visit, that in low evening dress " her breasts sometimes gave her a headache."

Men may have been so aware of them that perhaps she felt: Well, who are you sitting next to, me or my bosom; make up your mind because as it is I'm getting a headache.

Sometimes she closed her eyes while talking, as though resting them from a vast ubiquitous mirror of which each man's eyes were an extension.

Her flesh had the browny pinky radiance which is the mecca of cosmetic publicity and her whole body did look as if it had some kind of autonomy; it insisted to-day, for instance, on more light, air and general exposure than was the custom, insisted until for the sake of peace she had allowed it a little Italian number—a sort of cummerbund which put out various gay clamped hands, up and down, in the name of modesty;—the sort of thing which might have been made just for it (her body), she herself and some old voyeur millionaire—just the three of them together, on a yacht. And in fact it had been last year, in the Mediterranean.

Now it was in Newtown Sangoro, West Africa.

*   *   *

When she caught sight of her husband accompanied by a little boy she put her hands fastidiously to her cheeks and thinking of the visit she had already sustained, at eleven, from a " perfectly strange apparition in *total* white," the rumour of a snake in the shrubs at the back, and the endless sight of barbed wire and lobelias, she damned her environment as a cross between The Daily Mail Ideal Home Exhibition, Belsen and a Garden of Eden without Adam or a decent apple.

"But what a lovely surprise," she said evenly. "Two of you."

Children don't like bad mothers—even other people's. They like some tarts, of course, and proper tarts often like them, too much. But a straight bad mother, a woman who has made a tortured narcissistic hobby out of serious and vital matters like nipples and breasts fills them with a nameless economic anxiety and gloom.

Paul was young enough to get Isobel unconsciously in this way and nearly old enough to be disturbed by her in another. He shook hands with downcast head and the correctness that mocks.

Probably Isobel would have disregarded him as she did her own boy (except to snap and nag) but she saw he was a *beautiful* boy, somebody else's, perhaps Number One's, and now she had been complaining about tropical subtopian ugliness since leaving the plane at Santa Barbara . . . that is for eleven days.

"Cupid," she said, "who is he?" now sure he must be Number One's.

"This is Paul, Isobel. His father is the P.C."

Isobel said, "Who on earth "—she could scarcely utter it—" is the P.C.?"

It was so like him to presume on her acquiring, in eleven days, the kind of knowledge that even had it been available would probably have killed her.

"The Provincial Commissioner."

"My poor child!" she said, getting herself a drink. "Full many a pearl the dark unfathomed caves of ocean bear. Why d'you carry a fishing net?"

"For butterflies," said Meyer in a certain tone. "Is lunch ready?"

She disregarded him. She was looking at the child's face, looking and looking with a mixed expression which

I won't attempt to describe. " MacPherson," she said,
" are you Scottish—like me? "

Meyer said sadly, " Isobel! " and then to the child,
" You must forgive my wife." But the child had seen a
rifle in the corner.

" Where do you expect to catch butterflies? " she said.
" The camp is sprayed daily with DDT and penicillin
gas. You won't find any butterflies here. Only ten-foot
cobras, wire, suburban golf-courses and women dressed
as theatre sisters, white serge to the neck, who call on you
at eleven, one imagines to talk prices and wombs."

Meyer had gone out but her gleaming black eyes
followed. She began to toy with some hair. The sinuous
way she moved always struck me—so slowly and carefully
as though the whole thing, even this normal elegant move
of hand to hair, was precariously achieved against a great
weight of chaos. Her eyes closed an instant when he
was out of sight as though he had slashed her by going
out; then they came back to the child. " Tell me
where? " she said.

" Porokorro."

" Porokorro. I think you must be mistaken, my
child."

" Porokorro." Paul's eyes rested on the stock, the lie,
the sights of the rifle. His head looked sleepy. He said,
" How many rounds does it hold? How many? "

Affronted, she took the object in.

Then she looked back at him. " Do you really mean
Porokorro? You know no one's going there to-day.
There's a mutiny."

" I know. Wizard. Whizz-bang—eeeaiou ChLang."

" Would you mind not! " She took a moment to
recover. " Porokorro indeed. I don't think your father,
the Inspector, will agree. If I'm not allowed to go in

peacetime it's not likely a child will be able to go during a disturbance."

" My father's taking me. No—honestly, can I look at that? Can I? Would your husband mind, I mean? Is it loaded? "

" My husband . . ." she echoed ironically.

He went across and while he stood at a devoted distance from the weapon she looked him all over, deciding that he *was* almost certainly going to Porokorro with his father, *to-day*.

" William," she said when he came in, " I hear children can go to Porokorro. I've begun to think you lie amongst other things."

As she said this she stretched and closed her eyes as though she wasn't saying it but just stretching. She got to her feet and groomed her belt clasp and peered down one flank of her skirt. " If necessary I shall hire a Syrian," she said. (She had heard that some wives had got into trouble by going out of bounds in cars hired from Syrians.)

Meyer said, " Yes. You could do that."

She said, " I tried to interest Mrs. Scott, I told her I was going . . ."

He let her talk to herself—and now in a corner demonstrated the rifle, touching it expertly with his lean hands. But his lack of enthusiasm was even apparent to Paul, who looked up at him impatiently.

The boy wanted to see everything at once and to touch as many bullets as possible and he embarked on one of those child catechisms which suggest a visitor from another century who has only so much time to collect all the information he can.

" No—do tell," he said, " you see, because I've got to go back to school soon. I mean does it kick much? "

" I spoke," Isobel said.

Picnic at Porokorro

At this moment a camp messenger arrived on a bicycle. Standing before the open windows he held out a note which Isobel took.

"It's for you," she called to her husband, as though its whole interest had perished. "Shall I open it?" She did so and read satirically: "The picnic at Porokorro is on. I hope you can make it—and your Mrs. too. Bring something to quench your thirst. Mac."

William put the rifle down and came over.

She handed the note to him, saying, "You see, you do make difficulties—don't you? Not least for 'your Mrs.' A point that I'm glad to see has at last been taken."

"No, I don't, Isobel."

"We'd better eat. He doesn't say what time. But I shall have to change."

At lunch she proclaimed her liberty with every movement she made, also her right to judge Africa and Africans without consulting him first. Thus she ordered about the two boys who had been his servants for years as though they had much to learn, and treated them as though they were some kind of draught—doors left open. For when they came close she looked over her shoulder, uneasily, as though catching her death.

"I suppose they're really as intelligent as us," she said when the door closed.

"How was it—better?" Meyer said reluctantly.

"They touch the salad," she said.

"Well?"

"Well—is it well—when they refuse to use toilet paper."

He wondered what she had said in his absence.

"You see," she said, "you don't mind really, do you? In fact, you like it!"

He looked up at last and agreed to forget there was a

129   I

child present. " Isobel, the speed with which you find out this sort of fact rather suggests that *you like it*. You're excelling yourself here. Why do you want to go to Porokorro? That's another thing like the salad," he said, looking into her eyes, " which seems odd in a person who ' can't bear ugliness.' "

" You mean the famous beauty spot," she said with a little snort, " because it's a famous beauty spot."

" Oh—you just want to see the Falls? "

" I want to see it all."

" The Famous Beauty Spot. Porokorro." His eyes shone. *How* disappointed you will be. The back of Leicester Square on a Saturday night would give you more thrill.

" God! " she gasped, touched on the quick of exasperation, " you're a long German book! "

Minutes passed. Meyer talked to Paul.

Later there was a long silence which he ended by saying, " I'm sorry. Perhaps you are right, darling, to want to go to Porokorro. It is an extraordinary place— full of extraordinary stories. Epics of endurance and, yes, in a way it is beautiful like the Leonardo sketches of the Inferno. But you see it's not up to me. Wait. And let's go together. Let's hope Paul's father makes everyone very sweet and reasonable—here, and there too—and then we can fill our Thermoses with ice and scalding tea and go across in a hollow tree-trunk to-morrow and I'll introduce you to the warden who was in the Chindits. There is something moving in the way he lies. He is a grand baroque Johnsonian liar. He is telling you his dreams. . . ."

While her husband opened this vista, in a voice which sounded like a bleeding exhausted prayer for mutual tolerance, her face showed every sign of frustration. She said she had enough trouble with her own dreams—and she smiled with a sudden half grateful, half envious censure at the other non-official candidate for Porokorro who had, like herself, the advantages of youth and beauty.

For he was now stalking, without permission to leave the table, a brick-throated lizard peering round a pillar. The sun gleamed on the downy hairs of his upper lip and his blue eyes were rapt, secure in this or any home.

Meyer said, " He has the same hair as Robert."

She replied, " You can't resist it, can you? "

" What? " he said in some surprise.

" Blaming me."

She got up and left the table, which left Meyer alone.

From the next room she said, " All the time. Shall I have him flown out? " And there came the brisk rattle of a matchbox and then the rasping friction and sigh of ignition. Then she said, " I mean I could—if you persist."

The expulsion of smoke sounded like a curse—or the first rush of exhaust from a car already starting, going away, to Porokorro, anywhere.

14

Lunch at Barber's bungalow was outwardly like lunch
any other day. The ginger-haired, blank-faced Commissioner of Police Fadden, alone with his lack of social
grace or pretence of it, seemed the only one prepared to
be rather glum, vague and silent, in short relevant.

In fact he sometimes seemed about to burst out with
a general question: " Look! What *did* we decide? And
what is all this? Who *is* in charge? " Whereas, of course,
really he would have been the last to have done anything
of the kind because long ago he had been broken in to a
regard for discipline for its own sake. Nevertheless, a
certain simplicity and innocence seemed to put him into
a more open state of tension than the others.

MacPherson believed he himself was most fitted to call
the tune and he believed, too, that he had called it. He was
used to responsibility and outwardly made light of the
morning's decisions; but in fact he was tight as a violin,
as he talked of other things.

The Secretary, Joint-Hicks, was happier. A four-course
lunch reassured. Things were as they had always been.
The hand which offered a silver dish was the seal on old
certainties.

And then . . . Barber. Who would have ever guessed
there was someone in that room who saw both the
Secretary—and even MacPherson—with complete dis-

passion. For outwardly Barber was warmly engaged with them all. He was fruitier than the Secretary—the ceiling rang to their combined laugh when the Secretary told how the only broke Syrian in the colony had got home by selling his Boy's three bastards, girls, in French territory.

" And this happened *last week*? " Barber said with the passionate attention which always encouraged people who told him things to tell him more. Perhaps he even knew the story, as he laughed incredulously, " My God, why haven't I got any daughters? The Admiral only gives me sons."

The " Admiral," Mrs. Barber, had been a Captain in the Wrens. She was on leave. (He used to say " They've got a plaque in Portsmouth where she sat from '39 to '45.") She was jolly in a nice monotonous way and large. She seemed to consolidate behind him like infantry behind a flying armoured column.

Three white-coated boys moved swiftly with dishes and iced *vin rosé*. The room was invisibly, soundlessly air-conditioned but Barber excused himself for it by saying he'd had 'flu twice since it was put in. Had they ever shot lizards with an air-gun? He did it occasionally. It wasn't easy at 25 yards.

Fadden raised his hand to his mouth to silence the ghost of a belch but it didn't materialise.

There was something in the air, squadrons of angels overhead and no Admiral to dispel them with one of her determined, too dry, keen little questions to one of the men, " Have you been home this year? " supporting the question with her four-square imperturbability. She quite liked to be bored, that was her strength.

In his own house, without his wife, Barber made all feel precarious, an act of will, directed by strings. Wires!

That is what he suggested—a human soul looking out of a puppet's body, waiting for the twitch of the strings. Now, crouching like a trim flyweight over the business of hospitality, over the wine. Here he was no longer the magician of the office.

" Mac, you've got to tell how your predecessor shot his cook for the *Manchester Guardian*—what! " and Barber looked round to show himself already disturbed by more laughter than is good for you. " That's my favourite," he said, " in Mac's repertoire."

" Ach, they know that old story."

But they didn't.

" Well he was a loon, this newspaper fellow. Asking darn silly questions—about corporal punishment and bride-price and goodness knows what. Suddenly . . . Old Ben was eating his meat . . . like this, and chewed slower—slower—so—giving soft answers. Then he spat it all out and roared, ' Christopher! Fetch Christopher,' and the cook, Christopher, came. ' Christopher,' he said, ' the meat's tough! ' At once Christopher began to plead, ' No, sah—please, sah,' going gradually down on his knees—' Please don't—don't.' Slowly Ben drew a pistol out of his pocket.

" Bang! Christopher rolled over, clutching and gasping. ' Take him away.'

" The other boys picked him up.

" Ben went on eating.

" D'you know! That got into print. And when the shindy was at its worst Richardson was able to write a letter saying how he had an understanding with his cook how to get rid of people who asked silly questions. He said they practised once a week but it might have to stop. They were getting too good. A missionary had fainted."

Picnic at Porokorro

They were all grateful for MacPherson. In the absence of the Admiral he kept everything afloat.

When I think of this lunch party I wonder if, in the circumstances, any other people in the world but the British would have lived it out from beginning to end without reference to the business on hand. Even Mac-Pherson, who thought the only trouble was in *thinking* there was trouble, never asked any serious general questions about the last few weeks. If he had I can't believe the day would have ended as it did.

They ate four courses. Cream and butter cooking. The Administration are not rich compared to senior mining executives, but Barber made it all right. It is no exaggeration to say that he forked the perfect profiterolles *with distaste*. The fact is, he really was far more interested in power than in the things that went with it—except possibly the sport at which he excelled, shooting, fishing and cricket. I think he unconsciously hated women—real women. The Admiral had been more of a very pretty 1945 " spot height." Barber, D.S.O. (but merely Hayleybury) came back and took her at a moment when she was strictly an Old Etonian, objective on a wide, rich front.

I often thought it must have been a mysterious experience to have been the object of his intensity. The Admiral seldom spoke to him in public and never intimately. Sometimes she listened to his volubility with something like contempt in her eyes.

His laugh rang loud and often at lunch that day through the open windows, and the early returners to work after lunch, walking at the bottom of the flowery green on which he lived, heard it floating—and with it, " By God, I like that . . ." " No, go on, go on —do Umbopa, Mac—you must—you're not leaving here till you do Umbopa asking for money to buy a wife."

And why not? The Africans keep happy doing the same about us. But on the day in question the relaxation, the laughter, was to be remembered.

Heaven knows, there was real warmth in the way Barber pressed cigars upon them, the way he whispered almost like a ventriloquist that if any of them were ever up this way " Butlins was at their disposal." He was almost like Warner about the BMT. Here they could use anything he used—any time. " In November we're getting Phoozoo foam baths. They stop prickly heat." His face was a bomb of no-comment.

Then the note was brought in for him. From Gordon.

" Excuse me," he said and took it aside. While opening it he glanced through the window and saw that it had been brought by one of the Security Jeeps, and by one of the white staff, who stood looking up at the bungalow.

The conversation dwindled while glances were thrown in his direction.

The note was written in Gordon's schoolboyish longhand.

" *The three men who disappeared with the rifles crossed over to Bornu island this morning. They are said to be still there. The Cowboy is there too. Digging has stopped. More and more speeches. Palm wine galore!* "

Number One scribbled acknowledgment and turned to his guests.

" Well, Mac," he said, " bad men are reported on Bornu."

The remark was taken, as it seemed to be offered, in the spirit of the whole lunch—and Mac said, " You don't say! "

Barber said, " I do love Mac. You tell him a devil is waiting for him and he says ' Only *one*? ' "

Everyone laughed.

And a moment later to hear Barber say " I ought to go to the office," you'd have thought he would have kicked the whole BMT over in the name of a free-er, coarser, more open fraternity, which in the light of what happened is strange.

He scrumpled Gordon's note as though it were a routine circular and chucked it, scarcely crinkled, in a waste-paper basket near where Mac was standing.

Mac put his hand on his shoulder. " Mr. Tom Barber," he said, " yer staying a wee while yet: it's not often I have the pleasure . . ." He paused and stared with philanthropy into Number One's face. "Ai . . . the *pleasure* of telling the BMT what I think of it. . . ."

Another bottle of vine rosé was produced.

15

"But I *say*, darling," said Penny Scott as her husband entered wearing a Security Guard armband.

Hospital nurses greet their worst patients thus each fresh morning when they whisk in on the heels of the night nurse and scatter like a demonstration gun-grew to key functions, chasing away the low moments of the small hours, the humours of the night: "*Good morning, Mr. So-and-So!*" A challenge, almost a taunt. Live! And they drive the point home by shock—a brusque movement of the bed, or assault with a glass of medicine.

This was what Ian Scott got from his wife after even the shortest separation. Not that she did it on purpose; she did it with everyone. She had been, like him, in the British Council and before that at a drama school where animation was at a ghastly premium. And so she never hailed him in any other tone. His set-up, which she had coveted, disapproved of her—not only from a snob point of view but also—(which they made silently clear)—on apparently deeper levels which were nevertheless mainly class shibboleths although presented as moral and æsthetic objections. She was a "bore," "silly," even "maddening." So what was he? He was a little, little boy whose ear she could pull till his huge head rocked back and forth, back and forth—poor old bunny—he wouldn't cry, it was hurting enough but he wouldn't cry. *What a man!* Not to cry.

138

Picnic at Porokorro

Perhaps he was.

How cruel life is and perhaps cruel to describe their life together first in these terms. For like two mill-stones, in three years they had ground grating grooves into each other and propped each other up. Exacerbation remained but even this was *something*—a tension, an interest: without it what would there have been? The word is too dreadful and against that word I hear her breathless haste to say *some*thing—even the obvious thing, first before anyone else—(so that she literally dived to insert it)—even in the company of some expert or of a person who might perhaps not have uttered a cliché. Sometimes Ian looked as though mist were clearing above hell. For Penny could give a woman's mag. answer to almost any problem—and in the same brief terms, so good, so *right*. But the thing was she was a nightmare to herself, let alone other people.

Why?

Because she had provided the woman's mag. answer for herself: He was exactly like the illustrated *dark* heroes of women's mag. stories, and she had fitted him, like " the end " into her pattern, and he didn't work, either literally or in the larger sense. She had lived her fiction and it was proving a neurosis. They were left with one secret mutual bond: endurance.

" I *say!* " (One could almost imagine the squawk of the bed's casters.) And she sang: " Well—how did it go? "

He liked this to be asked: How did it go? A dreamy look came into his eyes.

Very slowly, as though remembering, he said, " Oh— much better, thank you, darling. With these people I feel I'm getting somewhere at last."

She tidied up round him.

" What did Bunny tell them ? " and she bent over him, cradled his head and rocked it suddenly.

" Ow ! " he cried.

" I'm so sorry, darling, what is it ? "

" Nothing, darling. But . . ." He got up feeling his neck.

" Oh, darling, have I hurt you? I'm *so* sorry. . . . Sit down. There."

He sat down reluctantly. " Was it too hard ? "she said.

She put her cheek against his. " Mmmmm," she said. ("Don't be too tired to show affection when he comes from work.")

The terrible thing is that he forgot now what had happened so recently to his neck and a moony, almost sleepy look came into his eyes while her flesh touched his.

Then he said, " I've to go down to Porokorro this afternoon."

" Oh, no ! Oh, good ! How clever. Clever bunny ! Then there is a riot ? "

" There's a little trouble," he conceded. " I'm going down where it is."

" You're not. I shan't let you, bunny. Honestly, really ? But really honestly ? But how wonderful."

God save us all. She was one of us—no doubt " doing all the wrong things." I know from one of the wives in whom she confided that she had written up to " Doris " or someone—Yours sincerely Well-meaning—and had been told to " give him Confidence." And perhaps she did. What standard of comparison have we to be sure that she didn't ?

The look of murderous bemused hatred which he very, very occasionally rested on her was probably nothing to go by. It often hinged on the most superficial and normal vanity.

" But *straight off?* " she said.

" What d'you mean, darling, straight off? "

" Won't you have to get used to things before you do anything. You know—go round? "

" Well—I'm going down there—to get used to things," and he laughed loudly. He had caught her out. " What, darling? " and still guffawing he said, " Silly darling " in tones of concise genial patronage.

Then he said gravely, " Did you call on Isobel Meyer? "

Meyer was kind to Scott—and even liked him probably better than most people in the camp. He used to say " I like Scott. He is not such a fool." Meyer dined often with the Scotts and used to talk till late at night. He had a good effect on Penny, quietening her—and giving her confidence—or perhaps giving her the feeling that this " having confidence " was not such a matter of life and death. Anyhow—confidence for what? There was a sensuous quality in his voice. Penny once said impetuously, " I feel I could tell him *anything*," as though she really meant, " Oh—*him* I *could* tell .... nothing."

" Did you call, darling? " he repeated.

" Yes I did. Extraordinary woman. After a few words she suddenly said she'd got a headache. She simply went out."

" Oh—I'm so sorry." He spoke formally. A headache was a headache. She must accept that. The alternative to accepting the excuse would be unbearable.

" I thought it rather odd," she persisted.

" Oh no, darling," he murmured mothily, " everyone has headaches. I'm sure she was very pleased."

Penny said, " D'you really think she was pleased? "

" I don't think you need worry about that. She is known to be a bit of a hypochondriac." He guffawed again at his temerity.

They went into lunch. A silent white-coated black boy approached from the sideboard with the entrée as they flipped free their napkins.

" Why you no change flower-water, Prescott? " she said.

" Yes, ma'am."

After a few moments Scott said carefully, " Did you like her? " He meant, " Did she like you? "

Penny sang, " Oh yes. Of course. Why not, Bunny? "

" Good, darling."

" She didn't tell me much except that she was going to Porokorro this afternoon."

He laughed louder than ever. " I'm quite sure she's not. Did she know about the trouble? "

" Yes—she said she was going with a Syrian. Can *I* come . . . with you? "

Very gravely, like a cardinal in public, he helped himself to Colman's tube mustard and in his whispy exquisite voice he said, " No—and I don't think Isobel Meyer will be at Porokorro."

But his face had tightened—as though it had been suggested his new job as Security Guard could prove social: a guide to a society woman who . . . well . . . he wouldn't say it.

He ate in silence thinking of what lay ahead. Apparently that reporter in common sun-glasses might turn up. Colonel Gordon had asked Ian to keep an eye on him if he did. He said: When the Black Watch took the Leitz Works in '45 it had been the Warcos who took the whole stock of Leicas in the offices.

" What is it, darling? " she said.

" Nothing, darling. Really . . ."

He put out his hand, smiling responsibly. And she took it, smiling too, across the table. " I've got to hurry,"

he said. " I've got to see a man called Roberts. At
2.30."

He was fussily devoted to punctuality. A schedule was
the chart and proof of his solid, practical orientation
and the grounds for his hope of a rise. He could say
" 2.30 " in a tone which would surely echo in high
places.

But unfortunately it only echoed inside himself. There
indeed it set up a great boom of transcendental triumph so
that afterwards his fervent eyes turned tired and ill at
the dimensions of his sacrifice; his whole life, he sometimes seemed to have laid down for " 2.30."

16

WARNER GOT back at about 2.15.

Apparently he tried to get in touch with Barber at once. He went to the head office and found it closed. A plant-operator posting mail in the air-box, which is clamped to the head office wall, saw him there and told him it was siesta time: he'd be lucky if he found a cat.

He then went to the mess, which was open but shuttered and all but dark. With difficulty he persuaded the bar-boy Attlee to let him use the camp phone.

" Then I'd like some chop," he said. " And two big shandies."

" I see, sah."

He went in behind the bar and was let into a little room with a rolltop desk, closed up and looking very locked. He was given the instrument by a white palmed hand looming without a sound at his side.

The next two minutes were like a soliloquy in a cave.
" Mr. Barber, please."

" Mr. Barber ? "

" The managing director."

" The managing director—yes, sah."

" Give me his house then."

" Bungalow."

" His bungalow OK his bungalow."

Picnic at Porokorro

" His bungalow OK. Number 28."

" Hallo," then a strange noise.

He once got as far as being asked who was speaking and he gave his name. The man never came back.

He thought: they're all the same. He came out and said aloud, " OK."

There was a shadowy figure by the bar.

" I'll try again after chop," he said to Attlee. " Got the shandies? "

" Bar shut, sah."

" Oh, for Pete's sake . . . Look at it all. . . ."

His mouth, his whole body yearned for cold moisture. He turned to the figure.

Attlee said, " For late chop see Mr. Jepson-Snailes, sah," and he began to swab the bar to show this was swab, not chop, time.

" Where can I find Mr. Jepson-Snailes? " Warner said, looking at the man a few yards away.

" What can I do for you? " the figure said unnaturally.

Many of us would resent the idea that we often speak truculently to each other in the BMT and quarrel in a repressed acidulous way over nothing—a mere word, before either party has made sure what the other meant. But this is the case.

People *press* here, press on each other, on anything.

Jepson-Snailes has reason perhaps to be the most " pressing " of all. He will bear the mark—the smooth yellowish hairless groove of the matchet slash—to his grave. I suspect he was always some kind of failure. He had been to a minor public school yet at the age of forty-five hadn't got as far in the BMT as many youths on the technical side who had started work at sixteen; and he had no wife or family and so lived in the mess with stray visitors or boys newly out, boys too young to be married

and have bungalows of their own. He was always reading
or drinking and pretending not to notice the proximity
of someone he knew until the person addressed him.
Then he affected indifference or tolerance. To look at,
these days, he reminded one of those farm mongrels who
fight unsuccessfully all their lives till finally they look
frayed and chewed all over and their aggression has
become a whine of defeat even before they attack. He was
a pitiful figure, but in argument always made a tyrannical
show of "experience," "dignity" and "reason." And
somehow it always came to argument.

The Company was "looking after him," and now to
his job running the mess had been added this part-time
supervision in the Separating House—in the wake of
Scott. He was thus mainly alone or with Africans all
day and all night, as he had been at the time he was
slashed. From to-day Silent Brown would be his only
frequent white contact.

He said to Attlee, "Give him the shandy."

Attlee turned the light on and for the first time Warner
noticed the immense portrait of the Queen, like a draw-
bridge pulled up, over the band dais.

"Jesus!" he said and gazed up with rapt distaste.
Then, "Could I get some grub?"

Jepson-Snailes said, "I very much doubt it."

Jepson-Snailes also now looked up at the Queen, and
then back at Warner, who said, "Big photographs seem
part of the international twitch. But I never saw one
that needed a crane. Not till now."

"I beg your pardon."

Warner weighed up the chances of getting it across,
then he said, "Nothing. Could I get grub?"

"The times are up on the board."

Attlee laid down the shandies with sensuous gentleness.

146

Warner drank frantically, exquisitely, and crashed the glass down, ready for more. " Mr. Barber told me I'd get grub here."

" At the proper time."

" Can I try begging? " He moved away towards the dining-room. Then Jepson-Snailes said, " You're a visitor —we might manage something. Through there. As a matter of fact, it's waiting. No one knew what the hell had happened to you."

When Warner was eating Jepson-Snailes came and sat near him with an expression of omniscient and hostile boredom. He offered no explanation for his company.

" Geological? " he said.

" Press," Warner said. " Daily ———. I think you knew."

The man's eyes closed and he reared his head away slightly as though from a stench. Then he just looked at Warner.

Warner said cheerfully, " How d'you get that mark on your face? "

" That's a long story."

" It's a long mark."

" What I wonder about you chaps is: do you try something else first. If it's a last resort—then that's different."

" What paper do you read? "

Jepson-Snailes would not reply—he just sat staring at Warner eating. At last he said, " I mean what's it in aid of this time? "

" I don't get you."

" The Assignment."

" A little floodlighting."

Jepson-Snailes couldn't work it out and thought Warner

was laughing at him, *patronising him*. His eyes slowly petrified.

Warner said, " What's the root of the trouble here? "

Jepson-Snailes smiled—like low sun on a corpse. One of his toes waggled. "'I can do that one," he said. " Little half educated monkeys, with chips on their shoulders."

" Or quarter educated baboons with diamonds in their fists? "

Jepson-Snailes smiled again and after a time said, " What's going to happen in Gold Coast? "

" Ghana's OK, isn't it? I mean it's better than France and that sort of thing. What are we worrying about? "

" The Ashanti will have enough of it one day. They'll get up and drive Nkrumah and his little coastal monkeys into the sea. If I had a gun I'd help them."

" They nicked you pretty deep, didn't they? "

Jepson-Snailes often looked as if he could strike the person he was talking to—and never more than when that person agreed with him. In fact he looked at Warner now rather peacefully and affectionately, as though the imminence of violence rested him.

" A chap got ten years for that."

" What did you get? "

" I . . . ? " Jepson-Snailes said vaguely.

" For taking his country's diamonds."

Silence.

" There's another kind of person who should get ten years—the people at home like you. You're the biggest bloody hypocrites outside America. You want it both ways. You want it five ways. All you're out for is yourselves."

" That's right: in the end it proved catching."

" What—proved catching? "

Picnic at Porokorro

Again Jepson-Snailes missed the meaning.

"We *got* ten years—thousands of years—now we're out. First morning out. No pal at the gate. That sort of thing. Have to arrange our own reception. No welcome. Even the probation officers have climbed the lamp-posts."

Jepson-Snailes looked at Warner with a butcher's regard for detail. At last he said, "I wish you'd been here the night the police changed sides . . . last year."

"That's all right: I'm here to-night."

". . . because I'd like to see them get you—just for a few minutes. No—but I really would—I really would. . . . You know what they put in your mouth . . . finally, your little black bastard educated democrats . . ."

"I've heard."

Jepson-Snailes got up. He leant forward till his face was near Warner's. "In your case I'd reverse the technique. I'd take your tongue and put it in the other end. And it could wag wag wag till doomsday in the same medium as ever."

Warner got up. He was pale.

As he passed the bar Attlee said, "You will phone now, sah? Get Mr. Barber now?"

He walked through and out without knowing where he was going.

The sun hit his eyes like a sore bright flame and he was cold all over with sweat. He stopped and looked about him like a lost dog in the middle of everyone, which was no one.

Attlee followed him. "Mr. Barber walk by to office, sah, just this moment."

Warner said, "Which is bungalow of Lieutenant Roberts?"

Jepson-Snailes's step sounded on the mess tiles, loitering towards the steel and glass door.

He planted himself, like a shop detective, where he could watch Warner out of sight, and stayed there for some reason till he was.

17

ROBERTS WOKE up as though from a noise. He listened. It was not repeated.

He stared at the new ceiling and couldn't think where he was; not even when his eyes were wide and intelligent could he think where he was. Amnesia lay on him like balm and for the moment he could not move, but kept sinking back to the nice place he'd come from, for sleep, at last, had been annihilation.

He had only slept two nights in this bed since coming to the BMT. Most nights he had been at Porokorro or one of the other sites, and before that all over the place for two years. So the ceiling might have been anybody's ceiling. And there was no help from the furniture either. For furniture in all the colony bungalows has much in common unless graced by a peculiar personal object—such as—and he now saw it looking at him—his panama hat with the ricketty ribbon perched on a very Designed, modern table.

The Hat placed him, placed yesterday and to-day—and he watched it long and quietly, still, as it were, from shelter.

Then he heard the noise which must have woken him in the first place—the sort of cough some chaps make when they haven't got a cough.

A man he did not know was sitting opposite a bottle of champagne angled in a sweating silver bucket. The man was rubbing his hands with a strange rhythmic motion that was somehow exquisite and responsible. Roberts remembered seeing his face in the mess—the face of a clergyman or a poet or something. Now the long hands desisted and one of them adjusted the signet ring on the other while the man's eyes rested on the window, on the distance.

" What ho there," Roberts said cheerlessly and got up, walking rather away from him as well as towards him, as people do in pyjamas.

The man rose to his full huge height, smiling with a kind of brilliant soft and condescending apology. " I'm *so* sorry," he said, " your Boy assured me . . ."

" But, sir, the pleasure's ours. Sit down again. Better be champagne, hadn't it? Struck lucky. Excuse me," and Roberts picked up a note beside the bottle. " It's about you," he said. " You're Ian Scott—I'm Roberts. Well there we are . . ." he was still reading. " Are you my successor? Is that it? "

" Good heavens, no." Scott was dismayed. " At least . . . well . . ."

Roberts got two glasses, taking the note with him. " Relax. I'm not sacked. Security—eh? Did you apply? "

" Well . . . not exactly . . . that is to say not specifically."

The sudden detonation of the cork shot the specifying sentence dead. Roberts smiled. " Sorry—go on."

" Well, I wanted a change."

" So you joined the cops. And you struck champagne."

" Yes," and Scott burst into one of his too sudden, too loud convivial guffaws. It almost had the confidence of charm. But not quite.

Roberts said factually, " Cheers."

After a little hesitation Scott responded, " Cheers."

They sat opposite each other. Roberts looked at his watch. It was two-thirty. He plucked his pyjama trousers above each knee and looked out of the window.

"I'm starved. What's happening?" He picked up the note again and read carefully. Then he said, "Well, are you in the picture . . . ?"

"I gather . . . you had . . ." Scott raised his mothy soft eyes to Roberts to see if he should proceed, "rather a nasty time yesterday . . . with some thugs."

He had showed he was in the picture.

But Roberts said, "Thugs eh? I'm a policeman. You know what we were taught at the police college? 'A policeman's no better than his worst informer.' Not a bad thing to remember."

Scott smiled with condescending apology. Then he said dreamily, "Well, I suppose a policeman *could* be *worse* than his worst informer." Scott was glad to have come upon a person who, like Meyer, enjoyed the play of ideas. He took up his glass in quite a different way, smiling and soon he added, "But I wonder how many cops *really* think they're as bad as their worst informer. I bet the man who taught you that didn't think so." And he guffawed. "What? . . ." he said and he repeated the thrust. "How many *really* . . ."

"Do *you*?" Roberts said.

"Do I . . . what?"

"Think you're as bad as an informer?"

"I haven't yet had an informer," and Scott guffawed again convivially, proudly, as though he had been quick. The debate was fun. "But cops are the villains nowadays," he said suddenly to keep it going. "We're the villains."

"And we could be, too. But what about the chaps that hire us?"

" Which chaps? "

" The chaps that hire the cops that . . . do the necessary. And the rest. I mean once you start in on that sort of thing then the set-up's a dead loss. The thing is you earn your screw and that's that. Correct me if I'm wrong."

After a due pause Scott replied in tones of gentle responsibility, " No—I don't think you are wrong." Scott was warming: the man was really consulting him. The man appreciated him. He wasn't bad really—spite of being a bit . . . well—to be bald: Charley.

" Well, say, chum—say if you think I am round the bend. I shan't mind."

" No, no, no, I don't think that at all."

" Thanks." And Roberts looked at him curiously. " What were you in till now? "

" The Separating House."

" And one day you started barking."

" Well—no," he said charmingly. " Not quite." He laughed more easily and frankly, and now with all the truth and gentleness of which he was capable he said simply " Nearly."

" OK. We're all human."

They drank. They made little contact. Every communication ended in a sort of stump.

Roberts got up. " And you don't know what's cooking."

Scott at once strained to be executive: he frowned and said, " The Provincial Commissioner's here."

" And they're still talking? " Roberts couldn't get his mind off the *chap's voice*. It made him more restless than ever, like seeing a batsman play a shot after the ball has passed.

" I heard a rumour something's going to happen this evening," Scott added.

Silence for a full minute.

" Something's going to happen, is it," Roberts had poured some more champagne.

" I wouldn't really know."

Then Roberts said, " D'you know what I think ? "

" What ? "

" They ask for what they get."

" Who? "

" The diggers."

" Oh yes, the diggers."

" You take up racing driving. OK you get killed. OK? "

" Yes."

" You don't blame the kerb? "

" No—quite."

" Well—you take up illicit digging—and you get killed. OK? "

" Yes."

" You don't blame the police."

" No."

" And I ask for what I get, OK? "

" Yes."

" OK, then."

Scott suddenly guffawed. " You ought to be a lawyer."

Roberts said wearily, " I was dumb at school. But do I look like a murderer? "

This question so astonished Scott that his face became quite blank.

Roberts said, " Skip it."

Then Scott saw: it was another joke. He laughed as he hadn't for weeks, not even on this relieving day.

Roberts turned away, and went and stood by the window.

Thankfully Scott thought here was a man at last who had enough confidence to relax, not to be "always on duty". Life would be better in Security. They would get on. He must come round to the house. As soon as possible. Yes . . . Life *would* be better.

Then from the figure at the window a cool voice said, "You want to watch that laugh," and then a moment later, "I mean just—you don't want to let it get the better of you. Fun's rationed."

Seconds passed.

At last Scott stood up. The perplexity of his face was terrible.

Roberts came back. "I'm sorry, chum . . . Ian, isn't it? Sit down. We've got to finish this . . ."

When he had poured out he said, "It's average hell, isn't it? I mean if a chap pauses."

But Scott was still on his feet and having thanked Roberts and made a rendezvous he said, "Good-bye."

"OK, then. Cheerio! On the dot, mind."

Roberts finished the bottle indifferently.

*　　　　*　　　　*

Barber's vin rosé—as we all of us know—is not the innocent stuff it seems. MacPherson's warm heart was overflowing. He couldn't wait to get down to Porokorro —to speak to those "damned rogues," many of whose fathers had "probably been up before" him, and with these expressions the subject suddenly surfaced beside them like an accompanying monster, but tame—as tame as you liked to make it, which was tame indeed.

"By God," he said, "get your parasol and yer bikinis,

yer sweet nothings and all get doon there. And now where's that damned rogue of mine. He'll get me the sack."

Barber scanned him with eyes like footlights: made Mac stand out in a great ambivalent blaze. He said, "I wish I could come. I'd like to see this, Mac. . . ."

MacPherson suddenly pointed a finger an inch from his nose and said, "Good lord—and to think I'm doon this for BMT. No' even for the British Empire any more but for the bloody Minerals Trust. While he stays at home and gives me that knowing look. Tom, remember? 'And Manhood is called foolery, when it stands against a falling fabric.' He'll come and dig me out afterwards. I'll get a BMT funeral and BF put after my name."

The others laughed as though agreeing, at which he said with some temper, "Well, ahm *no* doon it for the BMT—ahm doon it for *persons*. Not even for the Pipple, because personally I don't know of any such thing. You can huvv the Pipple. Neither the African Pipple nor the British Pipple. I'm doon it for One Person, and you can pu' tha' in yer pipe and smoke it, Mr. Barber—and the pairson migh' be bluck Digger or a pink and white policeman." There were tears in his eyes as he got Scotcher. Of course they were partly vin rosé—but—and this I think became known and was remembered with astonishment long after—Barber, who was standing as already described in front of MacPherson, hanging on his lips with only the usual elusive shadow of irony, suddenly too had tears in his eyes. Of course he admitted being a sentimentalist and wept copiously at bad films and when the British Fleet steamed in line ahead, or at George Orwell's descriptions of teatime in miners' cottages, but

157

in the light of what happened I can never forget his sudden tears at that moment.

MacPherson carried on a bit longer. He even told some more colony stories and sang a little song too. At some point or other Barber said, " And afterwards, Mac, is there going to be a difference? And if there isn't will you get Jim Fadden a proper police force? "

" I'd get him a bowler hat if I could. Look at him. £1,800 a year and a bloody army under him. Twenty years ago I covered his area with *one King's Messenger*—at two bob a week."

So it had come out at last.

Barber said, " I've got to get along . . ."

" Well, get along. Let everyone get along. I'm going to get along."

It had been MacPherson's whole faith from the moment he arrived to be purposefully " off duty "—in other words to live out to the full, even here, his contention that there was no trouble. Hence no timing had been arranged. They would " go down there after lunch." For him the " picnic " was not a psychological warfare trick—laid on with timings—but a restoration of a state of reality. There *was* no trouble.

" So—where's ma young devil—whoorin' round at Mrs. Meyer? "

" Steady, Mac! "

The lunch party broke up as it began, convivially.

" And what about the press? " Barber said. They were all on their feet.

" What press? " said Mac.

" The ————."

" Well, what about it? "

" It's here."

During MacPherson's silence Barber said, " You mean
you didn't know? "

" Why should I know? "

" We thought he must have come through your
people."

" Oh, Lord have mercy upon us."

" Amen," said the Secretary.

Fadden looked uneasy. He read the ————. He
thought it a clever rag, and lively. He couldn't do with
print when it looked up at you solid like porridge. And
he liked a good figure with curves. He had never known
one intimately. Life was dull enough. He coughed
evasively and looked at his feet.

" Well, let him come . . . why not? " MacPherson said.
" The more the merrier. I'll keep him along with me."

" Couldn't he be sent on a conducted tour in the other
direction? " laughed the Secretary. " Mac says there's
no trouble—but we can be sure there will be after the
Daily ———— has written us up."

" Och away—let him come. What's he like? " said
Mac.

" It's not what *he's* like—it's what his paper's like,"
the Secretary said agreeably.

" No, it's what *he's* like," MacPherson said. " If he's
with me, it's what he's like. So what *is* he like ? "

Barber took the question seriously. " I've only seen
him for a few minutes. . . . He's OK. . . . I think . . .
I don't know."

There was a dubious silence. And then MacPherson
added to his load. His eyes shone. All could be included,
all reconciled in the principle of his expedition.

" Bring him along. Show him everything. Put him
in my car—if it's come yet. Is it back? "

" Yes, it's back," Number One said quietly.

Several eyes were raised fleetingly to Barber's face. He knew such outlandish titbits of information. People sometimes looked at him with sudden surmise as though wondering what else he knew. There was a pause.

Then Mac said, " Good."

18

THE WOUNDED inhabit a private world. Other people
stand thankfully apart or spare a moment or an act of
pity before passing on—but having passed on something
sticks in their mind. A noise they heard from the con-
vulsed body nags as though " truer " than anything
they have heard for weeks.

Warner did not expect to communicate with those who
stood " thankfully apart." Perhaps by now he enjoyed
his inability to do so. He sucked the sweet of contempt—
as much as he sucked the sweet of his pain. He did a lot
of sucking and a lot of biting. But there were moments
when a little power came his way, moments when he got
a hearing and respect; then his thin mouth trembled as
he turned to *other people*—and felt now . . . now . . . see
what I do with this power—I give it to you back, won't
you always do the same with me, with everyone, and
won't the world then be better? But of course he couldn't
express this, or even act it. A medium wasn't available.
Besides, it was perhaps a corruptly partial truth. He could
never have enough satisfaction for generosity to become
a permanent sensation. They—the debtors—had
something like the national debt to face. He wanted
to see it faced. He wanted to be there for the total
pay-off.

And yet he had *hurried*, when he went into the mess

thinking the whole BMT was in his power. He almost ran to find Barber.

He knew very little of conditions here and had drawn immoderate conclusions from the words of P.C. Amanda. Like the Swiss chemist in Sangoro, he thought the powder train to another period of riots was already sputtering and flaming—*but could still be put out.*

Which lay in his gift. I do think he really felt he held our destiny in his hand.

There was the story, the scoop—but that would stand up without riots. He loathed his job—as Scott and Dickson could never loathe it in a thousand years. But he would make sure the story stood up.

It would be wrong to give the impression Warner *thought*; he didn't, he flowed—along with one tight complex feeling like a modern chord. Thought came afterwards, shored up banks, made bridges and said this was the right way.

He flowed into the dark mess, into Jepson-Snailes (instead of Barber) and then broke up, and in flood—so to speak—he flowed towards Roberts, a direction which must have seemed to him the very opposite of his original impulse towards Barber.

Why? He might have given six different answers in six minutes. After episodes that increased his natural tension he gravitated, perhaps, to *hubs*, and catalysts.

It was not difficult for him to find his way to the bungalow of Lieutenant Roberts, nor having found it to walk in, through the open windows—and catch him asleep sitting up beside an empty bottle of champagne.

Two-fifty, he noted, of an afternoon: the BMT police officer. . . .

He took a seat opposite.

Yes, the story was really beginning to " stand up."

Picnic at Porokorro

So great was his feeling of having the whole set-up from Dickson (somehow he didn't think of Barber) downwards —right down to Scarface the Paranoiac in a scissors-grip— that he did his nails with an orange stick and file. He took care of himself. The congestion of his head since the encounter in the mess was following its usual physical course—a feeling of elated galloping clarity in the mind accompanied by a sort of furriness on his brow, and hunger. Occasionally he paused and looked round. The bookcase was suitable for Penguin-sized books and in it he saw a collection of the violent kind of thriller—Chase and Cheyney and a book on etiquette—not a funny one in a mock-Victorian cover but one of the "How to get on" and "Help, your-personality" type. Many people might have been surprised such a book was read in our BMT society, in a diamond camp where you would have thought we would have evolved our own peculiar and suitable customs; but Warner was not surprised. It was just so much more confirmation.

Perhaps he was right. We had one member of the mess, I know, who was domiciled in Jersey and always wore a blue yachting mess jacket. He had ginger handle-bar moustaches and cool brave eyes. I think he was in the "little ships" and then in one-man subs. He had three daughters and his whole economic existence, domicile, habits and place of work was hinged to educating them privately and "bringing them out" in London, one a year for the three years after 1965. And he wouldn't even be there to see it—so he said—except perhaps now and again. So perhaps to a certain extent Warner was right to look at the book as he did, and to think the precepts would be impeccably "classless," we're-all-working-class-now sort of stuff.

And then Warner's eye strayed to a hat, a straw trilby

such as an octogenarian bowling club secretary might wear in Shropshire. It had a coloured band and looked heavily used.

"Christ," he said, "The Chamber of Horrors," and then at last he said loudly, "Wakey wakey."

Roberts opened his eyes.

The ease and depth with which he was now falling asleep I should think was due to shock more than fatigue. To be certain, even for five seconds, that you are going to be killed is a profound experience, something perhaps like giving birth.

He stared at the great blank fancy sun-glasses and saw the youth moving.

"Who are you?" Roberts said.

"Good kip?"

Warner had often been flung out of places. Sometimes it was a good thing to be flung out. It made you write a better story and sometimes even made a story. But it was no good being flung out too soon. Besides, he still wasn't sure if he hadn't come in peace—with vital information. Even now he wasn't sure.

He said, "Sorry I came in. Too hot outside." He put the orange-stick in his lapel pocket.

"What can I do for you?" Roberts said.

Warner said, "Warner"—and the name of his paper. He put out his hand.

Roberts repeated the paper's name incredulously and laughed. "And they let you in!" But he took the hand in a friendly way.

"No, I climbed in. Over the wire."

"Well, you'd better climb out again." Roberts raised the bottle to see if there was anything in the bottom. "It'll have to be whisky," he said. He went to the cupboard. "Who told you to come and see me."

" John-Jesus."

Roberts came back with the glass and put it down. He said nothing and sat down opposite Warner. The ice rattled and clanked into the glasses.

" And who's John-Jesus? " he said at last.

" One of your sleuths—out at Porokorro."

" Have you been to Porokorro? "

" He told me rather a seamy story. About an old man getting killed. We wouldn't want to publish it without getting the official version. That's why I'm here."

Roberts thought for a time and then said, " Have you seen Mr. Dickson? "

" Nay, more—I've seen Mr. Barber."

" Well . . . I think I'll ring Mr. Dickson."

There was a long long silence.

" D'you want to know what to say . . . is that it? " Warner said.

Roberts now on his feet paused. " Yes, I want to know what to say."

" Too bad. I thought you'd like to give your own version. As a matter of fact I got the official report—in Santa Barbara. But it's going to look pretty thin beside an eye-witness account."

" What d'you mean? "

" I mean isn't it? "

Roberts was still on his feet. Warner said, " Murder will out—isn't that what they say? "

After a bit Roberts sat down. Warner said, " Won't it? "

The length and nature of Roberts' silence at last dislodged Warner into speech . . . speech further and further all the time from his impulse to help—so the split lay now in his voice like a suppressed whine.

" But it was all an accident. That's obvious—or

165

isn't it? So why not come clean—before wiring the PRO. D'you know what a PRO is? A Public Isolation Officer. Helps no one."

Roberts still sat.

" Tell us about the accident," Warner spoke almost pleasantly. " If you don't—and if no one does—well— it looks bad . . . doesn't it? "

Almost dreamily Roberts said, " What are you going to cook up out of this? "

" Gem-camp whitewash is half champagne. How about that? "

Roberts put the ball of his bare foot against the rim of the table and examined a cut on his toe. He rocked the table slightly, once tilting it.

Roberts thought. All this time he was sincerely think-ing—almost as though alone. There was no animosity in his face. " Supposing," he said, " it comes out the police *may* have murdered an old man—I mean sup-posing you managed to give that impression, suggest it, which is about all one of you chaps legally could do— what I mean is, what would be the result of a show like that? "

" A good show—in the paper. Also, to my mind: hard news."

" Which would make the Africans angry."

" One doesn't want to do that. Good grief. One doesn't want to hump salt water all the way to the sea. There we agree."

Roberts' face clouded, following the metaphors which seemed to sizzle out of the man's brain like shreds of flaming iron.

" I wouldn't know about all that sort of thing," he said uncertainly. " I only know you seem to me the lowest yet. I don't even know why."

" But of course I *am* the lowest yet. That's the whole point. Before there's been Nothing. Fiction. Members Only. We're real."

Roberts made a noise with his lips and got up and went to the phone. He got Dickson and then he looked at Warner. " Roberts here," he said, " there's a reporter from the *Daily* ———— come to my bungalow."

Warner with his legs flung wide out could hear Dickson's voice croaking. He threw some nuts from a tin into his mouth.

Roberts said, " He's asking a lot of questions—could you answer them? "

Roberts came back and said, " He's coming himself."

" Well, I think I'll get along. Self-help is my motto. Also self-propelled. Sorry you couldn't make out. I might have helped."

" You might have helped? "

" Yes—I might have helped. That's why I came."

Roberts said nothing. I believe he really half wanted to argue with Warner, because he wanted to understand everything. To-day even a mote of dust, judging by the way he looked at it, presented problems which interested him.

But Warner got up and went out.

" See you later," he said.

19

Meyer was progressively nagged by MacPherson's invitation to come down with his wife " and picnic " at Porokorro. He knew the Provincial Commissioner believed in this picnic idea and would carry it out. But he also knew he wanted him, Meyer, to come down as a sort of Nehru—a neither black-nor-white man but professional friends-with-both man. That was why he had said, " Bring the Mrs. along too," etc., in case leaving *her* behind might prevent him, Meyer, from going.

Meyer was too much a friend of MacPherson to dismiss the matter from his mind. He always stayed with him when he went south. They had spent many happy evenings together in the delightful Residence above the town at Kaidu, smoking and talking on the veranda like those interminable raconteurs of Joseph Conrad, rather later in the imperial day, but often oblivious of date as far as mood though not as far as fact was concerned. MacPherson seemed to know the whole of Shakespeare and much native lore. He was out of touch with the atmosphere of present-day England. What he saw and heard bewildered him, so Meyer thought. He got depressed sometimes, and said he " would see it out "— not exactly specifying what " it " was; at other times he would attack the old for their attitude to " the times " and say that it was the greatest time of hope there had been for years—" even for God—cos ye'll damn' well pay for Him, and when you have to pay for a thing you appreciate it." But this was when he had had several whiskies.

Meyer admired the man's bull-like, tail-switching inconsistency and the courage of his lonely committal. "You're looking more sicklied o'er than usual," the Commissioner would say to him, and Meyer listened to the energy and kindliness with interest as though MacPherson were a scientific psychological fact which deserved examination and approval. He had seen so much of the opposite that he warmed to the P.C.—wearily waived, for once, as irrelevant the kind of thinking which would have taken a thousand years of insulation, security, class, Kirk, northern winters and the British channel into consideration. The man was good.

That was why he didn't understand his present behaviour.

He had credited him with more intelligence—or more friendship—than to have asked him down to Porokorro to-day. Because if it *was* merely a picnic then why did he try and *make* people come and if it wasn't then why did he try to take a friend whose bread-and-butter depended on a hard won position of neutrality ... though neutrality was the wrong word: he was not neutral. Had he been neutral he could never have allayed suspicion or gained anyone's confidence. And Mac should have been the first to understand this.

Now he thought again, as he had thought before, how strange it was that Mac had never asked him about his past—the camps, and never even left a gap, as it were, which would have been a kind of reference-by-omission. Had it been tact? He did not think so, for sometimes he would have liked to talk about that time—not to anyone,

169

but to *someone* if only to remove an hallucination, forced on him gradually from outside, that it *hadn't happened, and wasn't happening.*

The man was his only real friend in the colony. And here beside him was his son, the same age as his own son, which perhaps partly accounted for a feeling of responsibility—even towards that butterfly net. For it was true: Meyer knew where the best butterflies were to be found at Porokorro. It was also true that if they found the man known as "The Cowboy"—a Mandingoe from French territory—he would almost certainly be able to get more co-operation from him and elicit more truth from him than would people who didn't know him.

Only three weeks ago, the day after he had found "a double-decker" for one of the diggers—down there at Porokorro—his African clerk had let it be known that it was the "Corporation master's" birthday.

The "Cowboy" had laid on the dance.

So it was possible that to-day he *could* avert bloodshed. He admitted it was possible. But he would not go—nor if he could help it, would Isobel.

"Could we get butterflies here?" Paul said. The house made him want to get out of it.

Meyer tried to forget MacPherson and put all the friendship he felt for him into standing host to his son.

*   *   *

The Corporation Bungalow stands on the edge of the cricket field and so has more than its fair share of flowering shrubs. During the dry season there are boys watering there nearly all day long, dragging hoses and sprays from place to place. Sometimes butterflies frequent the place for the moisture.

Meyer wanted the boy to find his prey and counselled him like an equal.

I have seen Meyer engrossed in an infant still on the far side of speech at a BMT party, and everyone so bored with everyone else they became jealous of the happy understanding in the corner. The man people thought— if he would only be his age—had surprising information —about animals, Africans—even one's own boys. But he preferred to tickle the baby's toes or look out of the window.

As he left the bungalow he had no idea that Isobel was watching him and the child beside him.

Everything was fresh to Paul. His questions poured out. The seconds could not contain his interest. The pure trance of his eyes seemed to be at the service of each detail of our view—which for most of us at some time or other has seemed the very blank, back-end of life, gay as a loony-bin border, or a new grave.

They caught one or two quite ordinary butterflies.

Paul was impressed by them but William clearly had hoped for something better. " There is one," he said, " which I should like you to catch." And he described it, saying it was to be found near the Niéle river, in the forest. " It is difficult to catch because it flies high —almost like a bird—and only very rarely touches the ground. Indeed when it does touch the natives seem reminded of some superstition—they jabber and point."

Paul wanted to know more about this butterfly, parti-cularly about its size which he found difficult in crediting. He said he thought the biggest butterflies were in South America. His appetite was so whetted that he began seriously to inquire about William's programme for the afternoon. Could he not see his way to coming in the car with his father? Honestly, just once, he meant honestly, etc., etc., and he walked crabwise, looking up at William as though asking for next to nothing which would yet be everything.

Together they made a strange group. Our cricket field, in the dry season, is generous in mirages as many a bored long-on has witnessed. But this was the oddest yet. Why? —you may wonder.

There are only a few children in the camp, most of them infants or toddlers. When they reach school age we see no more of them.

I shall always remember catching sight of William and Paul on their butterfly venture. It seemed afterwards about the only direct contact I had with the events of that extraordinary—and yet so ordinary—day. I saw them skirting the cricket field and was suddenly struck as never before by the absence of children from our lives, and above all, from our thoughts.

I thought of the enormous expense of energy, human and mechanical, which affected every surrounding landscape as totally as hogs affect a field, affected the minute-to-minute sound of the air so that it hummed and vibrated and affected our movements and thoughts in such a way that imperceptibly we were conditioned to a tempo of personal or general emergency when in fact there was none that was not originally of our own making, perhaps none anyhow; and I thought how quick many of us would be to explain this emergency in terms of our children—when to all intents and purposes we hadn't got any, or if we had they were exiled and in no sense part of genuine feeling about the future, their future and the world's future—a destination which merely lay anonymously in the general buzz and clatter, like the destination of a rumbling steel ball in a fun fair game of chance.

Picnic at Porokorro

Paul whom none of us knew, a complete stranger suddenly at that moment took on all sorts of associations which you will quickly see scarcely belonged to him or any mortal except in the mind of some diamond employee whose leave was at that time long overdue.

The fact that he was with the obscure and impressive figure of William Meyer, who was never able to see his own son, also made a difference which is hard to evaluate. And that ludicrous butterfly-net—like a tiny flag . . . and their purposeful loafing, half-naked, amongst our desperate attempts at a picturesque boundary for the sight-screen to sit in. . . .

It is impossible to say how vividly I remember them.

*　　　　*　　　　*

If all the Blacks and all the Whites within a ten-mile radius of Sangoro had been put in a stadium the white contingent would have shown up as conspicuously, but no bigger than the orchestra or band. This numerical discrepancy, I think, had a bearing on what all of us felt like all the time.

The backs of several African camp-workers who were resting from watering the outfield, suddenly confronted William and Paul as they came tiptoeing through the shrubbery. Something about these backs reflected—not rest, but collective activity. They were all looking the same way—and upwards.

Beyond them, fifty yards away the pale yellow wall of Meyers bungalow was gapped as vastly as a breeding cage with immense modern windows, most of which were opened but darkened by straw sunblinds. Only one, at the top, was clear and deep as a picture with light and perspective. The picture was mobile, gently animated—Isobel Meyer stark naked, brushing her hair.

Picnic at Porokorro

" What? " said Paul. " What . . . who's that? . . ."
Because William had stopped in his tracks.

The Africans in front of them turned and one or two
made vague half-hearted movements towards their rakes
and watering-cans. A moment latter Paul was trying
to catch up with Meyer—ineffectually for the man was
moving towards the house quicker than Paul could walk.
So he ran—only to be asked, once they were inside, to
stay " down here and catch some more butterflies."

She was still combing her hair, using both hands so her
breasts moved sometimes into exaggerated prominence,
sometimes so they touched each other. Now her hands
paused above her head with the comb between them and
her fingers froze for an instant in a tableau which made
them like the ends of a gracefully, carefully tied headker-
chief, and thus it was she remained when she saw him in
the mirror.

At last having stared into his reflected eyes, a foot or
so in front of her, she closed hers and said, " What have
I done now? " By now he was walking across and with
a single movement had swept the thin curtain across the
window. " Do you have to? " he said.

She flicked on an unnecessary light like a curse and
went back to her face.

" I think you know you had an audience . . ." he said.

After one confident blank look straight at him she
turned back to the mirror; saying, " An audience? . . .
Really? I've never had much time for peeping Toms. If
they peep they peep. They're welcome."

After a moment he said, " Isobel—what are you
doing? . . ."

" Doing? I'm getting ready."

" To go to Porokorro? "

" Correct,"

174

Picnic at Porokorro

"Isobel; I'm asking you . . . please don't go."

He sat down near her. He was sure, if she went to Porokorro, she would do something to attract attention to herself, something which he would never be able to explain to anyone. And he would feel that the incident like the whole of their marriage was his fault.

"Would you give me my dressing-gown," she said.

"So you want it now," he said.

"You make me feel cold," she said.

He put it over her shoulders.

She had very thick and very white smooth skin which gave her body an enduring quality of puppy-fat. Now in her middle thirties, she could have stood on a pedestal in the Windmill; to be, he thought, a whited sepulchre of desire. Like her personality, her body ate and ate without nourishment. Tried to eat, disgorged, after tasting and then squirmed with hunger. It could not receive, and therefore could not give. She was wedded to some eternally conscious twisted version of herself which she could never let go of—not even in those moments when the blood demanded revival in anonymity —during childbirth, the act of love. He knew she would never grow old, only cadaverously "young." Her maw, her appetite for "happiness" and significance would increase till she nattered like a mad parrot of youth with everything lifted except her morale. By then she would be frantic with the eleventh hour intelligence that the audience, on which she had depended had never been anything but rows and rows of empty seats, a deserted hall—with perhaps not even the one face she had most actively spurned: or perhaps just that one gloomy face looking at her as it did now. From close.

And he thought: she is only here because another man has welched, escaped the scenes, the endless writhing on

the hook of herself; and she left my son behind because
he would be competition.

Oh, she shuddered at that gloomy yardstick beside her,
literally shuddered her plump shoulders. " Your eyes
are like dead plaice," she said.

" Did you know there were boys in view? " he said.

She caught her head and shut her eyes. " *In view*," she
echoed. " You talk like a travel brochure. And you know
I can't bear you to sit so close when I've got no clothes on.
I mean touch me . . . touch me . . . do something . . . or
don't . . . I mean you know so well really, don't you ? "
and she got up suddenly and wrapped the dressing-gown
about her as though suddenly in Spitzbergen and became
" decent." She went on with her face.

" You do ogle. You know that, don't you? I know
you think you don't, but you do. You're a voyeur.
You're fashionable."

" Isobel, why are you so determined to go to Porokorro to-day? Can I explain something to you? "

" You're not back on that? "

" Can I explain something to you? "

" Who's stopping you? " She made a little sideways
gesture with the pencil.

" It is very difficult for any white man to gain even a
little of the confidence of the African diggers. They would
sooner sell to Syrians. . . ."

" Why? " she said triumphantly, as though she agreed
with them.

He thought she really wanted to hear.

He said, " Partly because a Syrian is by being brown
or yellow not *quite* so alien, not so inimical as a white;
partly the Syrians can give better prices for the good
stones since they have no government overheads to pay."

" You won't bore me, will you, William? "

He faltered and then went on, " Therefore you must see it is doubly important for me to have the diggers' confidence. Any suggestion that I am on the side of the police in a business like this present palaver would do me harm . . . not even me . . . but my position—the Corporation, the job here and whoever fills it, now or later. So you see I ought not to go there to-day. Nor ought you."

" You mean you don't want to."

This was also true. He was silent.

She said, " You must be one of the last people to look ahead to to-morrow—when you won't be there; you look ahead about ten years with a thing that will be lucky if it lasts ten months. You'd do it with a tooth-brush."

He gazed into the floor. " There's no point in doing anything except in that spirit. I could only live in that spirit. Yes—you are right, Isobel—even ' with a tooth-brush.' "

She laughed impulsively, naturally—and cruelly. " You should do TEK—for ITV " and then, " I'm sorry you're not coming."

" And I'm sorry you're going."

" And why? " she wheeled on him. " I'll tell you: all men have a moslem inside them. They are jealous not of somebody but just jealous—like a kettle simmering— all the time. A wife takes a little initiative and there's panic. Purdah is in jeopardy. What can it matter to you if I go to Poro? "—she waved her hand wearily— " whatever it's called."

She was not good at rows or arguments. Her eyes burnt frantically as though she were cornered, even after a few quite friendly words. And then she flung her arms about

M

and "acted"; and seemed to be desperate to *mean* what she was saying.

Meyer was frightened for her sake. She was worse. He said quietly, " Could you take some other wife with you as you suggested . . . Mrs. Scott? "

" *Mrs. Scott!* . . . the woman in white? " Isobel was too outraged to frame a reply. The speed of her movement increased—as though with every word her husband was driving her more certainly and with ever greater personal abandon to Poro What's-its-name.

" You mean that poor little secretary. Why don't *you* come," she suddenly said, " if you're so frightened for my sake? I've scarcely seen you. (She was quoting him.) It's all right when *you* disappear for two days, but when *I* go out to tea there's uproar."

" Out to tea . . ." he repeated, but she interrupted him fast: " I'm afraid all roads lead to Rome:" she said. " Every tiny little thing shows we ought to lead our own lives."

Her implication that such a remark could still hurt or even mean anything struck him as mad and macabre; the most pathetic thing she had ever said.

" Dear Isobel . . ." he murmured.

" It's all because I didn't bring Robert. You don't believe what the doctor said. You *have* to put me in the wrong; you *have* to. . . ."

He got up.

" And now you're going," she said as though she might have known it.

" No, I am not going," he said.

She looked sharply over her shoulder, but he had come no nearer.

" If you do go," he said, ' just remember what the place is, and what it means to various people . . . Mac-

178

Picnic at Porokorro

Pherson and the Africans. It's true that life can be held cheap—so cheap you could not really offend, in our sense, whatever you did. There will be no polite people to wince at anything you say. They'll get you right in one—and that may give you a little thrill. You might want to throw yourself into one of the craters."

" I thought they were just looking for diamonds."

" Yes—that's all."

" I mean everything's so simple really, isn't it ? " she said, implying a larger debunking criticism of his tone, his face, everything he had ever said ever enjoyed ever looked forward to for years.

" I mean they're just looking for diamonds. And probably perfectly happy. You see, you *are* morbid. Perhaps you ought to see someone. No, William, really —I mean it." And she looked up, snapping a compact like a pistol going off, she took him in.

Meyer took two steps towards her. She saw him in the glass and the hand which she had moved to her face began to go slower. Finally it stopped.

He took a last step towards her and now looked down straight through the open V of her loose silk dressing-gown into the soft tiers of flesh congested now into long tyres and folds by her position. The powder on them looked like down. He put his hands on her shoulders and kissed the top of her head and then brushed it with his lips, and at the same time his hands tightened.

She perceived he was *smelling*. . . .

" Don't go, darling," he begged. " Stay—just stay."

His gentleness she experienced like a snake in the room.

" So that's it . . ." she said. " One might have guessed. I mean why not say . . ."

" Please! "

179

" I'm not in the mood."

" Were you ever in the mood? " he murmured. " Wouldn't you like to be before you die? Just once."

" My dear William, you persist in a big error."

She tried to move. She might scream. He let her move—then seeing she would get right away and probably dress as she already once had in the locked bathroom, he took her shoulders again and with ease held her down. He parted the robe from in front of her breasts and buried his lips and nose beneath her hair, in her neck.

She struggled.

" Stay," he begged, " this once. I believe we could change things—everything . . ."

Her eyes were tight shut and she was rigid all over. In a curious voice she said, " May one get up? "

And then at last when he let her go she said, " Thanks a lot," rose tying and tied the sash of her dressing-gown as though that was that: marriage—and she had conceived . . . as usual, a headache.

She said, " I suppose that sort of thing was appreciated by Fatuiyah? But you forget: she was paid."

" Oh—Isobel . . ."

" Well, isn't that what you said? Men's conceit in this matter is general. But yours wins two prizes—the handicap and the open."

He could not compete.

" Germans are so doggy," she said. " And their humour is like next week. The whole of it with several days' warning. Meanwhile you've left that child . . ."

Without any change in her voice, without any tears, she had begun crying. She turned away and sat on the bed.

" You've left the child." she repeated.

Picnic at Porokorro

" What can I do," he implored, " what is it you really
want ? "

And she sat there as though at last she agreed with
something he had said, sat there getting ready to go to
Porokorro, and crying, without tears.

20

TWO-THIRTY on normal days was a dead hour in the
BMT. The sun had it—alone, to itself, and drew out a
slow, brazen silence where damp, sweaty death was
imitated in the shade and on beds.

Only Number One walking down the deserted road in
the pale quiet glare, carrying a fly-swat like an Eighth
Army officer, rather as a symbol of authority than as a
utensil, and entering the deserted main building with his
own key, had lately become familiar to the sweeper
Africans who lay in bulky relief, like the remains of an
atrocity, under the big flamboyans. To-day they never
stirred as he went in, but their eyes, just open beneath
the tilted brims of discarded trilbies, or level with parched
dust, saw him.

Of course it was bad form to complain, bad form to
make heavy weather of heavy weather, bad policy to
show signs of strain, boring to keep efficiency anywhere
except out of sight, and dull to be serious. I think Tom
was like this by nature as well as by upper-class rote; for
unlike most public schoolboys of his generation he had
known that it was all work—even playing for Mr.
Leveson-Gower's XI in country house cricket, and
getting his blue; nearly all to do with power, not fun—
though of course he had made it seem more like fun than
anyone. Why not enjoy your medicine?

Though to refer it as medicine was taboo, something not uttered even to his own sons—those three schoolboys who could turn him ill by telling a lie.

Barber hadn't had the same start as most of his superiors. He hadn't been to Eton—except " after leaving Upping-ham," he once said. He had had a grand-paternal cottage—not palace or town villa. His father had said to him, " Remember: you've got a pistol in your back from the word go."

Yet the discipline of an assumed aristocratic equan-imity and of an unfailing Kiplingesque decency, with equal bouquets for Gunga Dhin and the general, was nowadays under a mechanical strain which perhaps no one but his wife and Dickson had any idea of. Some-times Barber was dramatically ill. " Some bug," he said contemptuously, dismissing it. He hated talking about himself. In fact he wouldn't. Like politics, the subject was taboo.

His wasted face was really sometimes that of a hermit of the rocks. Only in total secrecy he temporarily turned it to the wall and groaned intimately and with abandon to the Admiral—accepted the relief of collapse—with both hands, grasping, demanding all with a lack of humour which his public acquaintances wouldn't have recognised. When he came out he looked more like a moth-eyed misfit Roman centurion than ever. Craggier, yet even more sensitive.

His life was a cat's cradle. To-day, for instance, it wasn't only Porokorro. There still hung over him the labour dispute of the month before, unsettled, and the growing power of the BMT African union with whose leader he made tireless efforts to " really co-operate." He never admitted to what extent this " co-operation " was a game which each of them used to his own advantage,

but he knew the man as few—even white—TU leaders
are known by managers.

There were also staff problems which, if he could
divert Dickson, he handled himself—otherwise, before
he knew where he was, two people who worked in
the same room weren't on speaking terms, though their
job depended on mutual consultation. For this you
could partly blame the climate—and the wire; but also
the social climate in England, which was cock-eye.
Search him.

How long would Mrs. Meyer stay? He knew as sure
as the sun was hot that soon she would make trouble.
The sort of trouble which would lose him a Plant Operator
—a man it took personal London hours to find.

When his mind didn't focus on any particular one of
his many problems, the whole lot seemed to attack en
masse somewhere . . . in his breath, his spine. It was
like the game of grandmothers-steps played with real
murderers. So, in self-defence, he all the time selected
one problem for attention and then his eyes became bleak
and limiting, knowing that to keep sanity whole he must
keep this question apart, alone and not relate it to others.
Facts. Their autonomy contained a devil which lay at
the heart of the disease, but his survival, his job, was
the disease. *That* fact he accepted as the premise of all
others.

Why did he do the job if it was killing him? The purpose now seemed to be merely the feeling of being on top
and keeping three sons at Rugby. And habit . . . He
didn't go into the matter.

Over his desk was the production chart: carats per
week. The definite flattening out of the year-old downward trend dated from the beginning of Robert's
" Prangs." The small, unfinished, uplifted line caught

his eye for the hundredth time that day as he turned on the fan and sat down. The sight of it recurred on his momentarily closed eyelids; a tiny little line like the beginning of a road which he himself had engineered—towards solution.

He began to massage his face. He wished the Admiral were back. The Admiral! In Pitlochry, Perthshire. With animals. He couldn't stand animals. Animals were animals, different. He didn't get the overlap.

His " limiting " look now gradually settled in his wide blue eyes till he looked like a hypnotist and subject all in one. And he closed them. He stroked the skin of his eyelids, over shut eyes, as though to cope with lesser lesions were momentarily a way out.

The little line stayed, green, on the red screen of his closed eyelids. He wanted something simple—as simple as a single line. A new spine.

Perhaps if the Admiral had been back he might never have acted as he did.

Acted? No. No one acted. That is the one thing that strikes me, looking back on that extraordinary day. No one *did*—anything. The fashion was against it. You got round a table and a blind trend asserted itself another inch. The mouthpiece of the trend usually looked like a Little Algy sitting on the knee of History—garrulous but inanimate, unconscious.

Barber spent much of his life listening to the Little Algies with his dutiful, appraising, almost obedient stare and none of them, whether in the chair of the BMT or in the African Miners' Union, ever guessed that he cherished, without ever thinking about it, the dream of a change, the desire, perhaps even at the risk of their and his own personal destruction, for " a little common sense, a little freedom."

Picnic at Porokorro

I'm afraid he could not have been more explicit than this.

And yet whenever it came to his turn to speak he was that much more like Little Algy than any of them—simply because physically, too, he did somewhat resemble the wide-eyed, nervous dummy. And he "trended" better, as he did most things.

Who will ever know whether perhaps he didn't, that day, *do* something?

The sound he was waiting for came, when to pass time he had begun signing the morning's letters, some of which already risked being out of date.

He got up as Roberts came in and met him in mid-floor.

"Good. Feel better?"

He had spoken rapidly and offered no chair.

Roberts thanked him for the champagne. Barber didn't hear.

"The P.C. wants you to go out with him."

"Yes, sir. I got a message from Mr. Fadden."

"I know. I just wanted to make sure we hadn't given you marsh fever." Then Barber said, "Where's your hat?"

Roberts looked at the beret in his hand.

"No—THE hat. You're not going without that, are you?"

Roberts was troubled, embarrassed. He had not left it behind merely because of the presence of the Police Commissioner. He had chosen to leave it behind.

"Your men are used to it," Barber said. "They'll expect bad luck if you go without it suddenly."

This was possible. His chaps got the queerest notions and were more conservative than ye olde gaffer. What

186

Number One said could be an understatement as well as
sounding like an order.

"Do." Barber was suddenly like a girl with him.
"I want to see it. I've never seen it. They run a mile
when they see it, don't they?"

"They shout Hat-man," Roberts said, forgetting that
he had already told Barber.

"Hat-man!" and Barber sounded as surprised as he
had sounded in the morning.

"By God, I bet they do," and his footlight eyes dwelt
on the young man. "Taking Scott?" he added, as
though consecutively.

"Yes, sir."

"Has he been issued with a gun yet?"

"No."

"Good. We don't want anything—untoward, no
fireworks. We're on approval ... OK?"

"Yes, sir."

"You'll have the world and its wife down there. They
want you to walk on to Bornu Island site and sit there.
Then the top brass will go into the village—in beachwear and olive branches for a grand palaver. OK?"

"Yes, sir."

"There'll be a Beauty Queen and a representative
of the *Daily* ————. ITV cameramen, etc., etc."

"Yes, sir." Roberts smiled.

"Don't forget the hat. I think the P.C. would like it.
He's in the mood."

21

WHAT COULD have been easier for most of us, that day (or indeed any day) than to forget "what it was all about."

The only place we ever saw a diamond was when we happened to pass William Meyer's bungalow, after his return from a buying.

Then—on a table sometimes in full sunlight—he sorted the day's work on little rounds of white paper so that if you went close, to pass the time of day with him, you saw perhaps three or four perfect crystals the size of peas on the first bit of paper, then, on the next fifteen doilies, gradually inferior stuff till on the last lay a small pyramid of brownish " Boart," like gravel, which might be worth nothing.

One by one he held each stone up to his optician's monocle and peered into that often muddy and scarred little world of interior light. Millions of years ago these small objects were formed—probably in the glowing core of the earth's matrix, under the influence of colossal pressures and heat, sustained for periods so long as to be scarcely termed "time" in any human sense. Finally they were probably blown towards the globe's surface by volcanic action—and in the case of these Santa Barbara, alluvial, diamonds—confined to the rushing friction of river-beds for further thousands of years. The feat of imitating this process, in an inferior way, has been

attained by modern science—sufficiently well to produce
stones for industrial use—but the cost is still so high as to
put the possibility beyond the scope of any but a great
Power preparing for economic or physical war—and
Meyer often thought with bitter irony that the reason
why there were only three or four good 3-carat stones on
the first bit of paper and why the other stones were all
inferior examples of their kind was because the black
market across the border, in the neighbouring state
took the best diamonds, and that same black market,
three years out of four, had been sustained by Russian
demand (via smugglers, African politicians and Syrian
middlemen) and on the fourth year—when there was
stockpiling of grain in the United States after a surplus
harvest—by American business men, who then outbid
even the Russians.

And the reason why his Corporation could not compete
with those black-market prices was simply the system of
taxation which originated in the British political climate
—avowedly aimed at preventing the very kind of profit,
morality and political systems which it in this case most
aided.

There had been a time when Meyer had concerned
himself with all this and had even written a letter to
someone he knew in London who might have "done
something," but then the futility had struck him like a
vision: he came to regard the political utterance of his
time, both in the East and West, as so much Boart—
neurotic nightmare conducted in increasingly positivist
and absolutely devaluated language.

The problem of communication was central. In the
decay of the deeper subjective premises of language,
words lay open to the destructive criticism of those
who had, perhaps unconsciously, everything to gain

by the tower of Babel, which, happens when words mean nothing. The pained inferiority of such critics, *vis-à-vis* the constructive subjective systems of the immediate past, was then soothed; their emotional chaos spared from envy.

They prospered, these critics, and some of them knew well that in eliminating subjective factors they helped words to die—of their definitions, leaving the field open to the blind, colossal unworded pressures which were seldom frankly alluded to even by their opponents. And if these pressures—were alluded to, in extremities of protest, then at once they succeeded in crushing the isolated sane voice with one quick reflex of their blindly reacting mass.

The situation was now autonomous. The man-made environment was master; a colossal Moloch whose progressive meals would consume all the progress there had ever been.

Meyer turned inwards into his diamonds and remembered their birth and sometimes found one which a miser wouldn't have noticed, dark and drab as mud, a congestion you would have thought of flaws, if a diamond at all. But he knew that after a long soak in hydrofluoric acid it might emerge as a perfect crystal. The pressures of his time were natural and from the " inhuman " contradictions and stress, which stood beyond the power of any individual crystallised in the old culture to arrest or even minutely affect, there might emerge some now alien idea that would liberate man from the fatal stagnation and fascination of literal reductive material truth— which was itself as infinite and unknowable as any metaphysical truth. Who could tell—perhaps from the chance chaos of the Soviet ape-hill (a subject on which there were men actually regarded as " experts " and paid accordingly)—from that very least expected and least conscious quarter the resolution might emerge, the resolution or the—now easily realised—unconscious wish to be destroyed—utterly.

Meyer did his job. He lived in the calm and skilful evaluations of these brilliant microcosms, the full-stops of aeons, but he paid as daily price the profound melancholy of the sensuous hermit.

Perhaps it was a morbid equilibrium. Something savage rose in his heart as he worked, thinking of his one friend who had called him now to go on a " picnic " to Porokorro.

He would not go.

*   *   *

MacPherson found him with Paul looking on, Paul leaning his chin on his hands and holding his butterfly net as though that and the afternoon could still be taken away from him. Jerky rapt questions came from the child's mouth—" How much is that one worth? " How much this? Is that a double-decker? etc.

" Ye know," MacPherson said, " when you go round Cudburrys ye ge' a bar a chocolate."

Without removing his monocle William said, " Paul has a diamond."

The child opened his hand.

MacPherson grunted, " Fourpennorth."

" Well, that is what happens at Cadbury's."

" William, are ye coming to Porokorro, because we're off."

William took out the monocle and used the interruption as an opportunity to clean it. Before he could answer MacPherson said, " Because ye know I'm wanting you . . . in fact I'd like just the you and me to go. . . ."

Meyer looked down at his table load. " I must do all this . . ."

" You must do all that, must you? "

" Mac, I'm not a policeman."

" Nor am I."

There was silence.

" Surely you see if I start arriving with policemen and . . . and . . . offeeshals—whoever they are . . ."

And indeed it was extraordinary MacPherson *didn't* see it, or wanted so much not to see it that he made little less than an object plea to Meyer to come with him.

Waiting for a reply he turned red as though holding his breath and remained staring at Meyer in a " penetrating " way. At last he said quietly, " And if I went alone, would you come? "

" Come . . . where . . . to do what? "

A kind of cornered irritation was creeping into Meyer's voice.

" To clear off the licensed diggers . . . off BMT ground."

" Off BMT ground? "

" Off leased ground."

" Mac—if I were a . . . cog—in that way—as I am in this "—he waved his hand at his stones—" then of course. That would be my job. I would live by it. We would go together."

" But you wouldn't, would you, William Meyer?— you're too sicklied o'er, as I've told you. Nothing comes of nothing. That's you. I suppose you're a valuer. Barber's a miner. Me—if I'm caught murdering— judging from what I've heard to-day—I've got to base my defence on a single statement: I'm an Administrator."

Either vin rosé or tears or a mixture of both stood plainly in MacPherson's eyes.

" I didn't mean it like that.

" Well—how do you all mean it? " MacPherson said, becoming very Scots. " I'll tell ye something about you: it's pride. Ye'd sooner get strung up than dirty yer paw: well, I'm telling you: you're dirty: we're a' dirty. In the sight of the Lord."

" If there is a God," Meyer said slowly, " I have a better opinion of Him than that."

" Oh! so you've an opinion of God. You're taking a risk, man. Christ should be a feeling—of a discrepancy. No' an opinion."

" Yes—perhaps." There was silence. William said, " I'm afraid I have a mind. I cannot avoid using it."

" Congratyerlations, William. Have you a feeling? "

" Yes—I have a feeling too," William said, " one about the modern world."

" The *modern world* . . ." MacPherson snorted. " What's that? "

William smiled: " Perhaps, Mac, this is a new world to-day—a sudden exaggeration—like a flood or a cloud burst. Nature might compensate—terribly. For the moment we still think and feel as free individuals—don't we—you and I? Even you and I live in Ivory Towers. Shall we persevere as individuals? Shall we become criminals? Then which way will conscience walk? It is odd, isn't it, that the people for whom man is the highest value are the dislikers of " human nature "—of people as a whole, and the people for whom religion truly teaches the general sinfulness of men—that's you —are the likers of people."

" And what are you? "

" I? I'm a diamond valuer." He laughed as he said this, and then he said apologetically, " Yes. That's it—

isn't it? What am I? There should be some passionate answer—however deplorably inexact. . . ."

" Yet mean yer wai'in for bloody Godot."

Meyer smiled. " I didn't see it."

" I thought you wrote it, man."

" No. It wasn't me," William said in the literal way which distracted his wife.

" And so you're not coming to speak to yer pals and tell them to pull their finger out? "

" No."

There was a long silence. MacPherson prepared to leave.

Meyer said, " Good-bye, Mac. Paul will bring Isobel. She is very anxious to go. I hope . . . she helps."

" So I'm to be Cook's guide, too? " MacPherson said—with open reluctance.

" I'm sorry. I thought you said . . ."

" And your kid—is he coming? "

For the first time the face of the stateless valuer showed signs of pain.

" No, he's not here. I thought I told you . . ."

" Why d'you have a kid at all," MacPherson said suddenly, " if you thinks it all a washout? Did you want him? "

" Yes."

" Then you must be a sadist."

William looked at Paul. " No—I wanted children. Several of them. I have enjoyed Paul being here. I wish he could come again."

MacPherson was moved.

Meyer said, " There should be children. Perhaps to us the inheritance of the past is a wonderful, intolerable heirloom which we can never use and which yet occupies all available space. For them it may be different. I keep a diary. To-night I shall write: Paul MacPherson helped me sort my diamonds."

" By God, they must be in a mess then. Well, so long, William, and if you come south without calling I'll have you arrested."

Father and son went off, separating at the road, one to go to the cars consulting his watch, the other to " fetch Madam Meyer down here like a scalded cat."

22

Ten jeeps full of native colonial police in tin hats formed the core of the " picnic." They formed up outside the head office and people gathered to look at them.

In normal circumstances—on point duty, street patrol, immigration check-post—you will find our native police-man an eerie black image of his London cousin. The silver number and lettering on the grey shirt, " P.C. so and so," the flat British-made police hat, regulation stockings and general " shirt-sleeve order " is a straight tropical adaptation.

Such externals are easily copied but when on closer acquaintance you find yourself looked at by deep yellowish Manga, tribal eyes—suddenly broody with the uneasy restraint of a British constable, and you hear the familiar tones which conceal the pleasure of power and even of civic disapproval in an ominously polite verbosity—just as at home—then perhaps you believe that something has " sunk in," something more than you might have thought possible. And you wonder if you aren't in a black limb of Britain.

But this illusion is confined to very " easy " situations—speeding, parking and Customs. Let the emotional temperature rise a few degrees, or the situation become in any way unorthodox or unsupervised, then tensions arise in the Manga P.C. between his British façade and his deeper identity, to the advantage always of the latter.

Picnic at Porokorro

Our reason to him is not reason, and I think he unconsciously longs for opportunities to destroy it along with the forms it takes.

The gentlest and most intelligent Africans I have known were the most melancholy, as though they dragged God knows what impossible anchor on the course we have set them. And they were full of fear for the future.

*   *   *

MacPherson came up carrying a picnic basket and walked along the jeeps like a vicar reviewing the annual outing of some women's institute.

" My! " he said, looking at the tin hats. " My, my, my . . ."

The idea that the expedition was compatible with a leisured, cultured and " civilised " approach was implicit in everything he did or said. He at least would be guilty of no formality; and so when Fadden took it upon himself to introduce Warner, then press relations, like the tin hats, came into the orbit of his special attitude.

" Well, Mister Warner " (no doubt his anyhow paternal tone took added zest from Warner's almost adolescent appearance), " in taking you I'm taking a risk, the only damn' risk there is. But . . ." and he took the frail young man's shoulder in a semi-pugilist grip with one hand and bunched the other, with the picnic basket still in it, under his nose, " I'm the PRO, d'ye see, and you're out on a limb. Now if you file a trouble-making false story I'll find you . . . I'll find you and you'll feel it. . . . Now come along and be welcome—and for God's sake disappoint your employers. If you get me the sack I'll cut your throat."

Even the strongest critics of the popular press, of which there were several present, were taken aback. For Warner, however young he might appear, and however dependent he was upon the BMT and Government, was none the less the highly-paid representative and witness for several million Britons.

Some of us I know, especially the younger ones, examined Warner's face intently. There was an odd silence.

But Warner said nothing. He submitted to MacPherson's handling without a sound or a smile and thereby made a certain point. And some of us, without censure, put Mac's exuberance down to Number One's vin rosé —and to Mac's former omnipotence and experience, here, in this country.

" D'you no like me? " he said suddenly to Warner.

" I don't know yet," Warner said.

MacPherson became a shade self-conscious as though the thing could slip out of hand. " That's right—that's right, wait and see," he said indifferently and with a sudden touch of rank in his manner moved away.

Warner seemed to have retired for good behind the anonymity of his great lakes of smoked glass. Even his physical pent-up quality had abated.

Roberts, standing by the lined-up jeeps, watched him with open distaste and Scott was fastidiously unaware of his existence, and yet, such is the BMT terror of " trouble " with the press, none of us, not even Dickson, had spoken to him in anything like the tones of MacPherson; except of course Jepson-Snailes.

Only the scarred inferior Jepson-Snailes in our darkened mess—like the ghost of our secret feelings—had mouthed at him his absolute loathing.

*   *   *

Just before the column was due to move off Barber

passed by—perhaps by chance—for this was none of his business. Police were under Fadden, Policy under Mac-Pherson; the BMT had merely lent Roberts back—and provided information and lunch.

Yet Barber stopped beside Fadden and considered the column with approving deference. Suddenly he said, " Has Roberts shown you his BMT uniform ? "

Fadden, we knew, had felt increasingly bewildered by the cat's cradle of authority ever since arrival—but the vine rosé had now at last reconciled him to Wonderland. He smiled in a happily aimless way and looked inquiringly at Roberts. What was he expected to perceive? Or say?

Barber called loudly, " Where's the hat ? "

Roberts flushed slightly and stirred uncomfortably. He had been standing formally at ease, having recently given a formal order, " Embus," to his men. He was wearing the orthodox black beret and silver badge and his tin hat was slung in the formal position. To whom did he owe first obedience?

" Show me the hat," Fadden said.

Roberts came sketchily to attention and produced it from the jeep—the frayed beribboned relic of a Shropshire retired officer—an enthusiast of bowls and the Duke of Wellington.

The incident stuck in several people's minds because it was unlike Barber to have interfered at a semi-formal moment. Normally he minded his own business almost to the extent of ostentation; a *passion* he seemed to have for the privacy of others. (He almost went out of the house if a guest wanted to telephone.)

Yet now there was this stir which was his doing. Like a small stone dropped in stagnant water, the effect expanded only a short distance. But far enough. Mac-

Pherson was nearby. He caught sight of the hat and shouted, " By God! That's it. That's better." And he moved towards it.

Fadden smiled genially as though he knew what Barber, what MacPherson meant, which was more than any of the rest of us did.

" Why can't you put the whole bloomin' lot in boaters," Mac shouted, and then he said to Barber, " Does he wear it? "

Barber did not seem to know but looked intimately and waggishly at Roberts, who put the thing on in a kind of willed, hypnotised way.

Hat-man!

The police who had been leaning out of the side of the jeeps watching the affair of the hat with tranced, grinning interest (they had not been under Mr. Roberts for months) broke into excited talk which finally turned to muted applause.

Mac was delighted. " Have they all got one? " he said.

I think he would have back-pedalled more than a little if every policeman had produced a boater, but obviously he felt safe.

" My—that's better . . ." he said, and indeed the noise was almost that of a picnic.

He came back to Barber and Fadden and switched from public buffoonery with strangers to deadly familiar earnest. He chose them out with his pipe-stem as vessels for confidence, finding them worthy of it only after a long stare into both their faces. " Y'know, Barber—Tom . . . Jim—the African likes a laugh. I've seen a nasty moment—a very nasty moment indeed—*vanish*—because there was someone who could make them laugh."

Fadden shook his head in receptive incredulity and

moved a stone along with his boot tip. Now he thought
of it he was the same himself. He liked a laugh.

"A few more boaters is what we want," Mac said,
whereupon Mrs. Meyer appeared with his son and he
became petrified, looked there and then as though he
could have done with a laugh. "Stone the crows," he
whispered.

She was dressed for a Dior Beachwear Collection with
strange harlequin trousers and zips as easily pulled as
alarm cords. Her gay polka-dot shirt with " tailored "
collar was full as the two halves of a bellying sail and
her mouth a gory fat pout with sharp ends. Mosquito-
boots tied with floopy tape bows added a slightly vaude-
ville touch which seemed to call for a circus silver riding
whip and a top hat.

By an extraordinary coincidence her ornamental sun-
glasses were the same embellished " ivory " shape as
Warner's—a fact she seemed to notice at once. I say
" seemed " because you couldn't tell where she was
looking except that once her huge lens floated in Warner's
direction and dawdled an instant before she turned right
away, touching the back of her hair with a caressing
certifying motion and arching her back slightly.

No one had introduced her or seemed likely to until
Paul MacPherson moved his butterfly net in her direction
and said, " This is Mrs. Meyer, Dad."

Fadden now thoroughly proved that he liked a laugh,
but half-way through became aware of its isolation,
changed it to a cough, which became a real cough, then
a paroxysm of vin rosé, heat and perplexity so that he had
to remove himself, puce in the face, and bowed to one
side.

MacPherson shook Isobel's hand with cordiality.
" And where's William ? " he said, although he knew.

She let go of MacPherson's hand before he had finished with hers and then half turned one shoulder to him looking round for a fleeting linger at Barber, touching her hair again and said. "He's not coming. He's making little piles out of diamonds."

Barber did give her a smile. No one had yet ever described *publicly* anyone's role here as having anything to do with diamonds, let alone making little piles out of them.

And of course MacPherson was delighted. "The King is in his counting-house, eh?" In the distance Scott smiled too, as though to salute every fleeting proof that life was getting better.

"Well, *you're* coming anyhow, Mrs. Meyer," MacPherson said, taking his son by the shoulder and not looking at her again. (I don't think he did for the rest of the day), but still speaking to her: "And will you look after this?"

Unaware of the nature of her sudden success and half resenting it as not the kind she wanted, Isobel looked with increased self-consciousness at Paul as though they had never met.

Paul said, "She can carry the killing bottle," and he gave it to her.

"My!" said Mac. "Look at that then . . ." and Fadden had another paroxysm, this time openly, for everyone agreed to laugh—even Isobel: they looked a charming couple—a tableau of ancient and modern love —Cupid with his bow, and Tabloid Sex-Appeal with a killing-bottle.

Had the African police in their jeeps been British soldiers we may imagine what would have been their whistled reaction (once or twice, from the farthest jeep) to Mrs. Meyer, but the African P.C.s had been far more

interested in the hat and indeed were now mainly not
even looking this way, but peacefully at nothing. The
neglect was not the fault of Mrs. Meyer but just that
Africans don't look at pretty women as white men do;
perhaps because, in this area at least, every third Kuru
and Manga woman is beautiful and all are graceful and
feminine. And I doubt if " sex-appeal " could be trans-
lated to them.

*   *   *

Number One at this moment found his way unob-
trusively to Warner and, without looking at him but
keeping his eyes on MacPherson, said, " How are you? "
as though they had known each other a long time; and
then, " Did you find the chap you wanted? " While he
was speaking he continued to look at the preparations
for departure, at Mrs. Meyer, Paul and the Hat as
though in the stall of an open-air theatre, and as though
his questions weren't very important to either of them
but would be taken for what they were—small polite-
nesses—too small even to deserve an answer. He interrupted himself: " By Christ I should like to see this. Are
you going? "

" Yes."

" You'll probably have a wow of a time. They adore
Mac. He's a grand chap, Mac," and Number One
admired, stood admiring, conspicuously admiring the
architect of this plan. He grinned enough to save waving
as Mac turned in his direction.

" Mr. Barber," Warner said, with sudden urgent
nonchalance, " that's a place you've got there, isn't it,
at Porokorro? " The man of the world manner and
phrasing faltered and collapsed with a simple vehement
statement. " I went there."

"You've been there?" Barber said without moving his eyes.

"Yes ... I went there."

"This morning?" Barber said, his eyes remaining still.

"Yes—this morning."

"All quiet?"

"Yes ... all quiet ... but I don't know—I met an African guard chap ... he told me ... he told me something you might like to know ... I tried to find you ..." The pace of the words had increased.

Barber looked as if he were balancing something on his head: for a few seconds he didn't seem to breathe, or to hear or to move—except in response to some infinitesimal private concentration.

And then he suddenly shouted "Mac!" and moved into the centre of preparations. Warner saw him share a joke. Barber turned and did the embus signal for Armoured Troops, winding and stroking the crown of his head, at the same time getting it comically wrong, winding himself up and scratching his head—rupturing himself; Warner heard the fast, hard correct imitation of a frustrated CSM, and for a second caught his eye ... for less, much less than a second; for the time it takes something to start falling.

That was all.

Then they "mounted," and as Warner passed, Barber said to him, "As far as I can see you've got a scoop already. For *Punch*."

"It could be," Warner said.

Engines started up.

A lot more people came out of the offices to watch the cars ("the floats," as someone called them) move off.

I remember Roberts wearing the hat. Later this seemed important.

Picnic at Porokorro

More people came out of the offices and remarked on the hat; they stuck on it.

I think Roberts clung to it as to an age when leaders were distinguished as much as possible from those they led—and in revulsion from an age when leaders tried to go one better than the led in outward uniformity. Odd hats were the rage of both Churchill and Montgomery in the war Roberts missed, and before that there was probably—for him—a vaguely inherited, almost personal, memory of Nelson dressed to the nines in the face of death. And to-day (here at least)—what else had he against him except a leader called the Cowboy—on account of his hat.

And yet one could see that the title " Hat-man " had half curdled in his own mind, and it was only the combination of Barber and MacPherson—and perhaps the presence of Warner—which prompted him to put the hat on again even momentarily.

But once on, once approved by the various spectators and even recommended by MacPherson as the right medicine, I suppose from then on the wearing of it must have seemed to Roberts " an order," though he looked a bit sheepish as he took his place in the last jeep beside a broadly grinning driver.

MacPherson had " the guests," as he called them, in his car. He sat in front with the driver; Paul sat between Mrs. Meyer and Warner at the back. Looking out of the window at Number One, he shook his head in a rum way and winked, wheeled the thing open and said, " Won't the licensed diggers think they've got DT when they see us coming."

This allusion to the brilliant and unconventional dress of both Warner and Isobel Meyer and to Paul's blazer obliged Barber to retire a step with a non-committal smile. Personal remarks, for him, were taboo unless complimentary, and on this occasion staff and officials were concerned to say nothing of a young press man, representing millions, as sensitive as an ill-laid trip-wire.

And anyhow Number One was deafish at that moment to the small coin of conversation. Judging by faces it was he, not MacPherson, who was going to Porokorro. Though of course the strain in his face was never merely of one moment or of one thing.

When all the jeeps and cars were on the move I remember thinking that MacPherson had half made his point. The atmosphere had taken something from him. It did seem possible that whoever they met would " see reason "—if only the reason of divine folly.

When the last vehicle was through the check gate, Barber turned.

He passed me, quite close. I shall never forget his face. It suggested a watch opened at the back. Something had so stopped that all nerves—all little to-fro wheels and threads and dainty screws—were temporarily apparent. His whole meticulous system *stared*, stopped and unconnected, like the coat of an ill dog.

" By God," he said convivially, " what a party! "

23

THERE WAS no reason why MacPherson should have taken a journalist in his car. Most people "in his position" (we said) would never have dealt directly with Warner in such exceptional circumstances; they would have kept him away from Porokorro until it became clear how things would pan out.

Possibly Warner's extreme youth—which had stood against him several times that day—now appealed to Mac's fatherly disposition which believed ill of no immature person until it was proved. "You're working for the *Daily* ————," he said. "Well, I'm working for the b—— BMT—so we're in the same b—— boat."

I think this sort of easy talk, with its paternal undertone, had a strong emotional effect on Warner in his present state. There he was in the man's car beside his son as though he were a member of his family. As a result his internal conflict increased unbearably for he was a person for whom kindness is sometimes the subtlest cruelty, the final affront; the single drop of water in the desert. Yearning and desperate pride had often before in his life fought over kindness until he sat, as now, speechless and pale.

"By God," MacPherson said, staring at him, "I believe you earn more than I do."

"How much do you earn?" Warner said.

" You're a nosey blighter," said the older man, turning away. " You'd print it with a nought added on."

The effects of the good lunch were wearing off. Mac-Pherson looked back again over his shoulder as though he must have been mistaken. But no: there was his son with a butterfly net sitting between two people in the same kind of ornamental sun-glasses, one a man, the other a woman—and all this was his own cool plan for restoring civil order.

He said to Warner, " I'm mad bringing you along."

" Why? " said Warner.

" Because you'll get me the sack. What do you know about all this? "

" That's why I've come: to find out."

Mac wondered without resentment why the youth didn't call him " Sir."

" But if nothing happens what are you going to write? "

" Perhaps nothing."

" Ai, ' perhaps '—after your paper's sent you about five ruddy thousand miles! "

Mrs. Meyer had turned her attention even more to the outside scenery when the conversation, having started, persisted in ignoring her; until suddenly she looked round Paul and said, " Which paper do you represent? " When Warner had answered she looked at him with conspicuously dawning interest: it was one of her ambitions to be considered intellectually " on the ball " and without prejudice or class, inconceivable though this may seem.

" I think your paper is the liveliest and purest written," she said. " I always take it. That and the *Manchester Guardian.*"

" For the pure writing," said MacPherson, who even when referring thus to something Isobel had said didn't act as though she were present, " d'you know something, Mr. Warner—ma dearest possession for retirement is a home in a part of the country where your paper doesn't sell more than about two copies in ten miles."

" You mean where the people can't read yet, or where there are just two people? "

MacPherson looked at him oddly. " My," he said, " I do believe you're the sort of person I've read about. You're an Angry Young Man."

There was a long silence. For a time it seemed as if Warner might take offence and not answer, as though such a personal remark was the sort of presumption he knew well: a one-way traffic; OK just as long as it was one way.

Warner said, " I've met two angry young men to-day, one angry middle-aged man, and one angry elderly man."

" That's a lot of anger. ' Anger's my food, I sup upon myself. And so shall starve with feeding '—because yourself's a limited dish, unless you believe in God, Mr. Warner."

Warner was silent as though more than ever reluctant to continue the conversation. At last he said, " What difference would God make—I mean to the meal? "

" Why then you might sup on yourself for you'd sup on God—and then you'd have an infinite supper."

" Why then," he mocked, " God is yourself."

MacPherson paused. His brow lowered slightly and he said seriously, " God being within us all."

" God being conscience? "

" God being God."

" I thought God had had it. Or we've had God."

" I *so* agree," said Isobel Meyer restlessly. " I mean we've *had* Christianity. Let's face it."

Mac stared. " What's man without God? Shall I tell

O

you? A heap o' muck. Pipple who don't believe in God and stay sane must be of limited intelligence. What's a big town skyline without a steeple? Wrong—*wrong*. Man was always needing changing. A higher idea."

" Some other people say that too—but they don't dish you out pie in the sky."

" Might you be referrin' to the Communists? "

" I *might*," Warner said.

" I *hate* the Communists, I hate their guts, d'ye hear? "

" Sounds a very Christian sentiment."

" Mr. Warner, I'm no saint and don't pretend to be and I want no unnecessary suffering for any man. That's *why* I hate'm, that's why Ah'd *cut them out*—clean—like a cancer."

" And they say just the same about you—also without pretending to be saints—and you get all steamed up."

" Aren't you talking to cross purposes? " Isobel said.

" Ai—our purposes are cross right enough," said Mac-Pherson, staring at Warner as though he couldn't believe his ears. He leant further over and touched Warner's knee. " Did the Communists have a Good Man—ever? Did they ever have a man who taught love—who *didn't* teach hate . . . who taught we were all equal in one innermost similarity: the soul; all valuable . . ."

" Love," Warner said blankly. " Valuable, equal . . . Yes—in fact that's the main gimmick. Odd you should mention it."

" Take thon moons off," MacPherson said suddenly. " Ah can't see yer eyes. . . . OK—then keep them. . . . *Communism* . . ." He was speechless. " Blood," he murmured, " *seas* of it and hell—*hell*."

" There's been a lot of hell one way and another."

" And you—an educated man! King's English. University . . . ? "

Picnic at Porokorro

" Aren't you going to say Red Brick? "

" A scholar! "

" Got a gamma in my finals on Virginia Woolf."

MacPherson didn't hear. He just stared. Warner said, " Took her as my main question. Best thing I ever did. Title: the subjective cul de sac versus the way ahead. Onan-imity versus Anonymity. Gamma minus."

" My! God preserve us! " MacPherson murmured.

Warner said, " I mean well." He sounded delirious with the unsaid, the un-yelled.

Mac, suddenly factual, said, " Did you see the hospital at Sangoro? "

" I can imagine it."

" But why don't you *look* at it? " Isobel said, peering round again.

" Why d'you think that's there? " MacPherson went on.

" Because in the last ten years people have begun to see the writing on the wall: and because to develop the country, which had to be done in the war, financially it paid to have healthy workers, and families."

" You talk like a book. I knew the man who started that hospital, fifty years ago," MacPherson ended quietly. " He died in it."

" Sounds a good investment."

" He died *of* it, too, Mr. Warner."

" Most people in the world die indirectly of under-nourishment. They don't get glorified."

" If you could hear yourself . . ." Isobel said tensely, leaning round, " you'd know there was something wrong with you. I mean psychologically. Perhaps you . . ."

" *You* could *never* hear yourself," he interrupted, fast.

" Why . . ." she faltered, beginning to touch her hair and look out of the window. He gave her the shivers —what might he not do? " Now you're being personal."

211

" Because you couldn't. Your sort never can. If you did hear yourself you couldn't go on—*not another day*. You suck yourselves—like sweets—and when there's nothing left to suck . . ."

Isobel turned pale. Her eyes closed. She had a head-ache, instantly.

" Now, Warner, now," MacPherson said. " This was my fault. I started it. *I* made a personal remark—and *Mr. Barber's wine* . . . h'm—I'd better shut up. If I lose my job I'll sue him."

" You may yet have a good case."

This final wild and apparently nonsensical statement in his rather thin, high voice which was all the odder (" unreal," MacPherson thought) for being " Oxford," created a curious silence. The P.C. turned and stared quizzically, as much as to say " Go on . . . we're all ears." The frail mouth beneath the glasses had the mobility of a child's when it is accused and outnumbered.

" Valuable! " Warner suddenly blurted. " That's rich."

MacPherson turned away.

Isobel moved nervously. She wasn't at all sure what had been the argument but out of her seething inward emotion she suddenly drawled coolly, " I seem to have heard all this before somewhere—but I couldn't do with it: jealousy and self-pity simply make me want to go away like seeing someone be sick—I mean for the person's sake as well."

" Because it stinks? " he asked her deliberately.

" Yes, it stinks. I'd keep away unless of course one was a professional, a nurse—that is a psychologist—that's different. People like you ought to see a professional."

" Yet people like you do."

She turned from him—"coolly". Perhap he went to Ludo himself. Ludo was the soul of indiscretion. The thought made her weak.

"Well, what do you want?" she said unexpectedly and shuddering. "To be dead? Someone might oblige —for a mere pittance."

MacPherson said seriously, "He wants a pound of flesh, but let me tell him something—people who want a pound of flesh always want it from the same place. They want the heart."

"And if they are made to want it enough they get it," Warner said rapidly.

"Yes, and that's that. But, oh God, boy, it's not argument you need. You can supply that for yourself, any argument. It's a feeling—and feeling's a silt: it can't be donated, or even given in a three-year course."

"A nice feeling . . ." Warner said, and stopped.

MacPherson shrugged his shoulders and turned his head to look up the road which had closed in, and was beginning to go up and down like a switchback, each short almost sheer gradient ending in a stream. At last he said quietly:—"Better than a nasty one,"

Paul leant forward as though the All Clear had sounded and said, "Hufffff, I'm hot."

"Under the collar," said his father vaguely and pensively.

"Everywhere."

"You can get an *Atlas Anicus* while I'm talking to Umslobbergast," said MacPherson. "I've had a message that he's too fat to leave his car."

They began to pass files of Africans carrying supplies on their heads. Supplies for the licensed and the unlicensed diggers. The tall muscled figures stepped deep into the tall grass and foliage to give the cars way. Then they watched them pass with their large white-ful eyes slowly turning, moving in tenuous, unpreconceiving surmise.

Conversation in the car lay dead—stabbed to death. And from the corpse all eyes turned outwards uneasily and now with almost as little conviction as the Africans.

Some cars ahead were blocking the way.

They stopped and at once Warner got out of the car and went away from it—at first inconsecutively—until he found a collar-and-tie African near a little wayside shack selling sardines and beer. They began talking. They were talking before the others had all got out.

*   *   *

It was years since MacPherson had been to Porokorro. I think he was at once taken aback by the new dimensions and atmosphere of that fantastic landscape. He had thought the jeep track continued right the way to Bornu Island Ferry and of course it once did—but now he saw how it petered out a mile short in these reddish hills, rubble and ponds.

" Men at work, eh ? " he said as he got out. He avoided looking at his carload.

It was years, too, since he had seen this particular paramount chief—the Abu of Marraba, wedged in the Dodge pick-up which was parked in front. In his linen robes he so filled the back seat that but for his head he would have looked like a vast pile of washing. He waved glibly at once and was soon explaining his plight.

There was no alternative. MacPherson got in beside him and the Secretary, who had travelled in a jeep, got in front, screwed round with his hand on the wheel. There, when the doors were shut, the three of them sat, rather like those display dinners outside cafeteria, somehow irrelevant to the situation and its all encompassing hallmark, the landscape.

I think it was the oddity of the glass-case spectacle, more than expectation and awe, that lured quite a few diggers and porters to put down their loads and squat down beside the Abu's Dodge.

Fadden and Roberts had debussed the police farther back and were now lecturing them in two ranks. Roberts had no hat on.

Isobel stepped, almost naked as she was, into the *arms* she thought, of three almost naked men.

She stared round over their heads as though yes—this was what she had expected.

The great white expanse of her near-nakedness suggested some left-over dough for which there had been no room in the oven. Yet no one looked at her.

Her huge glasses roved like the eyes of a magnified insect in the barren desert of a microscope slide. She was acting interest.

MacPherson suddenly opened the door of the chief's car. " Paul—there! " He pointed to the bush on one side of the track. " Ye'll get yer flutterbies. Ten minutes now! D'ye hear? "

Isobel, staring out over the heads of the nearest squatters, eased her belt gracefully with her long lacquered nails and looked at Paul and then Warner.

When the child went she would be alone.

She called, " *Paul* . . . Wait! "

24

I DON'T think " Nature " enters much into the lives of
any of us in the BMT. We have no collectors, or bird-
watchers—only one man who studies animal or insect
interference with the business of extracting diamonds.
His office has " Hygiene " on the door and he comes
under Production. He conducted the spraying of the
nearby marshes with DDT and fixed the civets and
advises on ants. Apart from him I don't think anyone
gives " Nature " a thought. Why should they? The
nearest country on every side—supposing you regarded
nature as a " friend," or had some kind of anthropo-
morphic attitude to it—is a mutilated or doctored car-
case—including the " original trees " and " green belts "
of our own flat camp, which for some reason seems to
be the Mecca of snakes.

From the air the Diamond Protection Area looks like a
symmetrically diseased leaf.

There is, however, one piece of " Nature " which
comes wobbling in over the wire from the bush like a distracted slap-happy messenger, pausing only to be disappointed and go on again, each one seemingly more
brilliant, various and patterned than the last. Some have
trailing streamers to their wings, some antennæ like long
velvet spoons; some are winged with the spectacled, pre-
datory eyes and beak of their worst enemies, owls or

professors, and some are small, in dozens, like shards of rainbow leaping, shimmering and pausing in the great bronze pan of the heat. And some, large and alone, are discovered in a statuesque stillness, which seems life-giving or pregnant, but can turn out to be death—and are light already, as dust.

We have all of us commented on the butterflies, though perhaps only Meyer is—as Isobel put it once to another wife—" prepared to bore one with them." He complains we should see them in the bush, in the subaqueous light of the giant teak, above still purple water, floating past the open mouths of flowers like giant sea-anemones and extinguished in a sudden night of shade. Where he goes buying from the Licensed Diggers he sees a lot and particularly at Porokorro; and this was where Paul Mac-Pherson now had the chance of catching some, while his father in the Dodge conferred with the paramount chief, who was wedded to a chassis like an SP gun.

" Paul . . . Wait! "

Then Isobel called to Warner, " Shouldn't you go with Paul? "

Warner looked round as much as to say: Are you talking to me? And then when she repeated it he said he was very sorry but he had a job to do, speaking as though they had never met, let alone travelled in the same car.

He moved farther off, leaving her looking at his back.

The landscape which she had come to see seemed to take a step closer and breathe on her.

She said to the child, " Aren't you all right by yourself? " There would be snakes. What she felt about snakes wasn't a matter for words.

He stood resenting her: " Of course . . ."

The crowd of porters and diggers was increasing round

the Dodge. Some had squatted only a few feet from her bare legs and tight linen behind, which her beach jacket designedly overhung like an emphasising canopy, a neat circumflex for this her other, disagreeing face.

Now the car they had come in was backing. She would be alone.

No one was looking at her. A hundred yards away two men were washing in a half flooded crater and *there was something wrong* with one of them. With a twinge of near faintness she remembered a remark of William's: "Sometimes they should call it *bi-section*—not *circumcision.*"

She felt sick.

Now the man covered it with his hand.

Spit coagulated in a cocoon of dust a yard from her mosquito boot. A man grunted but it proved to be speech, for it was answered.

The child had begun to walk off in the bush, at every step risking a snake. A man said something nearby. Two or three laughed or did that basic affirmative grunt which never pleased her.

"I might have been warned," she called irritably, "that I would have to stand nursemaid to such a jolly little enthusiast . . . Paul. . . . Wait, where are you?"

But he turned and said, "Well, quick, please," and then went on without her.

He left her, floundering in roots and foliage which she tried to exaggerate in a petulant soliloquy. There, balancing, she made "responsible" remarks which suggested her talents fitted her for sociological discussion with Licensed Diggers but her sex, of which she was the sole representative, had destined her, not for the first time, for martyrdom to mammalian duty with,

in this case, the dangerous chores of ayah to a " PC,"
thrown in.

Soon he got too far ahead. She began to go slower
and then when she was out of sight of him and of the
diggers she compromised, she stopped, nowhere.

*   *   *

Paul's quest contained all the pent-up energy of a day's
wait, and of lunch with Mrs. Meyer; and all the com-
pression which the allowed ten minutes demanded; and
all the wild painful reaction from what happened in the
car—and from a feeling that dad was . . . what? He
didn't know. The child's incoherence took the form of
wanting to fling his arms round him. He didn't know
why. . . . In the car—and outside the bungalows—when
that man came up and told the other man to put the
straw hat on, and when Mrs. Meyer came . . . he had
wanted to take him away from all those people. Right
away. He hated them—the man who came up, the man
in sun-glasses.

Now he charged with his net, sometimes knocking
foliage and brushing grass in the hope of springing his
prey.

The sun came through the trees like in a dusty room,
great gold shafts with mist in them—and then . . . what
was it? A bird?

Now he stopped and stood staring up, looking for the
origin of the shadow which had fled from his feet like
something kicked.

Disappointed he looked once more at the ground.
There . . .! His eyes leapt up and this time he saw it:
not a bird, but a *butterfly*. A bird-butterfly.

It came again furrowing a beam of light. Then it became
light and all the colours of light broken up and arranged

in patterns, and from each wing a long streamer ending
in a black eye like the inside of a peacock's tail. It settled
twitching its wings as though balancing and then took
off again. But it was *vast*. . .

Now again it settled.

He moved towards it, till close. Then he simply stood,
paralysed with desire. Should he lunge or creep? It had
never been seen before this kind, never. He knew that it
was unknown to the world except to a few Africans.
There was only one of it left like this. The others were
different—not so beautiful. It was the biggest, the
furriest, the brightest and the chief of all the chief
butterflies. Professors would write to him from Japan.
He would keep the letters.

"You mustn't even breathe," he thought, without
breathing.

The child approached as though balancing along a
plank, his right arm holding the net wide and high, his
feet making no noise.

At the moment when he slowed to steady himself for
the great cupping swoop the thing departed like a leaf
in the wind and soared, sank, soared again, twiddled
over a bough and then sank as though shot—like a para-
chute seed straight on to bare ground.

This time he got it.

He remained for some time in the last attitude of his
triumph—partly to make sure that the prison was complete. Then he examined the prisoner through the net;
and then slowly, with love, he introduced it to its little
limited lethal snowfield, where it subsided like the
Sleeping Beauty. Then he gloated—incredulously for
minutes, talking of the streamers, swearing it was rare,
perhaps unheard of—the first or the last in the world:
captured.

Picnic at Porokorro

His rapt, downward, head angling scrutiny of his capture—engrossment in it—and occasional display of it (holding the thing up) made walking difficult.

But soon he broke into a stumbling run towards the car, still holding it up and beginning to talk.

25

MACPHERSON CAME out of the Dodge with no eyes for fabulous insects—no eyes for anything except the immediate implementation of his picnic which, while he was being held up by half an hour's deceit with the chief, had seemed to recede like a mirage.

The crowd round the lonely vehicle had increased to some hundreds of men squatting or standing. All those inexpressive dark faces with eyes like chinks of dream somehow managed to give an impression of being vitally concerned.

How many of those very men had helped to capture Roberts? How many knew the Cowboy? How many dug nightly on BMT ground?

MacPherson looked restlessly over their heads for a sign of Fadden. He experienced a twinge of isolation such as he had never felt on this continent before now.

Fadden and Roberts appeared up the path with the escort. They had called in at the Porokorro post while MacPherson was jammed in the Dodge. They had seen Sergeant Kahn and a Mr. Richardson who had been sent down at midday to take the place of Roberts. The talk ranged over every aspect of the trouble but there was no mention of desertions—even though it seems likely that Kahn and many of the Guards must have learnt from porters that the three deserters were now on Bornu Island.

Picnic at Porokorro

Personally I doubt if it would have made much difference, at this stage, if the desertions had become general knowledge. MacPherson by now had so sunk his teeth into his picnic plan that he saw every objection as an advantage: the stronger the objection then all the more powerfully did he transform it into cause for perseverance and optimism, on another level. *Credo quia absurdum est* was by now written all over his ruddy face, even in this most material, political context, even as he scanned his motley procession, including Mrs. Meyer and her basketwork shoes and red toe-nails.

He simply invited them when they had assembled to follow him across the mud, butterfly net and all, with a dour stare which called the role. " I hope," he said, " the Snark's not a boojum." And this was the only hint he ever gave of knowing how others might view the expedition. And he glanced at Warner, who had a forty-carat diamond in one pocket and " our safety in his hands."

More than ever Warner thought it lay in his power to save or destroy.

After the journey in the car, and in his youth and ignorance, he had every reason to take a dramatic view of his secret knowledge. He had so to speak more than three rifles inside him, more than a thousand " deserters," more than ten dead BMT " overseers " lying on parapets of warlike craters which teemed with shovelling " slaves." I don't think at any time he noticed the health of the diggers, nor their cheerfulness compared say to office-workers in the country he came from.

The diggers, for MacPherson, had stopped singing—that was bad; for Warner they hadn't started hating, and that was worse. He met MacPherson's eyes with an appearance of merely professional calm.

223

But the rifles were already going off inside him and the last looks of the dying BMT and police were directed hopelessly in the direction of the man whose warning they had scorned. He stood apart with such fastidious, proud and indifferent detachment that MacPherson asked the very question he hoped would be asked.

" And the press—is the press coming? "

" I'll follow."

" Ai—and you'll follow on too. I'm not sending out search parties. You stick by your Uncle Mac, Mr. Warner."

For a minute Warner looked as if he might decide to stay behind with the collar-and-tie African to whom he had been talking. Then a whole compelling complex of professional and personal reasons mastered his impulse to boycott this absurd Lord Mayor's Show. He went, certain as though it had already happened that there would be violence unless they made it " humanly possible for him to help them."

People have suggested that he was blindly struggling for a formula which would save his obscure, distorted, fanatic face and allow him to speak out and become " the saviour," and arbiter, of the expedition—on which terms only would he become part of it.

But perhaps he was already one of its cogs, beyond any possibility of freedom.

God knows what the licensed diggers thought of that strange procession which wended suddenly over their skylines and parapets. A white woman like Isobel must have been familiar from advertisements in towns, and in stray periodicals for wrapping. Hand in hand with magic weapons and medicines she was one of the new missionary stars rising in the west: cheesecake. She was on every product. They didn't know why.

Picnic at Porokorro

Warner was something new. They thought he was American because he didn't look British.

Some of the diggers, particularly those from French territory, had seldom seen white men, although the latest western water-pumps were roaring away like motor-bikes in several craters.

The diggers made their machines work as they worked themselves—without pause. And all the time both diggers and machines were multiplying and the sum of their activity changed the landscape.

MacPherson was astounded at the scale. The diggers' energy, which in the past had seemed so personal and piratical, used one against the other, took on suddenly, in his eyes, the dimensions and character of a vast, anonymous, co-ordinated tide.

He soon stopped. Sweat bedewed his glasses. He took them off and the lack of them made his eyes look wasted and perplexed. Having cleaned them he turned round and seemed to see his procession for the first time. A shadow of doubt turned into dry humour. Then he turned and went on with new resolution.

Once he fell down and was helped by a policeman. The trivial incident took on an exaggerated importance, for him and all who saw it.

More and more diggers stopped to watch, and the way they watched had a gradually cumulative effect upon him—for he felt now everywhere, even his own party, were watching *him*.

The next digger looked like Barber, and he thought: Barber was watching me. Merely watching; not helping. Why had no one told him the track ended where it did? What had happened to the Abu? He used to be fairly straight. Now his son was a lawyer, and he couldn't move . . . Said he had no influence with the chiefs since

Picnic at Porokorro

Ledgeco had appointed Wardens in the Protection Area Villagers. Another cat's-cradle.

And Meyer, even Meyer, had watched him, at arm's length.

Look at the quantity of these chaps. He had reported, only last week, that the Frenchies were *not* filtering back. He had had the D.O.'s word and passed it on. Now look at this—out of sight—on every side.

It wasn't the D.O.'s fault, he thought. He hadn't a chance to get out, with the paper work.

He must ask for a proper check again.

What could you do when " frontier " was a mere word, and the gaols were stuffed?

They marched on.

Picnic!

His face hardened and he began to call out cheerfully to some of the diggers.

" Bonjour, chef," one of them replied.

" Go away home," he complained, pointing at the man. " Allez."

There was laughter. But *good natured*. Yes—good, human-natured laughter. So there you are, he said. There you are. They're human. His picnic plan was OK. If he admitted a flaw it was that his son would get tired. Everything would take longer, far longer than he had thought. Nan would give him a wigging. Everything would be far more complicated. He would be out here in the middle of nowhere with a mother's outing at midnight. And Paul. The day had started in Paul's birthday honour. Now he was here, at Porokorro.

*   *   *

Warner soon realised the party was bound for the very spot where he had met Amanda in the morning. This

226

increased his inner tension. He might be pointed out as
the man who came down with " a message " from Mr.
Meyer: the man who had received Amanda's confession
—and diamonds.

Warner had got up at four that morning. There was
no woman. His head throbbed and sometimes he thought
nothing was real. He spoke but no one really listened.
They walked away like Smiling-Eyes Barber. He offered
reason and was met with heat: Hot-buttocks Dickson—
and yet was accused of heat: Roberts the Schoolboy's
Dream. F—— blind blockheads. He was surrounded
—and couldn't get in. He was surrounded by the job,
the paper on account of which he sometimes wished he
was dead; and yet was distastefully identified as the
personification of it by people who read it first of all
papers. The trouble wasn't in him. But it was no good.
He knew—because he had tried and it was no good. The
red ground crumbled, slithered beneath his tread. There
remained the gimmick, the story, the bye-line and the
spread which would OK an expense sheet for half a car.
Yes, there was half a car in this and all Fats Waller on
discs. He would merely look at Amanda as though he
were raving, which, since he *was* raving, would be a
suitable way of looking at him. And he hoped Scott
slipped into the crater and left five flatulent bubbles,
i.e., tradition to posterity and the diggers would dig up
the BMT like that tree, the BM Tree—Three MTB . . .
Three MBE rifles—he didn't care. They would be used
—when Nlongo the Bongo saw Roberts. He knew it
now.

He slithered and stumbled, his face as expressionless as
. . . an adult's, and as usual his eyes hidden.

He wanted to cry. The whole British set-up was like
a blackboard on which the master has written too much,

for too long—along the sides, between the lines, in the corners, everywhere. You couldn't just wipe it out and leave a sort of mist of bird-shit. You wet the rag with flaming hot water, you sweep off every mark. But then you find there's a white haze silted into the wood, going back perhaps to the Middle Ages, which crops out like boils every so often in people like Keats; or, when the Nasty Smelly Machines and People got smellier, going further back still with Pre-Raphaelite religiosity, to Godde and our Makere. Then when God was officially dead you got a new kind of subjectivity—this time based on private income and a parlourmaid: Virginia Woolf. The religion-neurosis in vacuo (Warner: gamma minus). So you got more hot-water, as you valued your life, and this time a scrubbing brush and you took out the tremulous private income, special view, subjective bird-shit with elbow grease and were left at last with something clean to work on. Then you had a chance of the new life: through facts. Then you could get around to the overdue admission that Art and God were powerful in proportion to the intensity of the subject's or the society's neurosis.

He hardly noticed when he reached Amanda's guard-post. He was floating, flying—omnipotent. He *knew*.

Now the party telescoped and stopped. The police were grouped on one side.

They had reached the Niele. Warner looked round and to mark a final thought he kicked at the fallen Guard-post shelter.

It was nothing, a mere fidget, at most a gesture of contemptuous recognition for the furniture of that day.

But Scott strolled up and stood near him.

Warner looked up and at last said, " Good afternoon. What can I do for you? "

" Good afternoon," Scott said. And remained.

Picnic at Porokorro

Scott's only instruction, " You can keep an eye on the Press," had been delivered by Colonel Gordon conversationally and humorously. But the suave gleam in Gordon's eye had said something more. Simply, quite genially, " I'm afraid we can't bump him off."

Scott had accepted the command and the unspoken regret with such alacrity that Gordon became thoughtful and soon said quietly, to the blotter, " I mean see he doesn't get in the way—or go swanning in the bush—or stick his foot through one of their shrines. Don't give the chap the impression he's being shadowed."

The moment Warner kicked at the shabby relic of BMT " property "—ten plaited palm leaves—Scott had moved up into his vicinity and stood at what he thought was a tactful distance. Not that he could seriously convince himself the rotten palms needed protection—simply the way Warner's foot went out, in a sort of trailing, nudging kick, at the fallen shelter constituted a comment; and although such a comment had not been banned by Colonel Gordon, it yet afforded Scott the very foothold which his pride had been waiting for; prompting him to suggest—by a movement, a way of standing close and looking at Warner—that he was on sufferance, and on a limb. All of which he did—with the vividness of disguised passion.

Warner examined him as though he were certifiable for a bleak second and then strolled off. He had other worries. At any moment he expected to see Amanda.

But Amanda was nowhere to be seen, and he noticed there was no surprise or consternation on the part of the police that the post was unoccupied. Had Amanda gone back to his H.Q. and reported his whole " confession to Mr. Meyer's assistant? "

Warner looked round with care. No one was looking

229

at him in any way accusingly—except Big Softy Scott,
Conrad Veidt, who must have lost his job at Moss Bros.

A few police began preparing some of the dug-out
canoes.

MacPherson was talking to the Secretary.

They were walking up and down like officers before
the forming up of parade. Most people kept their distance and the whole scene was the last thing MacPherson
had intended. He kept trying to break away from the
Secretary, who had suddenly button-holed him, asking
to be " put completely in the picture," asking nervously
what '' exactly the form was to be " when they got to the
island, and " what was his pigeon."

MacPherson was in a hurry yet had to reply in language
which made allowances. The Secretary was not gifted,
yet a family man like himself in the service, with the
Governor to answer to, and children to educate privately.

As he answered, MacPherson looked round and was
goaded to harshness by what he saw—because it was so
unlike the picnic he had imagined. Mrs. Meyer plastered
up to the knees in mud; Paul looking tired already;
Warner suddenly " a bloody red," who cadged lifts from
the people he'd like to see dead, and everywhere this
rocky, marshy waste. Even Fadden's detached obedience
suddenly seemed criticism, and the whole atmosphere,
of all those silent police officers a complacent I-Told-
You-So.

" Just nothing—just nothing—that's all you need do,"
Mac said with his eyes elsewhere and then suddenly he
broke off to shout, to assert once more his command over
his rebellious material. " By God," he said, " d'you
hear that . . ." and he invited them to listen to what
most had already heard—the distant sounds of revelry
on Bornu Island. " Somebody's found a diamond or got

married or something. Business as usual, eh? . . . eh?
Fun and games, eh?"

Tom-tom in Africa is as much a continual background
as the hollow knocking of the mortar and long pestle.
Birth, death, marriage, house-blessing, sickness, arrival
or departure are in sum as frequent as cooking and the
diggers brought their sense of celebration with them, to
this waste land along with the laws and customs which
had saved them from moral disintegration.

"D'you hear it . . . ?" MacPherson repeated.

There was silence.

"Eh?" MacPherson shouted to one Sergeant of
Police whom he had known before. "Kuru fellows plenty
palm wine, eh? Plenty copper?"

The sergeant lowered his eyes and said politely, "Yes,
sah."

"Well . . . ?" Then Mac turned in another direction.
"Roberts, where's that boater of yours?"

Roberts looked at Fadden, who was non-committal.
Then he put it on.

The groups of police were at once affected. They
began to grin. They cheered up. They moved their long,
pale, peeled riot sticks and their voices rose low and
undifferentiated like a swarm of bees. Roberts remembered the time when placing the hat on his head had
felt like positioning the rugger ball for a twenty-five-yard
kick. A charge. So did they.

Warner stared from the hat to the man who had asked
for it. He could see the old Scots Fuddy-duddy with a
haggis, reeling off Burns on a Burns' night. A man who
would have given up *Punch* lately, and occasionally
thrown *The Observer* out of his chair but shaken his head
like a confused doctor over Eden's voice and manner.
A good father to infants but a minus with adolescents.

Picnic at Porokorro

You couldn't blame the chap. It wasn't his fault. He
hadn't had a chance: fed crap since birth, found it paid,
as it did; so dished it out again caecula caeculorum—
Sir Adam MacPherson—modest Adam—who thought his
wife Mysterious Beatrice-Helen-Eve MacPherson. Club:
Heaven.

Should he open his eyes? Now? This moment?

Warner's thin face was orientated coldly towards the
ruddy older man who still held the centre of the stage.
Words began to form in his mind: " Mr. MacPherson I
think I ought to tell you you're taking a bigger risk than
you know—the diggers have rifles."

MacPherson was blowing his nose and bending his
ear fretfully to a further aside from the secretary. Now
he was folding over the result of the first blow and preparing for a second trumpeting evacuation of his nose as
though it gave him something to think about, something
to get on with while the secretary was talking. But it
made him look very ordinary and slightly tearful, weak
and old, and Warner had begun to move when Mac-
Pherson was suddenly touched and guided by the suave
Secretary a few steps away to consider a final eventuality.

At the same moment Scott moved not a yard to
Warner's left, where he had arrived without good reason.

Warner turned away—from Scott—to fill the time
till the Heavenly Twins came back. He kicked a stone.
He found himself in the very square yard Amanda had
given him the knowledge. His eyes dropped . . . searched.
The diamonds had gone. You don't say. His eyes rose
to the stricken landscape half expecting to see the man
hiding nearby, so bloody Christian-guilty by now and
responsible that at last he would be moving on all fours
in the mud asking people to step on him, which of course
they would—with pleasure—in return for a lifelong fee.

Picnic at Porokorro

But Warner's eyes, as they strayed from the distance, found instead only a piece of wood . . . familiar, and close.

He stared.

The *cross*. Amanda's cross.

It was tilted over and looked like the crazy ploy of a baboon. The junction of the two bits of wood was held by a piece of military webbing. He approached. The P.C.'s voice was droning again. He thought idly, as he kicked the thing over, that if you didn't have a little amulet full of moonshine and monkey-shit round your neck, then you gave yourself this kind of erection instead. There was no end to it. Typical: it wouldn't go first kick so he walked on it.

" Was that yours? "

He thought he must have imagined the utterance. The sense didn't fit anything recent.

But then it came from Scott . . . so why should it?

" Come again," he said and saw Scott's eyes. As in a dog, following an intruding dog—the sudden move of his kicking leg had triggered off a quick, aggressive movement forward which had tried to take the form of reasonable speech, a mere enquiry.

" Yes, it's mine," he said.

" Someone might have put it there. . . . One of the Guards. This is a Post here, you know. This is a Post. A BMT Post. . . ."

Silence.

Scott was ashen. He went on, " Couldn't it have belonged to someone? "

He could *persist*. . . . Warner gazed at the " noble," mothy face and identified the tone as that of a *restrained superior*.

" Isn't it possible he may come back? " Scott went on.

233

" No," Warner said, " I don't think it is."

" I see. You don't think it is possible he might come
back? "

" See my last letter."

" You know all about it, do you? "

" Yes—I know all about it."

" If I were you," Scott said, " I would mind my own
business—which round here, I should have thought, was
limited to news."

Suddenly friendly Warner said, " You know you want
to look out—I mean really—or you'll be back in the
grease at seven quid a week."

He turned from him and with a final kick sent the still
unflattened cross cavorting across mud.

Only Fadden, who was at a loose end, saw it happen.
Warner having kicked, had turned and was facing Scott
coolly with the great dark blanks where the eyes should
have been. Fadden remembered a sort of " eyeless "
quality in Warner's appearance at that moment.

Scott moved, rushed. Then Fadden saw Warner lying
on the ground, at the tall man's feet. Fadden thought
Scott must have hit Warner in the back of the neck or
head—for at the last moment Warner had turned calmly
away—not to avoid violence but presumably to paralyse
it by pretending the possibility didn't exist.

The mad impossible instant froze and was prolonged
as though time had gone off rails. A sense of emergency
and arrest was communicated to people who had heard
and seen nothing.

Moonlike faces turned—to each other—to what? To
it: the man lying on the ground.

Then everyone converged, with half hungry half reluctant speed, as toward a street accident.

The pattern of that afternoon which had been so

important to MacPherson now seemed to disintegrate in his eyes. He stared at the scene and at the red mud and at Warner's head and shoulders now bowed over his knees as though things had at last taken on an alien autonomy with which he could no longer struggle.

At last he made an effort. He began speaking, asking for an explanation.

No one seemed to hear him. Warner slowly found his feet and made his way through them all. Reaching an isolated spot he leant against a tree for a few broody seconds and then was profusely sick.

He stayed there until Isobel went towards him. Then he went farther off.

Fadden said to Scott, " I think you'd better go back. We'll discuss this later."

Scott looked mad and ill. He seemed about to say something important, enormously important—but the problem of where to start, in such a place and circumstances, resigned him again to a desperate, bitter and passive impotence. Besides, as usual, memory seemed to fail him. He looked in labour to give birth to one, only one, particular of memory. But it wouldn't come.

I say he looked " mad " because his huge soft eyes were lit with some inner version of what had happened— a version which by sheer intensity and privacy drew upon him the uneasy, side-long glances which are reserved for the possessed.

Two of his large beautiful fingers were tenderly clasped round his signet ring and one corner of his long tenuous mouth was raised in a vestigial suggestion of weeping— or snarling—and he stared at the place where Warner had lain as though he were still there—dead.

Then he, too, turned through the group and soon was lost to sight as he walked across the disused land.

26

"Boys WILL be boys," was Mac's attempted attitude. But it scarcely found utterance. A glint of childish venom now stood, at last, in the face of this kindly man.

His anger with Scott prevented him from looking even at his back, diminishing now on the causeway, in the distance; his commiseration with Warner was cool enough to fall short of sincerity.

"Four-fifteen," he complained at a large gold watch which he had dragged from his holiday wear. "By God— and here we are . . ." He couldn't finish.

Roberts got busy in his hat; whereupon the young Manga policemen stirred themselves happily. They did not understand what had happened between the two white masters, but things generally looked promising. The hat was the guarantee.

MacPherson, hearing their happy chatter, took, or seemed to take, new heart.

"They're good boys," he said, and he shouted a commentary on embarkation which had already started at Fadden's, not his command:

"Aye, that's it, that's right. Now, Mrs. Meyer, the Trousers, and Paul, the Net," he said, "will you kindly step aboard and I'll have the Hat with me too, and the secretary and two cops, Mr. Fadden—*withóut* golf clubs, if you wouldn't mind. Mr. Warner, the News, I think

you'd better travel with me in case someone else takes
a swipe. Now—are we right . . . ? "

Did he really feel he had once again got it all sensible
and in proportion?

The dug-outs were pushed clear of the tangled branches.

Certainly everyone was well fed, healthy, loosely dressed
and came in peace, almost to the point of absurdity. Perhaps they should have been travelling on scooters with
rucksacks and coloured designations of their point of
view sewn on to them; and televiewed even while it
happened. Never had there been such "individuality."

Now the lip-lap-lapping of the water along the sides
of the dug-outs had a soothing effect on everyone. They
looked at the banks as though at themselves, receding,
and a sudden silence descended as though suddenly a
good kind of self-consciousness had taken root in their
minds.

In this silence voices on Bornu could be plainly heard
and that, I think, was one reason why Mac suddenly
embarked upon a loud oration—hoping that the general
tone of his voice, at least, would reach the illicit diggers
—many of whom (as there were striking statistics to
prove) had been in domestic service with Europeans.

Often those digger boys must have had good masters
and listened without hatred to the drone of their after-
dinner talk on the cool verandas.

So Mac thought he would drone at 'em now and show
'em it was still the same people, the same mood of goodwill and common sense.

But he did not in fact drone merely to them.

With both hands he took this last opportunity of
putting a personal harmonious seal on his own followers
and of saving them from the welter of heterogeneous
minor conflicts, discords, babel of language and practical

anomalies in which they seemed to have been drowning ever since he got into Meyer's Rover in the morning.

" Now look out," he said publicly, " if ye sit on the edge then someone the same weight must sit on the other edge because if ye sit on the edge alone, then you put the thing out of balance, and you get a swim. But if you're prepared to get a wet bottom and sit in the bilge then you can have the apoplectic fit all to yourself, because you're dead centre and when you're dead centre you can do what you like: the boat just goes on. I well remember the day the Bishop of Letchslade, inspecting African Missions, crossing this very Niele—though farther south —Paul, this is one for you—had the sun in his eyes, and the Canon's secretary offered to change places. Well, I'd carefully arranged the bishop to be balanced, not by the Canon but by Umbopa, the Chief of the Manga, who was once weighed against an Ox by his admiring people. (The ox lost. I saw it.) When the Canon got up there was no difference, but when the bishop rose and crossed to the same side as Umbopa we went over so quickly that for a second I thought a granny hippo had scratched her back on us. Ai, man! that was a wet day. The crocs missed a grand feast that day. And how d'you think the other canoes fished out the Bishop and Umbopa? Well, they didn't; they towed them both—like buoys or bait—right to the edge."

The swift kissing of the paddles and the rustling of the water along the flanks of the dug-outs were small sounds.

When Mac stopped talking everyone noticed that the noise of revelry on Bornu had stopped also.

Warner's knees touched Isobel Meyer whenever she leant back the fraction more which made her comfortable. The contact was unpleasing to her and so whenever relaxation obliged it she tautened forward again.

Picnic at Porokorro

Crocodiles were sighted and Mac seized upon them as a fresh text. There were three of them on the far bank, great yellow brutes looking from far away like crinkly zoo scorpions in their glass-cases of yellow light and sand.

Far away they were but launchable, hungry and swift.

Roberts' field-glasses were handed first to Paul, who said, " Golly," and then to Isobel and Warner—the innocents abroad—while Mac discoursed:

" My, look at that! One hundred million years in those yellow eyes. He saw your grand-daddy, he did— a lemur in a tree. There's a conservative chap. Look at the scute on him. No compromise. Still the same. Like a little Andes. . . ."

Some people who had often seen crocodiles indulged at first in mildly proprietory and sophisticated glances, yet when they took a turn with the glasses they lost their mildly proprietory and sophisticated expression. The little plump arms and hands, the tree-trunk tail and the long yellow eyes in their craggy turrets bumped up, as Mac had hoped to suggest, out of everyone's personal memory . . . which of course was impossible and therefore all the more fascinating.

" They aren't often down as far as this," Roberts said. He was sitting in the bows, cocked up like a figurehead, in the Hat.

" Let's not rock the boat," said the Secretary as he got the focus right.

Isobel said, " How interesting." Her voice sounded wrong. " The one in the middle has got a cold. I thought there weren't any here."

There was no sound but the paddles. Everyone was looking at the crocodiles, which were getting nearer.

Paul said, " Look! They're moving."

Picnic at Porokorro

And they were—seeming to slide twistingly towards the water and then become part of it as though liquidated.

" They've been shot at, I expect," Roberts said.

" Don't let's catch any crabs," said the Secretary. All the Europeans were still looking at the place where the tails had disappeared. " They've gone," they said.

The Africans were looking ahead, at the island.

The talk became more and more desultory. Mac-Pherson was unable to sustain the first verve with which he had restored the tone of his picnic. The truth was simple: an act has to have an end. It can't go on and on. And so he suddenly fell back naturally, unconsciously, without noticing that he had done so, on the original feeling of that long day—the feeling of being old and with it the desire to show Paul Africa, the wonders of its fabulous variety, and to give him what he knew of it before retirement removed him, as it would soon, for ever from the field of his memories and expertise. For when he went perhaps Paul wouldn't manage back' here for years . . . perhaps ever again. And so he sat there looking for things for his son to examine through the binoculars —birds, animals, native sacrifices in the branches to the forest gods, or once a spot where a man he knew had simply picked up a gem stone in the sand, the last time he was here—" so keep your eyes open, son, and perhaps you'll pay for your own education."

Thus for a brief moment the twin, paired shirts, the big and little MacPherson and the spirit of leisure enjoyed a brief spell of the life which had been planned for it yesterday—up another river, without policeman.

And strangely enough everyone, even the African policemen who were paddling with harmonious vertical downward thrusts of the paddles, as Paul had seen in films of the old war canoes, from time to time co-operated in this search for more crocodiles, vultures, iguana. They even looked at their own familiar trees in a different way.

And so for a brief instant the picnic—when no one was thinking about it and when everyone, even its originator, had perhaps given it up—became a fleeting reality.

For a few minutes the rustle of the water and the absorbed curious silence of the people in the boats gave the impression of a unity, as though time had been suspended and as though in that sudden freedom they had all found the peace of healthy sleep.

      *   *   *

Suddenly there was a noise like a stinging, sharp hand-clap overhead, and in the distance a dry cough.

Only MacPherson and one or two of the Manga police who had been in Burma knew it at once, without thinking. Roberts was too young. He had to think, to grope with, repulse and finally accept a chilling intuition. Then he knew.

The second shot struck the water into a neat splash two yards to their left and went off with a furry noise.

Far away on Bornu there was another dry cough.

After a moment's silence several of the African police began to talk fast in their own tongue. Fadden stood up carefully and, facing his boatload like a clergyman faces a congregation, regardless of heaven or hell behind him, bade them be quiet, soothingly. And they were.

MacPherson, having survived a moment's pure paralysis, muttered, " Well I'll be b——d," and started hauling off his shirt. " Mrs. Meyer," he said, "and Paul, lie down. Everyone lie down."

Roberts stayed where he was in the bows, though he turned to face the island and very slightly lowered himself.

MacPherson stood up and began slowly, almost caressingly, to wave his unbuttoned shirt to and from above his head.

The paddlers had crouched too, and the dug-out began to turn in the current. In the continuing silence MacPherson said, " Keep paddling—keep upstream."

A sergeant in the third boat, who had risen like MacPherson and Fadden, repeated the order to his crews and the three dug-outs straightened.

Still waving his shirt, MacPherson shouted in Kuru, " Don't shoot . . . we come to talk peace. Don't shooooot."

His voice was old and anyhow not very strong. His second shout faltered as though weakening from the fear it was not carrying as much as from exhaustion.

Roberts stood up and shouted in English with much more power and carry.

There was still no third shot.

Heads were beginning to rise. Paul looked interested. He said, " Whew! " smiling, for it was a story. And it was over, finished.

Isobel's face was a mask. She said, " It's some joke."

Her mouth had the dead look of painted sculpture and her limbs were drowsy.

Roberts shouted again. The island could only be 250 yards away now and movement could be seen. MacPherson still waved his shirt and suddenly felt enough confidence to blurt out, " Damned silly loons." Roberts was in front of him, his hands moving like a semaphore. Roberts somehow got higher till he stood like a man-of-war figurehead in his fantastic hat.

Mac was sure now. He laughed wryly. " Crazy fools."

Then it happened. Three rifles—it must have been all three, people said afterwards—opened up. Of course, everyone had a different account of what happened. But

all agreed they remembered Roberts suddenly standing
hopelessly still and then throwing his hat into the river,
theatrically high conspicuously, far to one side. At this
the fire seemed to intensify. Wild, wild shooting. Sometimes the water spurted up so far away as to support the
amazed incredulity which everyone still felt. " They
can't be shooting at ME."

But of course—in spite of those remote little tufts far
downstream, far ahead and far to one side which made so
much more sense than the near ones—the diggers *were*
shooting at the three dug-outs which now broke like the
walls of a mined building in slow-motion, and parted in
the sway of the current while the paddlers crouched low
and jabbered.

MacPherson was kneeling now, glowering and creeping
forward to look round Roberts' legs. " Si' doon," he
said.

One rifle, more persistent as well as more accurate
than the others, filled their ears with crack-thumps and
the sudden little tunes that soldiers know. Sometimes
water splashed sharply cold over their skin.

Then one of the African police said, " The boy,
sah."

Both Warner and Isobel Meyer, nearest whom he was
sitting, noticed nothing. They turned to look at him as
though he might be feeling sick or doing something risky
for himself. And MacPherson, too, turned round ready to
be instantly firm or encouraging.

None of these people's faces changed at all quickly as
they remained looking at the child. Perhaps even at this
moment, even in someone like Warner in whom the
rifles had so to speak been going off all day and who had
experienced imaginary violence, there was an inability to
feel even the outer fringe of his much talked-of evils

when they became real. MacPherson was the first, after
the African guards, to know that his son was dead.

Yet he said "Paul!" quietly, invitingly—as though
tempting the child back across a chasm which he mustn't
look at if he was to come back. "Paul . . . Paul . . ."

He tried to reach him, climbing over people. Someone
muttered, "Careful . . ." with sudden temper and
shame.

The bullet seemed to have stolen him from under their
noses, under their very hands (Isobel had been touching
him). And stolen him out of his body, too—for there
was no mark on him of any kind.

He lay as though he had succumbed to the fatigue
which his father had begun to regret. His chin was
tucked down and his face had the luminous fragility of
porcelain, the elusiveness of beauty and the terrible
calm of absence. In his open eyes the image of the world
lay still and perfect, like threads in a marble.

The shooting stopped.

Some people say they remember the hat keeping pace
with the boats on the current and a group, in Mac-
Pherson's dug-out, crawling into shape round the boy
—the rows of hands like the markings on a long insect
feeling along the side of the dug-out, while MacPherson
tried to get to him without disturbing balance.

Fadden rose to his feet again to make the Africans
paddle and get up speed. He had been shot through the
wrist. He held it up with the other hand under the elbow
as though it were some kind of tiller and stood requesting
the paddlers to paddle, with his always ordinary face the
same as it had been in the morning, at lunch and now in
the evening.

The boats became a pattern again and there was
nothing but the spectacle and the sound of the aging

Scotsman and his child from which people withdrew their eyes and their ears.

At last they stared at the water, at the approaching bank, and most of them ticked off again and again with a sort of ashamed, reluctant, gluttony the fact that they were alive.

27

PERHAPS SOME of us in the camp turned round, like the people in the boats, and noticed the child only when he was dead. Until then few of us had " taken him in." Now we groped for some relic, some vestige of memory: he had charged into the car when he was asked to get in and had looked out of the window as though about to take off over the trees; we had seen him at Meyer's sorting table in the sun, still as a statue; he had a piece of plaster on one knee. . . .

The idea of a child being present had not perhaps seemed very real even to those who went on the expedition —I suppose because most people had more than enough to think about at each present moment.

And yet when the news spread that the child was dead people reacted, you might almost say, superstitiously, as though something worse than merely that fact was implied, something personal and far-reaching, darkened with an abrupt futility which no one dared express.

All our wills had been fully extended towards various " solutions," and then suddenly like a stab in the back, like a mortal thrust through some completely unengaged faculty—the day came to an end, died through a failure not of will, but of the imagination, which is to say faith. This failure was for some of us, at first, made more gruesome by the sideline figure of Meyer who somehow tinged it with the ghastly hue of the inevitable.

The car carrying the body moved with a ceremonious slowness which merely made a hideous parade of the whole hopeless fiasco. Bulldozers which hadn't been warned were held up with their shields a few yards from the side of the improvised hearse, and scarfed goggled Africans like stokers from the boiler-room of hell peered with unearthly surmise at this obstruction to the stupefying din of their exhausts, which shouldn't have paused yet.

From the window of the offices the car's slowness looked like the very definition of ugliness. Some people went on with their work without a word or a sign. Boys appeared at bungalow doors and stood grouped on the threshold as though for safety.

Barber never said a word when he took the boy's body into his house. People said afterwards how good he was to the Provincial Commissioner on that occasion. Nothing was too much trouble. The whole machinery of the BMT was put at the disposal of the MacPherson family and Number One himself supervised the minute and painful practicalities which attend a death.

The boy was laid on Number One's own bed. He insisted on this, and looked more like a little modern magician than ever standing beside that porcelain corpse; as usual he seemed rather larger than life; his great eyes shone with tears and—who can doubt it—were riven with responsibility.

I say " responsibility," but most of us merely thought that like the good officer he had once been he felt responsible for anything that happened " in his command." No more than that. No one ever suggested

247

anything more, least of all the reports which went in afterwards.

He offered to fetch Mrs. MacPherson in the Company plane; he offered to tell her himself. He behaved, as usual, in the most exaggerated way.

If you could point to any concrete result of Mac-Pherson's " picnic "—beyond his own bereavement—it would be merely a worsening in the health of Barber (who it is now suggested may " ask for a change "), and an increase in the number of fine-sounding formalities which stultify relationships between Government, the BMT, the NA, the Police and the Diggers—an increase in illicit digging; perhaps, too, a worsening in the camp atmosphere—which if you like is, on the one hand, " more unreal " than ever, more like a Thames country club, 1938, than ever, and on the other, more secretly apprehensive.

Amanda turned up and told a strange story which was eventually believed; how, after Warner had left him he had wandered into the forest and lived for a time in a Kuru village.

Scott and his wife have gone home. I heard he now has a job with the National Trust.

*   *   *

Warner went away that evening in one of Amfookha's Rovers. He saw Barber for a minute by chance before leaving.

It was outside the mess. Barber went up to him.

They stared at each other in a curious kind of silence as though each expected the other to make some kind of reference of open stark revelance to what had happened. But Warner's face by then had become rather like a diamond—the article which can cut (and shape) any material object.

Barber, after a tentative reference to the tragedy, stared and stared at him almost as though imploring this stray youth to consider that he, Barber, would do anything " within reason," perhaps even beyond reason, to " secure agreement " (about what?), but he met a perfect blank in the great sun-glasses where his, and Barber's, individuality and responsibility were now put aside as irrelevant, neither here nor there.

The fact that the victim was a child gave Warner, I think, a kind of satisfaction.

Then something closed in Barber's face too. There occurred in his eloquent eyes the *tu l'as voulu* of the man who is not a saint. They shook hands sparely.

The article which came out in Warner's paper two weeks later was what Dickson and others expected. " This ends in This." Two huge pictures—one of policemen in tin helmets carring white riot-sticks and the other of Paul MacPherson's small coffin and his mother weeping. The letterpress. bore no mark of Warner's tortuous, passionate and neurotic character. It was, so to speak, blank as his face had been: a formula—orthodox anti-colonial class-conscious propaganda with a selling slant of violence and sentimentality.

There was a codicil in jet bold sans 12 pt.: *Demand* for 1, hospitals; 2, enquiry into colonial police practices; 3, A Diggers' safety code; 4, a PAYE system for diggers.

It may, of course, have been largely put together on the sub's desk, because other articles we saw by Warner bore the individual stamp of his own fast, metaphoric, depreciatory speech, all with undertones of a child's sentimentality. But on this occasion his talent seems to have dis-

solved and suffered perhaps voluntary self-liquidation
and made way for a committee.

*   *   *

At eleven, that last night, there was silence, in the house
of William Meyer.

Isobel had been visited by the camp doctor and given
a sedative normally reserved for extreme pain. She lay
perfectly still upstairs with the fan ruffling the fringes of
a gossamer embroidered slip at the foot of the bed. It
sighed monotonously and swivelled back and forth as
though fulfilling all the restlessness which lay neutralised
by the pills. One of her lovely rounded arms was outside
the sheet—ending in long red nails which had embedded
themselves in a scrap of a handkerchief. They clamped
it, along with her own thumb, like the teeth of a trap.
The light sheet lay like a layer of snow over the perfect,
full shape of one breast. Her mouth was shut tight,
locked.

Downstairs William heard the first human sound for a
long time—the voice of MacPherson opposite suddenly
wrestling with what had happened as though now at
least he had worked it out as a trick played on him against
the laws of truth and therefore—by a further breach of
those laws—reversible.

" Oh God—Nan. . . . Y'see, William—it didn't
happen, it did not happen. . . . How could it have happened : I know these people. That's why I took Paul—
because I know them—y'see, that's why I took him. He
was all I've got—when you're getting on that's what it's
like. I was taking him—to Africa—and to my life's work;
I know it's all going—but I was taking ma future to ma
past—and I gave all I had to both . . . d'ye see that,
William ? But how could you see it ? I don't understand.

Picnic at Porokorro

I see—d'you want to hear what I see? I see sleek pigs
or bloody vultures on every side. I look into people's
faces and everything's just grand and normal and I see
just pigs and bloody vultures on every side. There's not
enough of something. What is it? There's less of something than there was—yes—even than there was. . . .
That's why Paul died . . . that's why." And the old
man's words trailed off and dispersed into hopeless
sobs.

The silence of William Meyer was strenuous and he
kept breathing deeply, leaning forward in his chair in
the direction of the distracted MacPherson. Always on
the brink of speech he always shrank from it.

The fan which ran on, facing this way and that, above
the motionless form of his wife and the handkerchief
trapped in her hand, the number branded on his own
flesh and this late casualty before him gave Meyer the
brief summarising vision of total experience which
drowners are said to experience. Something now was
required of him. But he had adjusted himself so often
and so profoundly that what was left of him could speak
only barely, to just support life, like the European bomb
ruins which made a home for cave-dwellers who soon
had good wallpaper. There was not much left in him.
The first harmonious images of life had died, it seemed.
of too much adjustment. Let him put it that way so as
not to blame the alien world emerging—nor, either,
his first memories which had given him the strength to
endure even the camps where under a steel sky all yard-
sticks, all censure and praise, died of a bitter relativity.
Did they rise again? The intellectual atmosphere that
followed the war had not been exactly an oxygen tent
nor heaven either. In fact the jet columns of Buchenwald
conifers which had become the literal spokesmen of

nature's moral neutrality, the daily amphitheatre, had
followed him figuratively into liberty beyond the wire, as
though interested in this victim of something worse than
their own dispassion. The ground was merely waiting
for another literal crop of those conifers. Prosperity and
lull had put a coat of paint on the huge omnipresent
offence; and only fear made babel slow.

All his past was now present in his utterly used face,
but from it he could extract no word for MacPherson
or the child, to whom he would have given his life easily,
for he himself had been born again perhaps against his
wish.

The self-imposed conditions of that renaissance had
been grim, and unsuccessful. He had submitted too
easily to the influence of any vitality, even spurious
vitality—Isobel's—when he met her; and then to
the commercial demand for his gift for human relations.

And yet something had remained.

" Yes . . ." he said awkwardly, " there is need for
something better. The expectation is right, and even natural
and perhaps ' scientific '—if we knew enough . . . But
. . . to-night . . . of course . . ." He couldn't finish but
made a falling gesture with his long hand.

MacPherson was past hearing.

He was suddenly old—and soon he made his way out of
the silence as though he had caught himself in the final
folly of that long day: talking at this moment of what
had happened with a stranger.

At the door he paused.

He was to go back to Barber's bungalow, where he was
expected for the night. But the camp roads are complicated.

Meyer rose and offered to go with him.

Picnic at Porokorro

MacPherson said he would manage.
He stumbled out into the night.

*   *   *

Meyer closed up the house.

Every window and door had special locks and at the minute they were all wide open to the ticking, creaking night.

The moon was yellow and the tall dry grass was whispering at the edge of the shrubs; he stood for a minute in the air which like shallow sea-water was hot and cool by patches. Then he went in, and when the triple locks were all turned he took a last look round as usual, and there was Paul's butterfly net, the killing bottle with some spare shoes and a mackintosh by the door. He put them all away out of sight in a cupboard so MacPherson shouldn't see them in the morning, if he came to say good-bye.

*   *   *

He did come—and Meyer never mentioned the things, not even the fabulous butterfly. Let him ask for it later, he thought, the day he feels a need for souvenirs.

But he knew that day would never come and so in time he had the butterfly set and put in glass. And he has it still.

THE END